ORDINARY BEAR

BOOKS BY C. B. BERNARD

NOVELS
Ordinary Bear
Small Animals Caught in Traps

NONFICTION
Chasing Alaska: A Portrait of the Last Frontier Then and Now

ORDINARY BEAR

A NOVEL

C. B. BERNARD

BLACK
STONE
PUBLISHING

Copyright © 2024 by Chris Bernard
Published in 2024 by Blackstone Publishing
Cover and book design by Larissa Ezell

All rights reserved. This book or any portion
thereof may not be reproduced or used in any manner
whatsoever without the express written permission
of the publisher except for the use of brief quotations
in a book review.

The characters and events in this book are fictitious.
Any similarity to real persons, living or dead, is coincidental
and not intended by the author.

Printed in the United States of America

First edition: 2024
ISBN 979-8-200-85051-8
Fiction / Literary

Version 1

Blackstone Publishing
31 Mistletoe Rd.
Ashland, OR 97520

www.BlackstonePublishing.com

For Kim above all . . .

*And for everyone I'd fight for,
and all who'd fight for me.*

"We carry nemesis inside us."
—Robert Stone

PART ONE

1

STAINS OF UNCERTAIN PROVENANCE

The bear stood on Farley's sofa ripping foam from the cushions, day-old seal blood crusted on its jaws and chest. The sofa—a shade of green not readily found in nature—had belonged to an oil company investigator named Hennessy. When Hennessy left Alaska a decade earlier for Sandpoint, Idaho, to marry a Russian woman he'd met online, Farley inherited the sofa along with his job, his company house, and the rust-hollowed Ford F-150 he drove. Some days Farley thought he'd inherited his lingering existential ambivalence as well. Too big for the house, the sectional extended the length of the living room and angled into the galley kitchen like a threadbare peninsula, blocking the fridge from opening more than a foot. It looked tiny beneath the bear, which dug through the cushions with a kind of joy, throwing stuffing behind it like snow. The real snow had melted early this year across much of the Arctic. The pack ice too. Watching from across the dump, Farley wondered if the bears had resorted to trying to make their own in the face of climate change.

This fucking world, he thought. Not for the first time.

That morning, Mayor Nell had stood in his kitchen and demanded he get rid of the sofa before Abril arrived from the Lower 48. "You can't expect your girl to sleep on them sofa, Farley. Sofa's covered in fleas. Sofa's got stains of uncertain provenance. Them rusty sofa springs give her tetanus if she rolls over at night."

Farley raised his chin at the mayor. "Uncertain provenance?"

Nell put a knuckle of chewing tobacco in her cheek and rolled it around thoughtfully. "What, Farley? You don't think I read library books?"

"New sofas are expensive," he said. "I'd have to ship one up from Fairbanks."

"I think you got plenty of good oil field money, Farley. Maybe spend some on furniture 'stead of food." She spat tobacco into the sink, which was nearly level with her shoulders. "Maybe then you don't get so fat, neither."

Well over six feet tall, and built like an Oldsmobile, he towered over all the Iñupiat in Nanuqmiut and most of the whites, too, not fat so much as thick, big-boned, though he conceded he'd gone soft since the army. After a few gin and tonics, his mother liked to joke to his girlfriends that her ob-gyn had needed a forklift to deliver him.

"It's all your *akutuq* and *muktuk*," he said, patting his belly amiably.

"Bullshit. Seal oil makes you smart. It's all them whiskey and frozen pizza that makes you fat."

"What if I sleep on the couch?" Farley asked, conceding the point. "Abril can have my bed. I fall asleep there watching the news most nights anyway."

The mayor spat again into the sink, leaving a dark spatter on the cracked porcelain. "I think maybe we find you a new couch for your daughter's visit so she don't get fleas for souvenirs. Jeffrey will help you get rid of your rotten green couch OK."

For the first time, Farley noticed one of Nell's sons—the mute one, Jeffrey—standing in his doorway and wondered how long he'd been there. Nell had been the village mayor for almost twenty years and he had no idea how old she was. Maybe forty. Maybe seventy. The high Arctic had a way of wearing people down. She had skin like a baseball glove, eyes that could strip paint, and eleven kids that spanned a range of ages from diapers to divorces. Dozens of her grand- and great-grandkids scurried around the village like voles. She ruled family and residents alike with matriarchal poise, and Farley knew there was no point in arguing with her. The discussion was over. He'd already lost.

Jeffrey helped him drag the couch from the house and onto a sled he pulled to the dump with his four-wheeler. Nell rode behind her son, arms wrapped around his stomach, yelling into his ears like a jockey as the quad belched black smoke. Farley followed on foot, having misplaced his truck keys. By the time he got there, his eyes still watering from the exhaust, the two of them were already standing around chewing Skoal and watching the big white bear shred the cushions.

"Bear's got something in his mouth," Nell said, spitting tobacco juice through her brown teeth. "What's he got in his stupid mouth?" Mute Jeffrey spit too, a kind of shrug. Farley squinted at the bear, which shook its head and sent a shiny black object skittling into a pile of trash and bones.

"I think it's my TV remote," he said. Nell smiled brightly, her teeth like rows of dirty ice blocks.

"Ha ha, Farley. You never checked them cushions? No more watching the news for you. Why do you watch the news so much anyway, Farley? What good did news ever do you?"

"I like to know what's happening in the world."

Nell looked at him crossways. The village transmitter got its news broadcasts two days old from a Phoenix affiliate cheaper than it would cost to pay the Anchorage stations for air rights, and the twice-a-day broadcasts were neither timely nor relevant, with overtly tanned blonds reporting stories about blistering heat, immigrant border crossings, and big-city crime. She scratched an armpit beneath her sweater and spit into the dirt thoughtfully.

"If you still want to know some stuff about the world, why did you move up here to Nanuqmiut anyway?"

"For the company, I guess."

Nell's spasmic laugh doubled her over, halving her to little more than two feet in height. Before it subsided, she slapped Jeffrey hard on the back. Farley watched him swallow his tobacco and turn the exact shade of green as the sofa.

2

A MAN'S GOT TO HAVE STANDARDS

Farley had seen Abril just a few times since he'd moved to the Arctic to work on the North Slope, and always at home in Portland. The first few years after he'd taken the job, he'd flown back for the holidays and rented a cheap hotel room on Burnside, where they'd eaten tacos in front of the wooden cabinet TV, watching grainy Christmas specials. That was the best arrangement he'd been able to get her mother to agree to at the time.

"You can't negotiate with terrorists," his lawyer had told him. "Just do what she says and it will be better for all of us."

It took two more years to convince her to let Abril visit him in Alaska—and then only under protest. Their split had been acrimonious. It hadn't even been a split, really, so much as the unsurprising conclusion of a few months together while he was still in the army, as if they'd pulled the pin out of a grenade the day they'd met. They both knew it would explode sooner or later.

If he thought of his life in baseball terms, Farley had expected a line drive, not a home run, but when she told him she was pregnant it curved wide and fast and dropped into foul territory with a thud. He left the army to be with her without asking if that's what she wanted. It was not.

Now she had custody, he agreed that was best, and they "co-parented" uneasily from different states with two thousand miles and a buffer country between them. For Abril to reach Nanuqmiut, they had to overcome a litany of logistic challenges and expenses together. Their particular form of co-parenting meant her mother resolved the former and Farley absorbed the latter. He purchased two tickets. She would fly with Abril from Portland to Seattle, Juneau, Anchorage, and then to Fairbanks, a complicated series of deplanings and connections made necessary by the remoteness of the destination and scarcity of flights. In Fairbanks, she would put Abril on the fifth and final leg to Nanuqmiut alone rather than risk seeing Farley for even a short while. The only plane in or out of the village each day was due around 2 p.m., which, historically, meant it might arrive anytime between 3 p.m. and Tuesday. Village custom dictated that if you had someone coming in, you waited until you heard its laborious approach before heading to the airport.

Many of the North Slope workers' shifts ran three weeks on, one week off. They lived in spartan dorms on the oil fields instead of in the village and flew back home to the Lower 48 for downtime. They knew to bring sleeping bags to the airport in case the daily didn't make it in and, realistically, knew it had a fifty-fifty chance. It wasn't just the weather, which could be unpredictable. It was that tourism as such did not exist in Nanuqmiut, so the flights carried mostly Slope grunts, geologists, wildlife biologists, and village residents returning from city doctor visits; the sole airline felt no urge to meet customer expectations. *We'll get there when we get there*, the unofficial motto. There was also the risk of a pilot making a detour that delayed the flight unexpectedly. Though many of the Arctic villages were dry, enterprising pilots would sometimes make unscheduled landings at bush airfields with a couple cases of booze they'd picked up in Anchorage to sell. The last thing Farley needed was to explain to his ex that their ten-year-old had gotten stuck alone in Kivalina for the night. She'd been looking for more excuses to hate him for years, and though he'd been quite generous with them, she hungered for more.

A half hour before the flight was due, Farley was looking for the keys to his truck when the phone rang. On the other end he found Pastor John McTeague, who spoke without preamble or greeting, his voice the deep baritone of a radio disc jockey.

"We've got a sofa in the rectory you can have."

Farley had stopped being surprised at the lack of privacy village life afforded a long time ago. News passed through at an alarming rate, rumors even more quickly—they called it the Bush Telegraph, but it was just gossip.

"There are no secrets in Nanuqmiut."

"Secrets are bad for the soul, Farley."

"What color is it?"

"The soul?"

"The couch."

"Well, now, I didn't realize you were in a position to be picky."

John and Rebecca McTeague had come from Alabama with the stated goal of serving Iñupiat who'd found Our Lord and Savior Jesus Christ and converting those who had not. Nearly two decades later, they remained preternaturally upbeat about their mission despite underwhelming results. Every other Thursday Farley played poker in the church rec room with Nell and John and a rotation of village irregulars. If John proselytized as poorly as he played poker, it was no wonder the villagers had yet to find salvation.

"A man's got to have standards."

"It's kind of a salmon color. It's got coffee stains from the AA meetings and it smells like smoke, but the mayor assures me it's an improvement over your current situation."

"I'll swing by with the truck as soon as I find my keys."

"You might bring your daughter to Sunday service while she's here, Farley."

"What for?"

"Just because *you're* going to hell doesn't mean *she* has to."

"Sartre said hell is other people."

"*L'enfer, c'est les autres.* You read Sartre?"

"No. An ex-girlfriend had it tattooed in a semicircle on her lower back."

"T. S. Eliot said hell is oneself."

"Did he?"

"Hell is alone, the other figures in it merely projections. There is nothing to escape from, and nothing to escape to. One is always alone."

"You're describing life here in the village."

"My wife would agree with you."

"So which is it? Is my hell *me* or *you*?"

"The Bible tells *me* what to think, Farley. What do *you* think?"

"I don't think they're mutually exclusive."

"Why not bring your daughter? What could it hurt?"

"I could make you a list."

John sighed audibly over the phone. Despite having ceded the moral high ground in nearly every way in his personal life, his religious authority gave him a judgmental superiority he wielded like a club.

"Anyway," Farley said, "isn't welcoming a sofa from the house of the Lord into my own home practically the same as welcoming the Lord himself?"

"Maybe a close second," John conceded. "If you come soon, I can help you load it into your truck."

"Roger that. As soon as I find my keys."

"Have you checked your sofa cushions?"

"You mean the sofa I hauled to the dump this morning?"

Pastor John chuckled. "The Lord moves in mysterious ways, Farley. Mysterious ways."

He heard the plane around 11 p.m. and set out on foot, reaching the airport as it taxied to the terminal. Originally part of the DEW Line, the air*port* was more of an air*field*. The military and the North Slope Borough ran it jointly with money the oil companies kicked in to keep the runway gravel smooth and the terminal lights on. Hulking radar dishes lined the field behind it, holdovers from the active service days when they served as an early warning system against Russian bombers during the Cold War. They looked both high-tech and dated, as if an ancient and advanced alien civilization had once monitored this planet but had grown too old and bored to care.

The terminal was a one-room Quonset hut with mismatched folding chairs, a couple of mattresses on the floor, and a wheelbarrow for baggage. Wilson Mequssuk sat on one of the chairs, smoking a cigarette. He worked airport maintenance and mopped the floors at night. Farley stood beside him to watch the passengers approach the terminal, the sun setting slowly behind them.

Abril stepped off the plane wearing an Oregon Ducks sweatshirt, a Columbia parka, and a pair of knee-high rubber boots.

"That your daughter, Farley?" Wilson said. "She don't look much like you."

"She got her looks from her mother." Abril's mother had been born in Haiti and had skin the color of an August night. If Farley's French Canadian and Irish roots had any input on their daughter's genetic makeup, it was subtle—she looked just like her mother but younger, unencumbered by the decades of bitterness and drama. He found it almost endearing.

"She looks smart, Farley."

"She gets that from her mother, too."

"So what she get from you?"

"Child support."

Wilson laughed abruptly. Then he pulled his Barrow Whalers hat down over his eyes and slumped in his chair. "Let ol' Wilson go back to work."

Abril approached and extended her hand. "Hello, Farley," she said. "It's me, your daughter, who you may not recognize because it's been so long."

"Hysterical. Did your mother teach you that?"

"No, I thought of it on the plane. Mom wanted me to tell you you're a miserable asshole who ruined her life and will probably ruin mine, but I thought mine was funnier."

"Yours *was* funnier."

"Only 'cause hers wasn't a joke."

When she leaned in to hug him, her arms barely reached around to his back. She felt so small, so insubstantial to him. So pure. Everything else in the village was rough around the edges, faded and beaten down, but Abril rang out like a bright note in a major key. She carried a unicorn backpack with rainbow shoulder straps and nothing else. Farley couldn't believe how light the bag was when he took it from her, a function of her size but also a rebuke about how brief her visit would be and how infrequently he saw her.

"Is this all you brought?"

"Mom says I didn't need any games or books because there's so much to do in Nanuqmiut, I'd be endlessly entertained."

"I see. Are the two of you taking your comedy act on the road anytime soon?"

"Oh, is there a road up here now? When did they put that in?"

"Your daughter is pretty funny, Farley," Wilson said from under his hat.

"She got my sense of humor."

"That makes sense," Abril said. "Because Mom still has hers."

Wilson was still laughing as they left the building.

3

THIS COLD AND MISERABLE WORLD

The sun considered the horizon but seemed unsure whether it liked what it saw. In just a few weeks it would not set at all, loitering visibly until August. With so little ice, the sea reflected more than usual, casting an orange glow on the village. Abril looked around the mostly empty parking lot.

"Where's your car?" she asked.

"I thought we'd walk."

"Seriously? It's so cold."

"It's summer."

"It's spring."

"Well, it's not winter."

"It's the Arctic, Farley."

She had a point. Though it was mid-May, the temperature would not climb out of the forties. He saw her disappointment but had no good response.

"Sorry, kid. No keys."

"Where are your keys?"

"Long story."

"The sun's going down too."

"Yeah, but it'll be back up in an hour."

"Won't we be home by then?"

"Depends on how fast you walk," he said.

Two cars leaving the airport passed them as they made their way toward town, their rusted-out exhausts and shocks roaring like caged animals. After that it was quiet. Farley could hear the gravel crunching beneath their feet. He could hear his heart beating. He couldn't hear Abril's heart, but he could hear her stomach and hoped he had food in the house. Frozen pizza, at least. He'd planned on shopping that afternoon but had gotten distracted looking for his keys. Then he heard another motor and Wilson Mequssuk pulled up on his Honda four-wheeler. When he shut off the engine, Farley heard the gas sloshing around in the spare cans bungeed to the seat rack.

"Shouldn't be walking home, Farley. Sun's going down. Getting dark."

"I've heard that's what happens when the sun goes down."

"Maybe leave the jokes to your girl." Wilson winked at Abril and she smiled. He wore a camo jumpsuit, old ski goggles, a safety-orange wool hat with the visor of his Barrow Whalers cap sticking out. "No joke, though, Farley. Bears been around town 'cause of the no ice."

"Statistically you're more likely to be killed by a moose in Alaska than a bear," Abril said.

"Is that true?" Farley asked. "About moose?"

"We learned it in school."

"Statistics don't kill you, Farley's daughter. It's the teeth and the claws." Wilson raised his hands in front of him, fingers bent, and bared his teeth comically. "Them polar bears, though. They been 'round all winter, still here spring and summer. Something's got them restless. That snowmelt, maybe. Maybe something else." He looked thoughtful for a moment. "Don't you worry, Farley's daughter. They eat your fat father before they eat you." He smiled to show he was joking but gave Farley a dark look. "Where's your truck, Farley? You get drunk again, forget where you park?"

"Is that what happened?" Abril asked.

"No. I just left my keys somewhere."

"Where'd you leave your keys, Farley?"

"It's a long story," Abril said.

Wilson nodded. "Always a long story with him. Don't worry. Ol' Wilson will send one of his idiot nephews in them Subaru to pick you up, get you home safe. Then Farley can tell all his dumb jokes."

Farley waved him off. "It's a ten-minute walk. We'll be fine."

"Hey, Farley's daughter," Wilson said. "Ol' Wilson got a joke better than any your fat father can tell you. Knock knock."

"Who's there?"

"Nobel."

"Nobel who?"

"No bell. That's why Wilson's knocking."

The streetlamps blinked on when they reached town, but the weak light only served to accentuate the shadows between them. The houses along the gravel street all looked of a style: single story, inornate, off plumb. Modified trailers or kit homes. Village houses had few windows, and only small ones; windows let in cold air and midnight sun. Some houses were brightly painted—often in multiple colors—while others were not even sided, their owners getting as far as the Tyvek before running out of money or calling it good. That particular phenomenon was so common in Alaska that he'd once seen a band at the Great Alaskan Bush Company in Anchorage that called itself Tyvek Vapor Wrap.

The door to the rectory opened as they walked by and Rebecca McTeague stepped out onto the porch—a handful of wooden pallets set on pavers to keep them out of the coming summer mud—in a bathrobe, her hair flickering like a tiki torch under the outside light.

"You must be Farley's daughter."

"I am."

"Why, you don't look a thing like him." Rebecca flashed the kind of smile that a predator uses to lure unsuspecting prey to its demise. "Lucky girl."

"Abril, meet the preacher's wife. She's married to Pastor John. He's married to God. It's a threesome."

His daughter gave him a look, unsure of his standing in this town, or with God, or with her.

"Abril, that's such a pretty name," Rebecca said.

"It means 'child of the spring.'"

"Oh! You were born in April?"

"October."

Rebecca cocked her head.

"I'm just kidding." Abril let her off the hook, but the preacher's wife smiled with discomfort, unused to being teased.

"You never came for the couch, Farley."

Abril looked interested. "What happened to *your* couch?"

"It's a long story."

"It's *always* a long story with your father." Rebecca's accent dripped down her chin like gravy.

"Well," Farley said, "you should probably know that it involves the TV too."

"Every village has an idiot, Abril. It may not surprise you to know that your father is ours." She winked to show she was joking. "What do you think of Nanuqmiut so far?"

"It's really different than Portland. I haven't gotten used to it yet."

"You never get used to this place. Never. If you do, there's something wrong with you."

Though Farley did not disagree, he felt the need to defend his way of life to his daughter. Before he could, he heard the crunch of footsteps on gravel and saw from Rebecca's expression that she'd heard it too.

"John?" She looked over their shoulders into the night. "Is that you?"

Farley's muscles tensed involuntarily, confusing him. Something paternal, maybe, triggered by Abril's presence or his army training, or something instinctual, a reaction to an event millions of years ago that had fused itself into human DNA. Into *his* DNA. The breeze shifted. He smelled rotten meat and moldering trash, and the hairs on his neck stood up. Clenching his fists, he took a step closer to his daughter and squinted into the darkness. More footsteps on gravel. Then Pastor John walked into the light wearing a bright red parka and the ear-to-ear smile of someone who has been drinking prodigiously.

"Farley!"

"Jesus Christ, John. Just because the Lord moves in mysterious ways doesn't mean you have to."

"And you must be Farley's daughter." Pastor John bowed before Abril, swaying precariously. "You look just like your father, my dear."

"Just how drunk *are* you, John?" Rebecca asked.

Farley barely heard them, his mind busy trying to understand why his muscles had not unclenched or why the pit in his stomach had not dissipated. Why his own early warning system had not stopped issuing an alert. He couldn't make sense of it, and that unsettled him.

Abril saw it on his face and looked at him with concern.

"Farley?" she said.

The word had barely cleared her lips when a bear loped out of the darkness, scattering it like dust. It brushed past Farley without slowing, grabbed Pastor John in its jaws, and carried him away into the night.

Rebecca's scream pierced something inside Farley. Abril had gone pale, frozen in place. He lunged for her, but before he could reach her—before he could even say her name—a second bear appeared, a dirty white ghost somehow bigger than the first, and faster too. It ran straight at him.

All his life he'd been aware of his size, of the space he occupied. How he had to duck to enter rooms, fold himself into cars and airplanes and movie theaters. All his life other men eyed him with suspicion, judging the thickness of his neck, the circumference of his arms and legs, the expanse of his shoulders, as if he posed some existential threat they did not dare articulate. He'd been in more than his fair share of fights with men for no other reason than they felt they had something to prove, endless Davids testing themselves against a reluctant Goliath. But when the bear grabbed him by the thigh and lifted him off his feet, he felt small for the first time he could remember. The first time ever. The jaws closed around his leg like a steel trap, teeth slicing through flesh, connecting with bone.

The bear shook him like a dog toy and tossed him onto the gravel, hard.

When it lunged again, Farley punched at it from the ground without strategy or forethought and hit it square in the nose. He swung again and again and felt his knuckles splinter.

The bear swiped him with a paw, rolling him over the sharp gravel. Farley tried to move, tried to get to his feet, but his legs would not respond, the muscles severed, flesh ribboned, bones snapped into shards. Only one eye seemed to function. He could taste blood, could taste the salt of the sea, the bile and excrement spilling from his gutted organs, but he could not get a deep breath. His ribs had punctured his lungs.

So much damage.

And yet, only a few seconds had passed.

He lay on the ground and watched with helpless confusion from this new and unexpected vantage point as the bear ambled toward Abril, who stood rooted in place, paralyzed with shock.

Later he would think back on that moment, would replay it over and over and over, considering and reconsidering how he had responded, critiquing his reaction, wondering what he might have done differently. He would hear Rebecca's wails rending the dry air of the village, would hear his own labored breathing whistling through his tattered lungs. Later still, when people would ask him what had happened—Alaska State Troopers, Fish and Wildlife officers, trauma counselors, village elders—he'd say the bears hadn't so much *run* out of the darkness as they had *materialized*. As if one second there were no bears and the next there were two. And how, like some natural law of converse truths being enforced, that's how his daughter had disappeared too. One minute she was there, holding her unicorn backpack outside the rectory, and the next she was not.

Gone from his sight.

Gone from her spot.

Gone from this cold and miserable world.

PART TWO

4

MAYBE VOTE DIFFERENTLY IN THE NEXT ELECTION

Almost overnight, a homeless encampment had sprung up at the bus stop across from Lissa's apartment. Tents lined the sidewalk, scavenged or bought or stolen, tarps on ropes strung between utility poles, their blue fabric shimmering in the breeze like a rippling sea. The occupants slept on wooden pallets above the rainwater that rushed the sidewalks. On cooler nights they burned the pallets to keep warm. Nights when the wind shifted and the smoke drifted across the street to push with gentle menace at Lissa's windows, she pushed right back, blowing cigarette smoke out into the night as she watched the camp after Olive went to bed.

Though Portland was no stranger to rain, the rain had come early this year and it felt oppressive. Lissa saw its effect on people around the city, who felt as if they'd been shortchanged, emotionally stunted by a shorter-than-average growing season. She couldn't remember the last time she'd gone outside without rain gear. She couldn't even remember the last time she'd seen the sun, or what it looked like. Gore-Tex had become a kind of second skin, one she and Olive shed each night and hung by the door, as if they'd evolved for the climate. Rain infiltrated their lives. Rain soaked through their shoes. Rain worked its way into the apartment on backpacks and hats. When Lissa slept, the rain spilled into her dreams, falling somehow even harder than reality's downpours. But the relentless rain had done nothing to dampen activity at the camp. All it had done was make the campers' fires smokier and their attitudes worse.

After weeks of observation from her window aerie—and an entire Ziploc bag full of extinguished cigarette butts she hid from her daughter—she'd begun to recognize the camp's individual residents. Not just to recognize them, but to *study* them like an anthropologist: the one with the tribal tattoos covering his entire face; the one who leaped to her feet and screamed at anyone who dared pass, real or imagined; the big, dumb-looking one with all the scars; the one who wore one of those pink knitted hats from the Women's March so filthy that it looked like every woman in Washington, DC, had stomped over it on their way to the Capitol. Collectively, they reminded her of the Joads passing through Dust Bowl resettlement camps in Steinbeck's Oklahoma. Only wetter. And less likable. She'd read *The Grapes of Wrath* in school, back when she still thought the world allowed people room to study such things as literature and art, before the pressing necessities of life compressed her days to learning and practicing only the most useful skills needed to pay rent and raise a child. She'd always loved reading but could not remember the last book she'd finished. She couldn't even remember the last book she'd started. She didn't have time for hobbies either, or friends. Hell, she barely had time to go to the bathroom and, even when she did, could not afford to give it her full attention as the task itself had to compete with Olive asking an endless barrage of questions from the other side of the door.

The world did not work the way she'd been led to believe. Her youthful naivete still embarrassed her. But a part of her missed it too. Maybe that's why she'd waited a few weeks after the camp appeared before calling the police, half-hoping it would migrate to another block and save her from Progressive Guilt. Anywhere but Portland she'd be a screaming liberal; here she always had to push herself to keep pace with the ever-more-extreme positions pushing people far to the left.

But hadn't the Joads been dealt a bad hand? Hadn't they been *seeking* work, looking for ways to keep the family together? The campers seemed only to want to be able to shoot up without shame, throw empty bottles at passing cars, panhandle aggressively, and piss into the street at will.

"The under-homed are not currently an enforcement priority for the department," the dispatcher told Lissa when she called the police nonemergency line. "Mayor's orders."

"Under-homed?"

"Ma'am. We're supposed to call them that now. Officially, I mean. Or 'people living outside.' Mayor's orders to leave the camps alone."

"My daughter and I have to pass by them twice a day to ride the bus. She shouldn't have to see that."

"Why don't you want your daughter to know about poor people, ma'am?"

"My daughter already knows about poor people. *We're* poor. That's not the problem."

"Then what *is* the problem, ma'am?"

"It's not poverty. It's behavior. They yell at us. Sexually suggestive things. Crazy things. They do drugs out in public. My daughter has seen more penises at the bus stop than I've seen my entire life."

"I'm sorry to hear that, ma'am."

"Is that supposed to be a joke?"

"No, ma'am."

"It's not funny. The situation is *unsafe*."

"Ma'am. I advise you to avoid the bus stop, then. You could take a cab. Or an Uber."

"That's too expensive. I'm a single mother."

"What about public transit?"

"That's what I'm telling you. That's why I called. They've taken over the bus stop entirely, like an occupation of enemy troops."

"Sounds like a TriMet issue. I can give you their number."

But Lissa had already called the public transit authority with dominion over buses, trains, and light rails. "I called them first," she explained. "They said it was a police issue. They told me to call you."

"Have you thought about moving to a better neighborhood, ma'am?"

Every day she took her lunch break at two and rode the MAX light rail into the city to meet her daughter at school. They walked together to Olive's after-school program at the Multnomah County Library, and Lissa took the MAX back to work at the Oregon Zoo. The trip took up her entire allotted lunch hour—either she ate on the train or she didn't eat at all. After work she took the six o'clock bus to the library so that she and Olive could ride the six-thirty home together. The bus driver had begun dropping passengers at the far corner to avoid the camp, which grew by the day in both size and depravity, spreading down the block like a homeless city so populous it had created its own urban sprawl.

A few campers had dogs tied to street signs in front of their tents. Pit bulls, mostly, or pit bull mixes. As an animal lover and vet tech, she didn't buy into the widespread panic about pit bulls—she'd met plenty of sweet ones—but nature had designed the dogs to cause damage, and in the hands of a shitty owner, they would. And that capacity for destruction seemed to attract an awful lot of shitty owners. The camp dogs barked at passing traffic, barked at pedestrians, barked at disembarking bus passengers. They barked at all hours of the day and night. Nearly every time Lissa passed the camp, some of the residents yelled at her to give them money, to fuck off, to get off their lawns. They shot up with God knew what and flashed their genitals while pissing on the glass bus shelter.

Some nights she rushed Olive across the street and into their building with a coat over her eyes like a celebrity being perp-walked into court rather than expose her to someone's exposure.

A few days ago, the camp had begun to expand beyond the sidewalk, encroaching on the shoulder of the street with a stable of shopping carts parked at the curb stuffed with purloined and scavenged goods: pillows, sleeping bags, backpacks, gas cans, tires, coolers, license plates. Anything at all that might be used or sold or bartered. If a camper filled a cart, they stole another from the Fred Meyer and tied it to the first, and so on, building caravans four and five carts long piled high with trash bags and objects they pushed down the street like some nomadic tribe. Like a Mad Max movie.

"Move to a better neighborhood? How am I supposed to do that?"

she asked the dispatcher. "I'm a single mother making fifteen bucks an hour with student loans to pay off."

"Ma'am. I don't know what to tell you. We have our mandates. Our hands are tied. Maybe vote differently in the next election if you want tough on crime."

Each night on her bus ride home from work, Lissa noted the other homeless camps throughout the city. There were many of them, of varying sizes and configurations. Some included the shells of stripped cars or vans, one a ramshackle cabin built out of pallets, and one even boasted a bright-blue porta-potty some enterprising resident had stolen and engineered a way to relocate. But the one on her block had grown dramatically bigger than the rest, with dozens of residents arriving seemingly every night. She'd been keeping track of their comings and goings in a notebook. Methodological. Scientific. She noted and recorded an increase in drug use, a parallel increase in the flagrance of it. People shooting up on the wet curb during what passed for daylight, smoking heroin beside a fire lit on a public sidewalk, dealing in the great wide open. The rain seemed to provide cover for their activity. Rather, it facilitated their boldness by keeping everyone else under cover and out of sight.

She called TriMet again. They referred her to the police. She called the police again. They referred her to the mayor's office. She called the mayor's office, but her calls went unanswered, the voice mailbox already full. Her next call would be to the newspaper or one of the TV stations. Fox News, maybe. Though she despised the network and all it stood for, its highly calibrated sense of alarmism and opposition to all liberal points of pride meant it would at least pick up the story and rally an army of aggrieved flag wavers to bombard city hall with complaints and grievances about the mayor's embrace of the under-homed.

She had *some* empathy for the campers. Hell, at any given moment she was only a paycheck or two away from eviction herself. And she recognized a high degree of mental illness among them from her observation.

Addiction. Veterans suffering PTSD. She'd always felt something for the homeless. If not empathy, exactly, it wasn't pity either. Not exactly. Like most Portlanders, she saw them as a necessary part of urban life and a symptom of the city's laudable progressive tendencies. But the problem had grown until it overran Portland, and soon the homeless were panhandling relentlessly in city squares, sleeping in the doorways of shops and markets, squatting in neighborhood parks, and bathing in urban creeks and ponds.

On the TV news and in the local papers, the statistics staggered her. Portland alone had almost four thousand homeless residents, and enough shelter space for just half of them.

And now they'd taken over her bus stop. Their behavior had inured her to their plight. They'd sanded the edges off her empathy, and she feared they were making her a bad person. Housing advocates said the homeless deserve dignity just like the rest of us. Lissa wanted to believe that. But where was the dignity of the man with his pants around his ankles grinning up at her window while shitting into the storm drain across the street?

5

A LANDSCAPE LITTERED WITH BONES

After being airlifted out of the village on a medevac, Farley spent three months drifting in and out of consciousness in an Anchorage hospital, medicated against pain. Pain racked him anyway. Ghost bears scuttled through his feverish mind, mauling him, snatching Abril over and over again and again and again. Each time his brain settled or his heart rate slowed, the sedatives doing their work, another bear appeared out of the darkness of his memory to decimate him once more.

The Alaska Department of Fish and Game flew field biologists into Nanuqmiut. They were joined by Alaska State Troopers, Fish and Wildlife feds, and hunters from the village. National press picked up stories from the *Fairbanks News-Miner* and the *Anchorage Daily News*, and network camera crews descended on the village, breathlessly awaiting word.

But within a few days of the killings, a buffet of walruses appeared on the spit. For weeks after that, their blood covered every bear near the village, making it impossible to distinguish the human-killers from all the others. An ursine "I'm Spartacus" moment.

Officially, the task force comms team called the joint effort a "Search and Rescue for Abril Hebert and John McTeague." But it wasn't a SAR. It wasn't even a recovery operation. John and Abril were gone, along with all hope of finding them. Best case, it was a revenge mission—if the search teams found and identified the culpable bears, they would put them down. Once bears had a taste for blood—once they started to think of humans as food they could pluck as easily as cocktail shrimp from an hors d'oeuvres tray—they had to be destroyed.

Destroyed. That was the state's word for it. Actual humans outside of a bureaucracy might use different words, Farley thought, but they all meant the same thing.

As the days wore on, the search and rescue ops diminished in frequency. And then one day they ended altogether, and that was that. The feverish media coverage died along with John and Abril, and all that remained was the pain.

When Farley had first moved to Nanuqmiut, he'd stood out. Not just for his size but for his temperament and personality. He was markedly different from the taciturn, noncommittal Iñupiat community, and the locals eyed him with unease. Until Mayor Nell arrived on his doorstep one day. Not just the mayor but also the unofficial village matriarch, she'd designated herself as the Welcome Wagon too. Invisible beneath the peephole she could not reach, she'd had to knock a second time when Farley failed to answer.

"Some people believe that when bears go back to them dens to hibernate, they remove them skins like a coat," she'd told him when he'd answered the door. "Underneath, them bears look human."

The oil company that had hired Farley provided housing in the village because it required him to live off-site, outside the barracks, to discourage relationships with the people he'd be investigating. Human Resources had provided a binder of materials to prepare him for transitioning to Arctic village life; he'd read it on one of the legs of his inaugural flight north. It barely touched upon Iñupiat culture but devoted what felt like a worrying amount of space to the presence of polar bears in the region. Nell told him the bears held a special place not just for the Iñupiat but for all Inuit, who knew them as Nanuq, king of the *iqsinaqtuit*.

"Those who inspire fear in humans," she said.

Still, Farley did not immediately make the connection she seemed to want him to make.

"What does that have to do with me?"

She spit tobacco juice into the dirty snow on his front stoop, a motion he would later come to associate with her.

"Some people see big old giant like you walking 'round them streets and think maybe one of them bears forget to put them coat back on before he go looking for food."

After the task force left town, Nell's sons and some of the other village hunters kept up the watch. Though the Iñupiat people had a complicated relationship with polar bears, they mostly did not mind shooting them. Bears provided food. Fabrics. Artifacts. Oil. In all, the hunters took eight of them that summer, but no one recovered John's and Abril's bodies.

How do you find a few bones in a landscape littered with them?

A month after the incident, while Farley was still in the hospital, his phone rang, the ringtone a second-chair instrument in a symphony of beeping medical equipment monitoring his health and progress. The world had all but ceased to exist for him outside the borders of his pain and grief and guilt. Painkillers. Hospital food. How much television could a person watch before it crossed the line from entertainment to torture? He'd murder somebody for a bottle of whiskey and a cheeseburger. The phone vibrated on the bedstand, the effort to reach it a cruelty. A war crime. How did it still hold a charge? Maybe a nurse had plugged it in under the mistaken belief that he had anyone who loved him. He stabbed at the screen and laid it on the pillow beside his head.

"Do you think the dead know they're dead, Farley?"

He didn't recognize the number, but he recognized the voice immediately. Though it had changed, sharpened, honed by grief, it remained honeyed even in its pain.

"Rebecca."

"Do you think they wander the earth like spirits? Ghosts? Just following their old routines? Going to work, brushing their teeth, tinkling and messing, forever frustrated that their loved ones are ignoring them, unaware that they're not part of this world anymore?"

Farley did not know the answer to her questions. Nor did he know any grown woman who talked about pissing and shitting as "tinkling and messing." Maybe it was a southern thing. Or a religious thing. Rebecca had not been fond of him in Nanuqmiut. But neither had she seemed fond of anyone, including her husband, John. Including herself. She'd carried herself as if the world itself were somehow an unbearable burden, the effort of breathing too much to ask, her own heart's efforts to beat inside her chest an imposition. Farley doubted she would be any more fond of him now.

"Did you know John had three brothers, Farley? One of them became a marine. A war hero, killed by a sniper in Afghanistan. The bullet splattered his brain into a billion pieces all over the inside of his helmet. They put him back together for the wake. I looked at his body in the coffin and he didn't look dead. Just asleep. Peaceful, almost. All I could think was that maybe they could hollow out *my* head and scatter my brain and it wouldn't be so bad. Not if I could feel as peaceful as he did."

Her southern accent sounded stronger, more pronounced, as if she'd been tempering it as long as he'd known her but now it had overrun her voice like weeds in a neglected yard or cobwebs in an abandoned house.

"Another one of his brothers died in a car accident. Someone driving the wrong way on the highway, drunk or tired or stupid, hit his car head-on. The state police said the force equaled a rocket ship going into outer space. The *G force* or whatever it's called."

Po-leece. Gee fo-ahs.

"His body tore right out of the seatbelt, flew through the windshield, and landed so far from the wreck that at first they weren't sure he was part of it." She paused. "It was a Cadillac."

Farley said nothing because there was nothing to say and, anyway, because it did not matter to her. But when nearly an entire minute passed and she did not say anything else, he became emboldened, maybe, by painkillers or pain or boredom or anything but curiosity.

"What about the third brother?"

"He's an actuary. In Akron. Do you know what that is, Farley? An actuary?"

"Yes."

"Can you imagine that, then? The one brother who lived spends his days calculating the odds of dying in all the different ways. All four brothers were athletes when they were younger, Farley, healthy and active and so alive. But now the actuary is the only one left. If their mother weren't dead herself, she'd have him under armed guard twenty-four hours a day, don't you think?"

She had not asked Farley how he was doing, and he did not tell her. He didn't know what she wanted or hoped to accomplish by calling. Maybe she blamed him for John's death and wanted to accuse him. Or maybe she just wanted to commiserate over their shared experience. How many people on earth could understand what she'd been through? How many had seen what she'd seen, felt what she'd felt? On this entire planet, maybe a handful.

Fewer.

On this entire planet, maybe him and him alone.

"Do you remember how it happened, Farley? How fast it happened? How John and your daughter were there and then they weren't?"

"Do I remember? Goddamn it, Rebecca, I still have staples in my wounds," he snapped, painkillers and patience both wearing thin. "Do I remember? It's all I can fucking think about."

In her silence, he heard her breathing, heard splashing, as if she were in a bath or swirling a drink around a glass, or both. He heard something else too: tears. She was crying. Then the tears turned to sobs, rising in substance and volume.

"Rebecca," he said. But it took just a few seconds to recognize his mistake, to realize they were not sobs, that she was not crying, that she was in fact laughing a ruthless, humorless laugh.

"They haven't found John's body, Farley."

"Not yet."

"Not yet? Fuck you, Farley. Fuck *you*." Whether because of the alcohol or the anger, her primness of speech had vanished. "You know why they haven't found his body? Because that bear swallowed him whole and shit out the bones in the dirt."

If they'd been together in person, face-to-face, Farley thought he could choke her to shut her up, throttle the life and breath out of her just to stop the words. Because the words didn't just recall what had happened to her husband; they recalled what had happened to Abril too. They'd never found her body, either.

He began to fear that he would forever be haunted not just by Abril and by John and the bears that took them but by Rebecca too, and when she laughed again he *knew* he could choke her. But for a reason he did not understand, a reason he could not identify—a reason for which he hated himself—he could not hang up on her.

"John's skin was the texture of an old basketball. You know that? He had moles on his back that looked like gunshots. Like he'd been shot with a paintball gun, but instead of paint the bullets were loaded with shit."

"Jesus, Rebecca."

"I bet he gave that, that, that . . . *beast* . . . indigestion. I bet he gave it some awful gas, Farley."

More sloshing, as if she were slipping under the bath water or pouring another drink.

"But you know what?"

He waited. Tethered to the bed by tubes and electrodes, what else could he do but wait?

"I was married to him for eighteen years. I knew his body like the back of my hands. And I'll *tell* you what. That bear probably used John's dick as a toothpick."

6

THE LAST PERSON
I COULD EVER MISS

The hospital released Farley in August. Though he faced months of physical therapy and carried a doctor's firm referral to a trauma shrink, without pause he flew back to the village on the first available flight. As he tested the new limits of his body and the boundaries of his injuries—deplaning twice, limping down the aisles with his cane, collapsing into the tiny seats of the puddle jumper—Farley held on to an almost frivolous hope that, despite what he'd seen, despite what he knew, despite the months that had passed, Abril might yet turn up alive.

That hope kept him afloat, buoyant with possibility. Until it popped like a balloon just a few hours after he landed in Nanuqmiut and Farley crashed headlong into misery and pain.

After that, all hope was gone. Twin bears of despair and physical agony filled the empty space where it had been—where Abril had been—like a den for hibernation. Those bears tried to kill him from within, mauling him all over again, leaving him alive and wounded, deeply scarred, devastated by guilt, having already taken away the only thing he loved in this world.

Thinking he might need Abril's mother's absolution, he flew to Portland to seek it. His plane hadn't even taxied to the gate at PDX before he realized what a stupid idea that had been. On protesting legs, he shuffled to the baggage claim and, from there, hauled his only luggage—a camo dry-bag backpack big enough to carry a body—to the taxi stand. He watched the driver try to lift it into his cab and fall over beneath the substantial weight. A compact man, a midsize sedan. Farley helped him back to his feet and wedged the pack into the trunk.

When they reached Nirva's house—a Hawthorne neighborhood craftsman she shared with her new husband, a lawyer named Sawyer—he unfolded himself from the Ford with some difficulty, shouldered his pack, and limped up the path. The front door opened. His ex stepped onto the front steps and overhanded a hot skillet at him, still sizzling with diced calabaza or hanks of goat for soup joumou or whatever it was she'd been cooking. The pan failed to reach him and the food spilled out onto the lawn.

"You missed me," he said, leaning on his cane. The weight of his pack drove the tip into the damp grass, and he stared at the growing divot, unable to look her in the eyes.

"You're the last goddamned person on this earth I could ever miss, Farley."

Her voice still had the Haitian lilt he'd always loved. Even now it felt good to hear it. Or maybe he just could no longer distinguish between good and familiar, like when an old song he knew came on the radio. She'd been crying when she opened the door, had probably been crying since the Alaska State Troopers called about Abril. Had maybe been crying long before that, even. Maybe since she put their daughter on the plane in Fairbanks, or since she agreed to let her visit him at all. Or maybe since she met him so many years ago, tying her future to him before she recognized him as the anchor that would root her in place.

Is misery infectious? If something as common as a cold is contagious, why not sadness?

She stepped closer.

"Does it hurt?" she asked.

"Of course it hurts." He looked up, defensive, but she stepped closer still and touched the scars on his face with a gentleness that surprised him. "Oh, that," he said. "It's fine." He couldn't remember the last time he'd been touched by anyone not changing a bandage or connecting an

IV and hadn't realized how much he missed it. What would it do to a man to go weeks or months or more without being touched by another human? What would it do to someone to never touch or be touched by someone they love again? Something told him he would find out the hard way.

"It looks bad," she said. Her voice held empathy. Or sadness.

Or pity.

Abruptly she pulled her hand away. Somehow the temperature dropped in the yard. In Portland. In the whole Pacific Northwest.

"Why are you here, Farley?"

"Because I'm sorry."

"You're sorry?"

"I came here to tell you I'm sorry."

"You're *sorry*?"

He recognized the challenge but did not know how to face it. This was new territory for him, all of it, and all he could do was wander, lost.

"We should . . . There should be a service."

"There was."

"A funeral. Something."

"There was."

"For Abril."

"There *was*, Farley. Goddamnit, there was."

"There was?"

"Yes. *Yes*."

He repositioned his cane, shifting his weight to take the burden off his devastated muscles. "When?"

"July."

"While I was in the hospital?"

He waited for her to explain or elaborate, waited for her to apologize. She did not.

"Why? Why would you have it when you knew I was still in the hospital?"

She said nothing.

"Why would you have it when you knew I couldn't come?"

She reached out again. Like an addict who'd been given a taste, he shivered anticipating her touch. But instead of touching him, she slapped his cheek. Hard. Her eyes burned with anger, or worse.

"Because you don't invite the killer to the funeral."

Slumped beneath the weight of his preposterous backpack, Farley began to cry. The tears irritated the fresh scars, clinging like rain to a dry riverbed and following them down his body. The scars ran the length of him. The scars held him together in the place of what once had been, pain where once was connective tissue, a circulatory system of grief pumping through his body. But he could not remember, now—had he ever been anything else *but* damaged?

He lifted his head—all the effort he could muster—and managed somehow to meet her eyes.

"I'm sorry, Nirva."

"I believe you, Farley." She reached down to retrieve her skillet. "Now get the fuck off my lawn."

7

WELCOME TO THE GODDAMNED NEIGHBORHOOD

After leaving Nirva's, Farley wandered Southeast Portland on foot, walking for hours, limping beneath the brutal weights of his pain and his pack. He walked until his muscles and bones and scars screamed in dissonant harmony. His hand blistered where he gripped his cane.

The Portland he wandered felt like an immeasurably different world from the one he had left a decade earlier. Once so familiar, it now felt foreign. Alien. The city had grown, and he'd lost all sense of scale living in a tiny Arctic village. The sheer chaos terrified him: endless traffic, idling cars and buses, bearded men hurtling sidewalks on long skateboards, women on motorized scooters carrying yoga mats and shopping bags. No longer a small charismatic city, Portland had become a migraine. The constant stimuli battered his shell-shocked brain. In need of a drink, a rest, a bathroom, something to numb the pain constricting his heart like a python, he stepped into a dive bar he remembered from late nights home on leave. As soon as he walked through the door he knew it had changed too. While it still *looked* like a dive bar, the decrepit furnishings and vulgar art felt like an affectation, like buying jeans with pre-ripped knees. He remembered a clientele of professional drinkers: bottom-feeders, bar fighters, relics, lushes. But now the stools and dark booths were occupied by young people with tattoos and piercings, asymmetrical haircuts, their faces lit by smartphones and laptops.

He found an empty stool and leaned his pack and cane against the bar. A woman in an anachronistic black top eyed him and his gear with suspicion and approached cautiously to take his order.

"Canadian Club," he said. "Neat."

"This is a cocktail bar."

"I just want a whiskey."

"We only do cocktails and craft beer."

"You're a bartender?"

"I'm a mixologist." Dark tattoos covered her pale arms and the backs of her hands and she wore lipstick the color of a maraschino cherry. "How about an old-fashioned?" she asked. "Toronto? Sazerac? Remember the Maine?"

"I just want a shot. Canadian Club. I can talk you through how to make it."

She glared, impassive. A hipster sphinx.

"Irish coffee? Hold the coffee?"

"I'll make you a Manhattan."

"Shaken," he said. "Not stirred."

"You never shake a Manhattan. It bruises the rye."

As he walked the streets some more, the alcohol warming him from within, he had to admit, she made a damned good drink. But what had happened to this city? What had happened to the world? What would become of him now that nothing remained to tether him to it? And still he walked, pressing on without promise or purpose or pause, letting the city continue to reveal itself to him until he understood that the chaos was *why* he'd come. Not for Nirva. Not for rest and recovery. He'd come because he knew the city would assail his senses. It would not allow him a moment's peace, and he did not want peace.

He didn't deserve it.

"The human body is remarkable," the surgeon had told him in the Anchorage hospital. "It will heal if you give it time. What doesn't heal will adapt. But go too far too fast and it will adapt *poorly*. You'll damage the other parts of your body that step in to compensate."

Already he could feel it, his misaligned back, feet cramping his boots, how his shoulders felt like he was still being bitten.

The pain was what he wanted.

The pain was what he deserved.

He'd taken a disability settlement from work, surrendered the company house, left the truck for Mayor Nell. She'd need a ladder to reach the cab—if she could even find the keys—but he had no use for it anymore. He did not want it anymore. He had no home to return to in Nanuqmiut and did not want to be there, in a landscape littered with bones and memories and ghosts.

Before he left, he'd rented an apartment in Portland through an agency, sight unseen, a month-to-month lease to see him through while he sorted things out with Nirva. With himself. After wandering most of the afternoon, summoning the pain, augmenting it, embracing it, he found himself standing in front of his rental as night fell on the city. A small two-bedroom in a nondescript Southeast Portland apartment building in the neighborhood equivalent of a flyover state: no restaurants, bars, or shops to serve as destinations, just bus transfer stops, proximity to the train station, and easy access to the parkway and highways. The steady roar of traffic and noise rose and fell in waves but never stopped. Forklifts raced around a nearby industrial lot, beeping like a race of metal creatures communicating. Music spilled from passing cars, the heavy bass roiling his stomach when they stopped at red lights. Some people loved the noise. They loved the bustle of the city. Farley had loved Portland despite it, the way you tolerate a lover's flaws, but his years in the village had stripped him of any immunity he'd built. He would never again find peace in a place like this.

Which made it perfect.

Fatigue washed over him like an incoming tide. He'd been walking all day on a broken body, a good ten miles with his cane and heavy pack. Though he wanted nothing more than to lie down and sleep, the idea of finding the super, picking up keys, and settling into an empty apartment felt beyond him. The idea of crossing the street felt beyond him.

"Are you moving in?" a voice behind him asked.

Farley turned to find a disembodied head and neck popping out of the fly of a ratty sidewalk tent that sat on a tarp for a ground cloth, like a turtle with a nylon shell. The tent was one of about a half dozen set up alongside tarps lashed to the fence, sleeping bags on cardboard spread on the ground. The beginnings of a homeless camp.

"I am." Farley looked back at the building, wondering which windows were his.

"That's good, man. That's good. These camps, they're like restaurants. Nobody goes into the empty ones. Right? We need people. We need tents. We need a *presence*. That will attract the others."

Farley looked at the man again, slow to recognize the misunderstanding.

"Safety in numbers, right, man?" He had a voice like he'd taken a shotgun blast to the lungs. He wore filthy Carhartt coveralls, construction boots with duct-taped toes, a wool hat over a deeply lined face. Farley wondered what he'd been through, what he'd seen. The man stared at Farley's face without embarrassment, but without challenge either—at the milky eye, the scars—maybe wondering the same thing.

"The more of us there are, the harder it'll be for the fuckers to kick us out." He smiled a mouth full of teeth so crooked they seemed to be fleeing one another. "Lemme ask you something. What do you do with a spaceman?"

Not understanding the question, Farley wondered how he'd gotten so deep into this conversation without following any of it. His fatigue had begun to swallow him. After moving up his legs and torso and past his shoulders and neck, it seemed to have reached his brain, which felt addled and inadequate.

"A spaceman?"

"Yeah." The man grinned through knackered yellow teeth, his eyes wide with expectation. "What do you do with a space, man?"

"I don't know."

"You park in it, man!" The man laughed silently, a wheeze that became a cough. When he regained his breath, he nodded. "That's a good one."

Farley said nothing. A wave of exhaustion that felt existential had begun to wash over him, his maligned body shutting itself down. He turned to leave, or tried to, but his body failed him and he stood rooted to his spot.

"Do you have a tent?" the man asked.

"A tent?"

"Oh, man. You must be new to this. Don't worry, I'll look out for you. I've got an extra tarp you can use. But just for the night. I need it back, OK?"

He extended a filthy hand. Farley shook it tentatively, too tired to resist, too tired to explain.

"I'm Wayne. Everybody calls me Insane Wayne."

"Why?"

"It's just my street name, man. Everybody's got a street name."

"So you're not crazy?"

"Oh, yeah. I mean, yeah. Absolutely. But my real name's just Wayne. What's yours?"

"Farley."

"Farley. Cool. Do you have a street name?"

Farley shook his head no, the effort both dizzying and excruciating.

"OK, Farley. I'm glad you're here, man. Set up anywhere you like. I'll go find you that tarp. Welcome to the goddamned neighborhood."

Unshouldering his pack as the man left, Farley dropped it to the ground with relief. All day it had seemed to grow heavier, impossibly heavy, until it felt as if he were carrying all the world's sins. Or at least his own. Now that he'd put it down, he could not convince himself to lift it again. Instead he lowered himself beside it, no easy task in his condition, and sat on the sidewalk.

The hard concrete pressed through his clothing, through his tender flesh and distraught muscles and straight to his bones. The discomfort embraced him.

Wayne returned with a small green tarp, leprous with holes and rot.

Stains of uncertain provenance, Farley thought, letting his sadness, his exhaustion, his pain overtake him.

"I can show you how to rig it if you want," Wayne said. "We can tie it to the fence."

Farley waved him off and wrapped the tarp around his shoulders like a cape. Without another word, he lay down on the cold ground right where he'd been sitting. The relentless traffic, the exhaust fumes, the overbright streetlights felt like a lab experiment to test his capacity for suffering. His grief dwarfed it all.

Within minutes he was asleep.

The next morning he awakened in the same position, confused about his whereabouts. The day came into focus around him as he struggled to his feet, his entire body stiff, wet with dew or rain or both. Everything hurt and he felt awful.

That cheered him immeasurably.

He folded the tarp into a tight triangle, like a flag, and returned it to Wayne, who sat on a five-gallon bucket outside his own tent smoking strenuously.

"Oh, hey, Farley. I wanted to tell you, man. There's a pretty good army navy surplus store on MLK. They've got, like, a consignment cellar. You can get used camping gear there if you can scrape together a few bucks, man."

Farley thanked him and limped away to find breakfast. He found a coffee shop a few blocks away where he used the bathroom and fed himself before returning to his building. Once again he found himself standing on the sidewalk in front of it, looking up, unable to persuade himself to go inside. People came and went around him. They passed him by, parted around him like the current around a piling, but he did not move.

He could not move.

After a while he left. All day he walked and walked and walked. Each step ripped through his central nervous system like a fire alarm, each step like triggering a landmine, his waterproof pack of sins bearing down on his disintegrating muscles and tendons.

Before it closed for the day, he bought an old military bivouac tent and used sleeping bag at the army navy store Wayne had told him about. The ancient tent was made of canvas and weighed more than it should. The sleeping bag smelled like something had died in it. It felt aspirational. He would use his pack for a pillow because he only planned to sleep in the camp for another night or two. Just until he felt like he'd punished himself enough.

But how much was enough? What amount of punishment would be sufficient? How long would he force himself to suffer? And what would it take to forgive himself?

He did not know if he could.

He did not know if he wanted to.

8

A BOOMERANG THAT DOESN'T COME BACK

Wayne stopped by on Farley's fourth night in the camp to see how he was getting by and found him sitting on a milk crate in the rain, eating a slice of pizza, hood up against the drizzle.

"Wait 'til it rains for real. By November you'll have enough mold growing on all your stuff for a salad bar to go with that pizza."

Farley pulled his hood down and slid the pizza box toward him. Wayne lit up.

"For real? OK, man. Thank you. Let me get a chair."

Farley had seen him making the rounds like the camp's unofficial mayor, checking on the others, welcoming new arrivals, trying out new jokes. He'd also seen him stand alone at its edges for long fugues, rapt in conversation with someone who was not actually there—or someone only Wayne could see. Whatever mental illness he suffered, from the outside it *looked* like suffering. He looked haunted. Farley could empathize.

Wayne returned with his bucket and grabbed a slice from the box.

"Lemme ask you something," he said. "Why don't fish make good hockey players?"

Wayne's jokes reminded him of Wilson Mequssuk. Wilson reminded him of Nanuqmiut. Nanuqmiut reminded him of everything he'd left behind and everything that had happened. Nearly every conversation became a kind of flowchart of grief, funneling him inexorably toward misery, just as every breath racked his body with pain.

"I don't know. Why?"

"Because they're afraid of the net." Wayne laughed wheezily and took a bite of pizza. They ate in silence for a while, a condition that seemed to suit them unequally. Wayne grew increasingly restless with each minute that passed until he could no longer stand it.

"How'd you end up on the streets, Farley?"

"It's a long story."

It's always a long story with your father.

"It always is, man. I bet it has something to do with those scars?"

"More with the ones you can't see."

Wayne eyed the pizza box until Farley nodded and he took another slice.

"How about you?" Farley asked.

"Well that's a long story too." He bit into his pizza and chewed it thoughtfully. "I had a family. A house. A good job. I even married my high school sweetheart, Mary Jo. She was a cheerleader, man. Prom queen. I had it all." Wayne picked something out of his teeth. A piece of crust. A flake of oregano. "Then Kevin started talking to me."

"Kevin?"

"Yeah."

"Who is Kevin?"

"He talks to me sometimes."

"What does he say?"

"At first he just whispered and I couldn't really tell. I wasn't even sure he was real. But his voice got louder. Real loud."

"What did he want?"

"He wanted me to protect my kids."

"From what?"

"Well. From me."

"How?" Farley asked, regretting it before he'd even finished. Wayne shrugged.

"By sending them to heaven," he said as matter-of-factly as if he were describing a toothache or a hangnail. "I didn't want to do it. And I resisted for a long time. For as long as I could. But Kevin kept getting louder and louder, and after a while he was too loud to ignore anymore."

Farley took another slice of rain-damp pizza and chewed it vigorously.

"So I got out of bed quietly, without waking Mary Jo. I walked down the hall to their bedroom. And I tried to crush my youngest boy's windpipe."

Farley stopped chewing, but Wayne bit into a slice of pizza with yellow teeth and pulled it away, stretching out a long, sagging bridge of cheese.

"I didn't let go until his brother got me in the back of the head with an aluminum bat. I was glad he stopped me, man. I loved those kids." He folded the remainder of his slice and popped it into his mouth. "But I was just following orders," he said, his words distorted by the mouthful of food.

"Whose orders?"

"Kevin's."

"OK. Who does Kevin work for?"

Wayne shrugged. "Someone with a higher pay grade, man. Someone who doesn't like to be let down."

Farley nodded. He'd been in the army—he knew about orders, knew that sometimes you had to do what you were told regardless of how you felt about it.

"So what happened?" he asked.

"Courts put me in a psych ward. Mary Jo left and took the kids. I didn't fight it, you know? I didn't want them around me, man. It wasn't safe." After the hospital, he said, he drifted from group homes to shelters to jails. Petty crimes. Crimes of survival. His parole officer kept him in meds and made sure he took them. Met him twice a month with a county-assigned social worker to buy him a warm lunch, feed him pills, assess his mental state. "My boys," he said. "They're doing good now. I can't talk to them and the courts won't let me even know where they are, but that's OK. Teddy—he's my PO—says they're doing good now."

When Wayne's county-mandated care team showed up at the camp a few days later to check on him, he introduced them to Farley. They seemed sincerely fond of Wayne and genuinely concerned about his well-being. Teddy took him aside to chat privately, leaving Farley with the social worker, a tough-looking woman with Slavic features.

"How do you know where to find Wayne?" he asked her.

She did not look up from the folder full of papers she was studying. "Oh, he calls in and lets us know where he's camping."

"He's got a phone?"

"You must be new to the streets," she said. "You can buy disposable cell phones at most drug stores, cheap. Get one. Keep some minutes on it in case you ever need to call for emergency help or anything. Or, you know, if you have family somewhere to talk to. You can charge it at most coffee shops, the library, or the bus station. And do yourself a favor. Stop by one of the shelters as soon as you can. They've all got informational packets to help you survive out here. Help you learn from other people's experience. Like if you have any cash, get rid of it—buy one of those Visa gift cards you see at the grocery store. They're rechargeable. Works just like a debit, but easier to carry, easier to hide."

"Is it true what Wayne told me?" Farley asked. "About his kids?"

"You wouldn't think him capable of it. He's filled with such kindness." She shivered at a chill either imagined or remembered. "Can you imagine spending your whole life in the shadow of your own regret like that? What it must do to you?"

"Yes," Farley said. "I can."

For the first time she looked up from her paperwork to study him. He saw how his answer landed, saw how she took in his size, his scars, as if noticing him for the first time, and did not hold it against her when she stepped away.

Each day more campers arrived. Farley kept a sullen distance from the others, and they from him. Many seemed to know one another, at least in passing. He thought of them collectively as a kind of urban nomadic tribe, wandering the streets for food, cast-off or stolen goods to barter with, someplace to sleep. They gathered in groups not because they were socially inclined but because of the safety a pack provided. Safety from city or transit police who might otherwise roust them. Safety from drunk college kids who might harass or hurt them. Safety from missionaries and advocates who might pester them with offers of salvation. Safety, even, from one another—of the new arrivals, a few were what Farley's mother would have gleefully called "Real Pieces of Shit." One in particular worked hard to distinguish himself as such from the moment he appeared with his foul-tempered pit bull in tow. Younger than Farley but no longer young, he wore an oily rain slicker with a brown hooded sweatshirt camouflaged against the rain-streaked tents. Beneath the hood, his tattooed face looked angular and mean. Sores pocked his cheeks and forehead. He made no efforts to hide his drug dealing. He bullied other campers, threatened people who walked past the tents on their way to dinner or work or the bus shelter, and drew unwanted attention to the camp. Sometimes he'd disappear for a few hours and return with a shopping cart full of things he'd stolen, which put all the other campers at risk.

One evening, while Farley was sharing a couple of sandwiches he'd brought home with Wayne, the new arrival appeared behind another camper's tent, dropped his pants, and squatted onto the sidewalk right out in the open.

Farley nodded in his direction. "Who's the new asshole?"

Wayne looked over and winced. "That's The Ferryman."

"The *Ferryman*?"

"That's what he calls himself. It's his street name, man."

"What a douchebag."

"He's bad, Farley. Bad." Looking troubled, Wayne squinted like he had more to share but said nothing while they watched The Ferryman finish his business and wipe his ass with the other camper's rain fly. When he saw them watching, he glared defiantly their way as he pulled up his pants and buckled his belt.

"Oh, hey, that reminds me—let me ask you something, Farley. What's brown and sticky?"

"No, Wayne," he said, but already Wayne wheezed with laughter.

"A stick, man. A stick. Get it?"

By late September the rain had begun in earnest and showed no sign of letting up, the wet season an oppression that would last until the Rose Festival the following June signaled the beginning of summer. The cheap sleeping bag Farley had bought was rated for fifty degrees; from his military training he remembered that the rating signified the temperature at which the bag would keep him *alive*, not *comfortable*. It blocked some of the cold but not most of it. The tent canvas blocked some of the rain but not all of it. Neither blocked any of the city noise that kept him always on edge, always irritated. Each night he lay in the shadow of an apartment for which he was paying rent. Each morning he awakened from a sleep tormented by dreams of bears. Each night he lay back down on the hard sidewalk in his bivvy and huddled against the weather. Each day he wandered far and wide across the city, seeking . . . something.

He did not know what. Not exactly. He wandered without destination, but not without purpose—the walking *was* the purpose.

So was the pain.

"Where do you go every day, man?" Wayne asked one morning as Farley packed his gear. He carried it with him in case the camp got rousted in his absence. They could have his bivvy, they could have his tent, but his pack held the only things he still owned in this world, such as they were. Besides, carrying the extra weight made each minute of the day hurt that much more.

"Just going for a walk."

Wayne nodded thoughtfully, considering what he'd said. "Lemme ask you something, man. What do you call a fly without wings?"

Farley shrugged, or tried to, already bent by the weight of his pack.

Wayne's persistent joy felt like an anomaly in a camp otherwise governed by a fear both tangible and taut. Living on the streets meant living with the near-constant anxiety of being exposed to the elements, to society's pretenses and expectations and judgments. Though The Ferryman's malignant presence engendered a new tension among its residents, a different kind of fear, even, most of them kept their heads down and their mouths more or less shut. They greeted one another, polite but disengaged, standoffish, their detachment both a precaution against the risk and the accumulation of their preoccupation with the more pervasive, existential fear of trying to stay alive. Finding food and keeping warm was an exhausting and relentless task. Only Wayne seemed to embrace those around him as a true community.

"A walk," Wayne said.

"What?"

"A fly without wings is a walk, man."

Farley saw how people who passed the camp were both afraid and scornful of its residents, rendering them at once threatened and a threat. The campers, like the rest of the homeless throughout the city, lived not just outside but outside of society. Most were just trying to survive. He lived among them without assimilating. Each of them had a story, he knew, each a particular stanchion that had folded, collapsing a bridge that plummeted them into this river of desperation. Though his own misery paralleled theirs, he did not feel the desperation—at any moment he could end this farce and move into the heated apartment he'd already paid for. He lived among them, but he lived apart from them too because he did not fear the other campers, he did not fear discomfort or pain, and he did not fear for his life.

He'd already survived.

And the truth was, he thought survival might be overrated.

9

ANY QUESTIONS SO FAR?

Though a small city in terms of population, Portland nonetheless occupies a great deal of physical space. Sprawling one hundred and forty-five square miles across the Willamette River, which bisects it, the city itself is divided into quadrants, each of which is in turn divided into neighborhoods. Each neighborhood manifests its own personality: industrial, artsy, boutique, professional, poor. Farley walked them all, wondering about the lives of the people he saw in them, wondering what gave them purpose. How did they find meaning in this existence? How would they cope if all of it were suddenly taken away? He walked past coffee shops and bars, past antique shops and hardware stores, past sushi dives and strip clubs, past all-night pizza counters and takeout waffle windows.

His only plan, as far as he could articulate it, was to walk himself *back* from the brink of death by walking himself *to* the brink of death.

He'd been back in the city about a month when he found himself slowly winding his way up the twisting road in Washington Park in the northwest quadrant. The urban park climbed steeply through wooded hills, and the hills and their dizzying grades brought a new kind of pain to his broken body. Straining cyclists grunted past him, climbing like wheeled and hairless mountain goats. Goats in Lycra suits that looked painted on. As an endless parade of taxis and rideshares and city buses passed by, the drivers raised their eyebrows at him—he *looked* like he needed a ride—but Farley waved them on, instead leaning into the grade and the agony and walking up and up and up. Slowly, painfully, he wound his way past tennis courts, past the Japanese garden, past an open-air archery range, past rose-framed vistas of the city sprawling east toward Mount Hood speckled with tourists taking panoramic photos of the view. His mother used to call Portland "A Half-Mile City." It looked great from half a mile away, but the closer you got the more readily you saw the grime and graffiti, the boarded-up windows, the torched cars and street beggars and filth.

Struggling for air as he neared the summit, blind with the despair of his limbs and muscles, as the road leveled out at last, Farley found himself in the parking lot of the Oregon Zoo. He hadn't been to the zoo since his mother took him as a kid. Hadn't public sentiment turned against zoos years ago on the shouts of animal activists and environmentalists? How did Portland, a liberal bastion that had outlawed plastic grocery bags and drinking straws while decriminalizing drug use, reconcile a zoo? In possession of both an empty stomach and a full bladder, he paid the entrance fee as a uniformed security guard watched overly close and, ticket in hand, walked through the gates.

Once inside, he bought a few hot dogs at the commissary and wandered until he found an empty park bench in front of an empty exhibit. When he unshouldered his pack and sat, leaning his cane against the bench, it felt liberating in a way that made him think he might never get to his feet again. They could build a cage around him and charge admission if they wanted, but he lived there now.

He regretted that choice almost immediately when he realized that, of all the exhibits in the zoo, he'd found his way to the polar bears. The bears weren't out, so he ate his hot dogs and stared at the empty habitat. Designed to look like the Arctic, with fake ice pack above a large swimming tank, it all felt familiar in a synthetic way. A cave-like tunnel wrapped around the tank so visitors could watch the bears swim from behind plexiglass, but he didn't want to see them in water. If he was going to have to face those fuckers again, he wanted to see them on land.

Before he finished his hot dogs, a small tour group arrived led by a guide with a microphone and a tiny speaker strapped to her belt. Wearing a Columbia raincoat and knee-high rainboots with brightly colored animals on them, she put her back to the fence and began her lecture.

"Unlike brown bears, black bears, panda bears, or koala bears—which aren't really bears at all—polar bears are marine mammals. Does anyone know why?"

She looked around the group expectantly, but no hands went up.

"Because they spend so much time on the sea ice," she said, undaunted. "They're also excellent swimmers. They can maintain speeds of six miles per hour in the water. That's about as fast as the fastest human swimmers. But even Olympians can only maintain those speeds for short periods. Polar bears can swim for days. They can swim underwater for as long as three minutes. They have webbed feet and a layer of fat four inches thick that both keeps them warm and keeps them afloat in the icy water."

As he listened to the guide speak about the bears with such reverence—to her they were objects of science, marvels of nature—Farley felt the anger growing inside him.

"Here's a bit of trivia for you," she said. "Cow's milk is about three-point-five percent fat, but polar bear milk is about *thirty-one percent* fat. That's how the mothers are able to keep their cubs warm and help them grow so quickly."

She looked around the group, which still looked bored.

"Any questions so far?"

No hands.

"OK, let's continue. Bears are sexually dimorphic. Does anyone know what that means?"

Finally a hand went up, confident, sure. The guide pointed at a middle-aged man in a leather jacket sodden with rain, his enthusiasm evident.

"It means they have he-she bears. Like, hermaphrodites."

Her face puckered involuntarily, like she'd bitten into a strawberry expecting sweetness but instead it tasted like bitter rhubarb.

"No. No, that's . . . no."

"Or, like, they go both ways?"

The guide stared at the man, doing whatever mental yoga necessary to bring her smile back to her face.

"'Sexually dimorphic' means females and males of a species show different characteristics," she said finally. "Like humans. Male polar bears can average nearly a thousand pounds in the wild, and females about half that. But that's just the average. Individual bears can actually get much bigger. Males can weigh as much as fifteen hundred pounds—as much as a smart car. And the largest one ever recorded stood more than eleven feet tall on his hind legs."

The ones that came for Abril and John had been males, Farley thought. They must have been. He'd never seen anything so big. Legs thick as oaks, snouts like cast iron. When the bear grabbed him, it felt like getting hit by a train.

"Polar bears follow something called Allen's rule," the guide said, "which states that cold-climate animals adapt with shorter limbs and appendages than warm-climate animals. Their paws are covered with dermal bumps called *papillae*. Like treads on bike tires. Those bumps give the bears traction when walking on ice." She mimed a bear walking, shoulders arched, legs spread apart. "They have two layers of coat, underfur and guard hairs, which, along with those four inches of fat I mentioned, do such an efficient job insulating them that they're more or less invisible to infrared sensors. Pretty cool, huh?"

He'd been somewhat immunized to the presence of bears fairly quickly upon his arrival in the Arctic, though not until the initial shock of seeing them in the wild wore off. They wandered Nanuqmiut like stray dogs, coming and going with both regularity and impunity. The oil company had put him through a two-day training on Arctic survival to earn an NSTC cert needed to travel without an escort on the North Slope. Most of the certification was safety and hazmat-related, but one of the six sections of training had been devoted to the Arctic environment. Carry Arctic-rated gear at all times. Maintain high situational awareness—what they'd called "head on a swivel" in the army. Both brown bears and polar bears roamed the Slope, and if you worked there, you learned to watch for them. The oil companies used thermal imaging to detect them, and employed bear guards trained in a hierarchy of nonlethal discouragement methods—flares, noisemakers, bean bags—on patrol. When "nonlethal discouragement" failed, they shot problem bears.

The Iñupiat relationship with bears was more confusing; it seemed to vary with the context. Culturally, they gave the animals a mystical history and role in their lore but, at the same time, saw them as food.

"Polar bears are apex predators, perfectly adapted to hunting their prey," the guide told her group. "They have forty-two teeth—the same amount as dogs, but ten more than you or me—and deeply scooped claws that make it easier to dig through ice to get to seals."

Finally, the audience looked interested. Nothing like bloodlust to pique curiosity. A hand went up. The guide pointed at a boy not much older than Abril would have been.

"Do polar bears eat people?" he asked, somewhat predictably. Farley reached for the scars on his face, which had begun to burn.

"Well, that's a good question. The short answer is yes, they do."

A collective gasp rose from the group.

"Most species of bears have attacked humans on occasion, but for different reasons. Brown bears—you might think of them as grizzly bears, though there are other kinds of brown bears as well—attack humans only when startled. If you surprise one in the woods, for example. Or when it's eating something it's killed. But polar bears? They're *stealth* hunters. That means they sneak up on their prey. So most humans attacked by polar bears aren't even aware of the bears' presence until it's too late."

Farley's legs had begun to ache too, and he found himself clenching his muscles so tightly that the bench rattled against the ground beneath him.

"*Brown* bears rarely eat humans. They maul them and flee. But when a *polar* bear kills a human in the wild, it *will* eat them. That's just its nature. And nature is a powerful thing."

One of the kids in the group pointed at the habitat. The bears had arrived. The voices of the crowd rose as everyone rushed past the guide to get close to the fenced-in enclosure. Farley didn't get up, didn't move from his seat. He didn't move at all. In fact, he found himself somewhat paralyzed.

Not by fear. By something else.

Slowly the bears came into view. From his bench, he caught glimpses of them through the crowd. The two zoo bears did not look like the same species the guide had just described. These bears did not look dangerous or fierce; these bears did not look like apex predators. They looked lazy. Ignoble. Jolly. Fat. They rolled into the pool, played with beach balls, chased each other playfully around the habitat. These bears looked domesticated, their coats yellowed with age, nearly green, almost unrecognizable from the bears that had changed his life irreparably.

"Algae growing in the guard hairs causes the discoloration," the guide explained. "That's a side effect of the warmer temperatures here in Portland as a result of climate change."

The crowd clearly loved the zoo bears, but Farley hated them. He hated every bear in existence, polar, brown, black, and otherwise—even koalas, which weren't even bears. He hated every bear seen and unseen, known and imagined, hated every single goddamned bear in existence because of the actions of two of them. He wasn't naive—he knew they had not acted out of malice or intent, but out of hunger, instinct, nature—so he hated nature too, hated it for designing bears that way and hated the world for accommodating them. He hated humanity for causing the climate to shrink the sea ice and force the bears onto land to seek new avenues of food. He hated the oil company that had employed him for profiting off the land and contributing to climate change.

But most of all he hated himself for not stopping the attack. He hated himself for being here to remember it when Abril was not. He hated himself because all he could do was sit there on his bench staring at those yellowed bears with mustard on his lips, seething in all his impotent and pathetic hatred as the crowd cheered and laughed and pointed.

10

A PILE OF TATTOOED PAPER
AND DIRTY RAGS

One of the zoo's giraffes needed an impacted molar removed, and since the procedure required an entire team of people, Lissa got pulled in to assist. She did not often get to help with such procedures. Her usual assignments more often involved collecting massive stool samples, monitoring skin infections, or restraining animals during vitamin shots or blood draws. Excited to participate in something new with one of the more exotic animals, she rushed over to the Africa habitat and made herself available.

Once the animal—a male Masai named Nolari—had been anesthetized, the senior vet called Lissa over to hold the animal's tongue while she reached in past it with a gooseneck inspection camera and light. The thick and purple tongue stretched the length of her forearm and shimmered weirdly as the bright light passed over it.

"Why is it purple?"

"To protect it from the sun." The vet was a woman not much older than Lissa but effortlessly confident, with a dimpled chin and blue eyes, her voice muffled by her proximity to the animal's gaping mouth.

"So it's a vestigial feature here in Portland?" Lissa said. The vet laughed and looked at her as if wondering who she was, though they'd worked together for three years.

"Feels that way lately, doesn't it? The rain is more oppressive this year than usual."

"Why is it so slimy?"

"The rain?"

"The tongue."

"Good observation. Gelatinous saliva. It keeps the tongue from getting scratched by thorns when they eat in the wild."

"That's . . ." Lissa started, unsure how to finish. What was it, exactly? What word would impress the vet?

"Cool?"

"Yes! It's cool."

"Yes. It is." The vet smiled at her before sticking her head back inside the giraffe's glimmering mouth, and it was the closest thing to the sun she'd seen in weeks.

———

Brimming with excitement, Lissa told Olive about the procedure on the bus ride home that evening. "Giraffes have the same number of teeth as humans—thirty-two—but they're arranged differently," she said. "There's no top teeth, just dental pads. Big flat things. Because they don't use their front teeth to chew like we do. They use them to comb leaves from branches. They chew with their molars, which are concentrated in the back." She pulled her mouth open like she was landing a fish and pointed to her own molars. "These teeth," she said, her words slurred and muffled by her fingers.

"Gross, Mom."

"It's not gross. It's . . . cool. It's how they eat."

"Not them. *You*. Putting your hands in your mouth on a public bus is gross."

Lissa looked around at the filthy seats and handrails, the rain-soaked passengers, the trash littered around the cabin. Conceding her daughter's point, she pulled hand sanitizer out of her purse.

"Did you know that giraffes give birth standing up? The calves can drop as far as five feet. That's higher than you are tall."

"*That's* cool," Olive said approvingly. Rubbing her hands vigorously,

Lissa flushed in a way that made her feel needy and wondered if her daughter's approval would always matter so much to her. Or everybody's approval.

As the bus neared home, she saw the sprawl of the homeless camp come into sight like a dystopian Oz.

"Put your hat on and get ready to run," she said. "Our stop is coming up."

"I know, Mom."

"Maybe we'll get burritos for dinner."

"We had burritos *last* week."

"We also had ice cream for dessert last week, so I guess that's out too?"

Olive rolled her eyes. She could be infuriating, Lissa thought, zipping her raincoat. She struggled with the elastic to adjust the hood, which had a tendency to fall forward over her eyes. The bus pulled to the curb at the corner before the stop, avoiding the camp entirely. Despite their height disparity, she had to walk quickly to keep pace with Olive, who ran down the aisle and out the doors into the rain. Rushing to follow, Lissa stepped off the bus into a puddle deep enough to fill her boots.

"Damn it."

But Olive didn't stop. She walked quickly along the sidewalk by the curb, deftly navigating the obstacle course of the homeless camp as she weaved her way around shopping carts, torn suitcases full of junk, a teetering stack of pallets. Lissa hurried to catch up, wet feet squishing in her boots with each miserable step.

When they neared the corner, Olive veered to push the crosswalk button. Before she could reach it, a bull-headed Staffordshire mix with legs thick as Lissa's own leapt out from behind a tent, barking ferociously. Lissa had seen the dog from her window, threatening passing cars and frightening pedestrians. As it lunged, Olive froze in terror, little arms frozen at awkward angles like broken wings. She'd been bitten by a friend's Vizsla at age two, punishment for the high crime of trying to pet it while it ate. Lissa understood the animal's instinct but found it heartbreaking too, a noble beast reduced to defending a Tupperware of machine-processed kibble from a toddler. Olive had gone white as bone when she saw her own blood pooling on her hand, and now Lissa watched that fear resurface in her daughter's wide eyes and stepped in front of her.

That only annoyed the dog, which barked louder and more fiercely. The barking cut at her like a scythe. When the dog lunged again, so did she, her maternal instinct putting her at risk to protect her daughter. She saw that the dog was tied to a sign pole with a length of filthy rope, the end of which it had not yet reached, and snatched Olive away by her backpack.

The dog lunged closer still, slobber pooling on its thick snout.

"The fuck you doing to Smoke?"

She hadn't seen the man and it took her a moment to register him. His black eyes bored into her so intently she could almost feel his stare. Even with his tattoos buried beneath rain gear, she recognized him from the index of the camp's residents she'd begun to keep. She'd called him The Asshole for the way he seemed to bully others. He waved a baseball bat whose metal surface was pocked like his skin.

"The fuck you doing to my dog? Huh?"

Without waiting for her to answer, he swung the bat, connecting hard with the sign pole. The dissonance of metal on metal blurred with the bone hum of the dog's barks, nauseating her.

"I see you up there watching." He pointed the bat at her windows like Babe Ruth calling his home run. "You like to watch me, bitch?"

He stepped closer still, pure menace. Lissa backed away—a flinch, really—just as Olive came up behind her and they collided. Too late, she turned to grab her daughter and watched her fall backward into the street. Olive landed face up in a puddle slick with oil, where she lay like a fallen angel amid the floating condoms, candy wrappers, and cigarette butts.

Lissa heard the horn, looked up to see a truck bearing down on them, and had time only to scream. The wall of water hit her like a fist, cold and dark and sudden. Water entered her open mouth and nostrils, forcing itself into her eyes and ears. It worked its way down the collar of her coat and chilled her instantly. For a single, terrifying moment, she could not see, the world sodden and out of focus, chaotic.

Then the wave crested and subsided. The truck was gone. In its place stood the biggest man she'd ever seen. He held Olive in his arms, water pouring off them both.

"Olive!" Lissa's voice fought its way out of her throat like an escaping animal, finding a measure of strength when it saw the light of day. "Let her go! Let go of my daughter!"

The man held Olive out at arm's length, presenting her to Lissa.

"Take her home," he said, his voice deep and loud and rough. "Dry her off. She'll be fine."

Olive felt cold and wet and deadweight heavy in Lissa's arms. Her limbs hung limply at her sides, her blue lips trembling with shock or fear or both.

Relieved of his burden, the man stepped onto the sidewalk and brushed past Lissa toward the outraged dog. Sensing something on him, or scenting it, the dog stopped barking and whimpered, backing down with its ears flat against its head and its stub tail tucked.

"The fuck you do to my dog? The fuck you do to Smoke?"

Lissa couldn't track what happened next because of the speed and her angle of view. The big man said nothing but took another step toward The Asshole, dwarfing him. The Asshole swung the bat and she heard a dull thud. Then, as if he weighed nothing, she saw the big man lift him like a pile of tattooed paper and dirty rags and throw him through the bus shelter wall.

The glass splintered into a million pieces that fell to the wet ground like rain.

The big man turned back to her. She saw the scars across his face, the one milky eye, the other dark as a bruise.

"Go," he said. "Now. Go."

11

YOU WERE LOOKING AT MY SCARS

Lissa called in sick to work for the rest of the week to stay home with Olive. Though she watched her daughter closely for signs of lingering trauma, she showed no adverse effects—not outwardly, at least—and even seemed to enjoy the idea of a minivacation with Mom. They ate boxes of Kraft macaroni and cheese, frozen burritos, sleeves of canned tuna. Olive spent hours in front of her favorite cartoons while Lissa watched out the window as the Portland Police Department, the transit police, and volunteers from a housing advocacy nonprofit cleared the homeless camp.

When she called the police the night of the attack, the dispatcher told her the camp was scheduled to be cleared that week anyway. "It's part of the mayor's broader initiative to sweep the camps in more visible public locations in an effort to encourage the under-homed to seek out shelters and other sanctioned locations," she said.

"I don't care why you do it," Lissa told her. "Just get them off my goddamned street."

The effort took some doing. The crews closed the bus stop temporarily and brought in a dumpster that filled quickly with bags of trash and human waste. Under supervision, the campers packed up their gear and left with their carts to find somewhere else to haunt. Lissa hadn't noticed it right away, but a truck from the Multnomah County Animal Welfare Department had also joined the fray, collaring and removing campers' dogs.

She did not see the giant but wished she'd had a chance to thank him. She would keep an eye out for him. Even in a city the size of Portland, it couldn't be easy to hide someone as distinctive as him. Nor did she see The Asshole—at least, not at first. After the garbage trucks and the social workers and housing advocates had left, after the last police car had turned off its lights and pulled away from the bus shelter, after the sidewalk had been cleared completely and pedestrians reappeared for the first time in months, she watched mindlessly from her window until one of them stopped, turned, and stared directly up at her from across the street.

She jumped in her seat.

You.

He lifted a hand and pointed at her. Then he dragged a finger across his tattooed throat. Lissa quickly pulled down her shade.

"Fuck you," she said.

"What'd you say, Mom?" Olive said, looking up from the TV.

"Nothing, honey. Go back to your show."

After the weekend she hired a babysitter to pick Olive up at school for a few days and bring her home rather than sending her to after-school care. Lissa couldn't really afford the luxury, but it let her get back to work without having to rush off. Having missed a few days at the zoo, she expected to be punished, and having time for extra credit might help.

On her first day back, she held Olive's hand tightly at the bus stop as the rain fell around them. Though the glass shelter had yet to be repaired, a TriMet crew had swept up the broken pieces and taped the edges. Lissa shuddered, wondering what had caused the stains that lingered on the sidewalk where the camp used to be. She'd never been so grateful to step onto a filthy bus.

When she arrived at work an hour later and saw the assignment board, all her fears about punishment were confirmed. With resolve, she passed the morning collecting fecal samples in an unpleasant blur of fur and shit and paperwork. For the first time she could remember, she didn't need to leave for lunch. The rain had stopped so she grabbed her sandwich and set out to eat outside in the zoo.

Though the elephants were her favorite animals, they weren't out that day. Lissa sat on a wet park bench in front of their empty enclosure, eating her tuna and mustard on a hard roll. When she stood and brushed the crumbs from her lap, a handful of juncos alighted on the ground to peck at them. Why would a bird with the power of flight choose to spend its days at a zoo, she wondered? Maybe just to taunt the caged animals with its own freedom. Maybe as a show of solidarity—*chins up, comrades, your free brothers and sisters are working on a liberation plan.*

As she walked back to the medical building, Lissa saw a crowd gathered around the marine mammal habitat for the seal and sea lion show. To avoid it, she cut through the polar bear exhibit, empty except for a single person. He stood alone in front of the plexiglass, staring into the habitat, and to her surprise she recognized him immediately.

The giant.

She would get to thank him after all. But as she got closer, she had second thoughts. He stood quietly, staring in at Tasul and Conrad, the playful resident bears, with a look of such contempt that it frightened her. Who could hate the bears?

He'd saved her daughter's life. She wanted to return the favor, wanted to pay him back for what he had done. But what did she actually know about him? Did she really want to invite some kind of relationship with a filthy, homeless giant who had shown no hesitation to become violent? Second-guessing herself, she studied him from afar. He wore the same dark clothes, dirty from the street, leaning on his cane as he stared into the enclosure. The bears ignored him completely despite the intensity of his glare, swimming in their pool, rolling around on the rocks, flipping over the truck tire given to them as a toy.

She watched until the end of her lunch break. During that time, he did not move even once. As far as she could tell, he did not blink. He did not seem even to breathe.

When she left, his expression still had not changed.

Maybe it was best not to thank him. Maybe it was best just to keep her distance entirely. She walked back to work without saying anything at all, leaving him to glare at the bears in peace.

The rest of her day passed as a blur of blood samples and teeth cleanings. Her mood had been diminishing steadily since lunch, and though she wanted to blame the giant and his dour aura, she knew it was her own cowardice about talking to him that rankled her.

Though she'd intended to work late, when the zoo closed at six she all but sprinted across the grounds to catch the bus home. Worried she would not find a seat, she took a shortcut she knew behind the condor exhibit to beat the crowd gathering at the bus stop. She had the sitter and did not need to be back at any given time, but the worry had become muscle memory, repeated each day as she faced the prospect of being late to gather Olive from after-school care. Late parents accrued additional fees—fees she could not afford. Forty-five bucks for fifteen minutes, enough to make her wonder whether the fines were meant to discourage tardiness or raise revenue.

When the bus pulled up, she filed aboard with the others and got the last empty row to herself. The doors closed and the bus lurched forward. Then it stopped immediately. The doors opened again with a hiss to let one more passenger aboard. The bus dipped as he boarded. He filled the aisle, ducking to keep his head from hitting the curved metal ceiling. As he made his way toward the back, clutching his cane, lurching with a painful-looking limp, he saw the empty spot beside her and groaned himself into it without making eye contact or acknowledging her at all.

Lissa did not necessarily believe in signs. Still, it seemed she'd been given a second chance to thank him. She would not miss another opportunity.

But before she could say anything—before she could even say hello—he crossed his arms around his cane, slumped in the seat, and closed his eyes.

Why was he even on her bus? Did he not know the camp had been rousted? Maybe he would step off at her stop only to be surprised to find the sidewalks cleared, the tent city gone. She decided he'd probably set up a new campsite nearby, on the same bus line; he didn't look like he could walk very far. She tried to muster the courage to speak to him as the bus made its way through the park toward Route 26. Why was it so difficult? This man had saved Olive's life. Maybe hers too. His size, his scars, his living situation—none of that mattered.

Say something.

Overcoming her nerves, she took a deep breath and turned to him to speak.

At that exact moment he began to snore. His chest filled with air, his expanding body threatening to push her against the bus window. Each breath arrived as a long, deep rumble, thunder rolling in over the horizon; each breath left as a quack, a ridiculous, comical flutter of lips loud enough to scare birds into flight.

She put her hand to her mouth to prevent her laughter and studied the man with curiosity. Up close he was even bigger than she'd thought, with ears the size of her hands, a broad chin, shoulders like the headboard of Olive's bed. He smelled like sweat and car exhaust and rain. She studied his scars, thick parallel lines that raked one entire side of his face, including the eye, raised above the skin and shining and red enough to look new. The eye itself was white. Milky.

It was also open, staring at her. She sat back against the window, startled.

"I'm sorry. I didn't mean to stare."

"You were looking at my scars."

Lissa nodded.

"It's hard to see anything else."

"No . . ." Lissa trailed off; to finish would be to lie. "Can I ask about them? How . . . how you got them?"

He returned her stare for a long moment.

"No," he said, and closed his eyes once more.

Having missed her opportunity a second time, Lissa decided she would not say anything else. She felt rebuked—either he did not recognize her or he did not want to talk, or both, and she would honor his wish. At least for the duration of the trip.

But as the bus approached her neighborhood, she panicked anew. To get up from her seat, she would have to wake him. She cleared her throat like a cat with a hairball as her stop neared but her efforts yielded no response. The man sat perfectly still.

"Excuse me?"

She tapped him on the arm. He did not rouse, asleep and oblivious to her escalating panic.

Lissa put a hand on his arm. She'd always been aware of her own legs—not ashamed, exactly, but aware of them, of their thickness, the meatiness of her thighs and calves. In sixth grade a misguided gym teacher with a shoeshine-brush flattop and formaldehyde breath had bestowed her with a lifetime of mild self-consciousness by referring to her as "Thunder Thighs," a nickname that her high school boyfriend—Olive's father—latched on to in a way she would have held against him if it weren't buried deep on a long list of emotional transgressions. But at their thickest, her legs were thinner than the man's arm. She squeezed it gently.

Nothing.

She shook it as politely as she could. Still no response.

As the bus braked at her stop, Lissa knew she would have to take the only recourse still available to her—she would have to climb over the man's prodigious lap. Complicating matters, he'd jammed his long legs against the seat back in front of him to fit in the tight seat, with the cane between them. They arched high off the ground, a potentially insurmountable obstacle between her and the aisle.

She looked up, saw the driver watching impatiently, and got to her feet. Facing the back of the bus and holding the overhead rail for support, she pivoted, lifted one leg as high as she could, and stepped carefully over him. But even when she stretched her toes, on pointe like a ballerina, she could not reach the floor on the other side of his legs. Now all the eyes of the other passengers were upon her, the driver watching in her rearview mirror with train-wreck curiosity. Lissa was an unqualified gymnast hung up on the Olympics vault, and the judges awaited her next move.

Still holding the rail with one hand, she grabbed her work bag from her seat with the other and tried to pass it between herself and the man and into the aisle. But its weight threw her off-balance, and for a long moment she teetered and swayed, knowing she would fall. She contemplated retreat. But there was no going back. Instead she went all in, pushing off with her inside leg and leaping over the man's lap onto her other foot.

For a few perilous seconds, her fate—like her body—could go either way. Then, to her relief, her foot touched the aisle floor.

But now she found herself with two new problems: the first being that she was straddling the giant, holding the overhead rail as a bus full of people watched; the second being that he was now wide awake and staring at her, his own face just inches from hers.

"Sorry," she said. "It's my stop."

"Mine too. Remember?"

Lissa nodded, embarrassed.

"May I?" he asked.

She nodded again. Putting his hands on either side of her waist—they nearly encircled her like a belt—he lifted her without any hint of effort and set her down gently in the aisle. Some of the other passengers applauded.

Grabbing her bag, an embarrassed Lissa hurried down the aisle. Once outside, she waited for him on the sidewalk. She saw him wince and try to hide it as he stepped off the stairs into the rain. He brushed past her without stopping.

"Hey," she said, following him toward her building. "Hey!"

He approached the door to the lobby, opened it, and stepped inside. She followed him in.

"This is my building," she said.

"Mine too."

"You live in my building?"

"Yes."

"Since when?"

He pushed the button for her floor. "Since I got back to Portland."

"But you were sleeping in that homeless camp. You had a tent there. I watched that camp for weeks. I called the cops on it. I called TriMet. I *studied* that camp. You were there almost the entire time it was."

The doors opened on her floor and they exited together. Despite his limp and broken gait, he walked quickly with long, pained strides, and Lissa hurried to keep pace. Then he astonished her again by stopping in front of her apartment.

"This is my apartment."

"Congratulations." His voice heavy with annoyance, he turned and opened the door across the hall.

"You live *across the hall* from me?"

"Is there something you want?" His manner brusque, impatient, she saw in his eyes that he just wanted to be left alone.

But she could not let it go.

"I thought you were homeless," she said. "You lived *in a homeless camp*."

He looked at her and she felt the ferocity of his gaze, recognized the pain in his eyes.

"Just tell me this," she said. "Why would you sleep in a homeless camp if you're not homeless?"

The man ducked his head to fit through the doorway and turned, awkwardly, to face her. Taking a deep breath, he shut his eyes and rolled his head around until his neck cracked. With a long, slow sound, he released his breath again.

He opened his eyes.

He shut the door.

12

THE ASSHOLE LIVING IN CAPTIVITY

Farley walked all the next morning. Whether the miles he had been forcing upon himself over the past weeks were making his injuries better or worse, he could not tell, but with each day he felt stronger on his feet, more comfortable with the realignment of muscle, tendon, and bone, more confident in the tectonic shift that had devastated his body. Still it hurt—the pain a song he sang himself, with each verse adding more voices, a richer instrumentation, a faster backbeat—but now, at least, he recognized the melody.

He'd been walking without really paying attention, but that afternoon, to his surprise, he found himself back on the hill at Washington Park and made his way once more toward the zoo. At the gate, he paid and bought himself lunch—burritos instead of hot dogs, a side salad that felt like it had been taken from one of the animal exhibits—and took his seat in front of the bears. All afternoon he glared into their enclosure until he heard the announcement over the loudspeakers that the zoo would be closing soon.

When he got to his feet to leave, it took some effort, his body slow to respond, on the verge of betrayal. But it did not fold beneath him, and one tentative step at a time he made his way toward the exit.

As he passed the Steller Cove exhibit in the Pacific Shores habitat, a sea lion approached the glass and stared at him with cartoonish saucer eyes. It followed him as he walked, drifting effortlessly without any visible sign of effort or propulsion. Farley stopped and stood close to the glass. The animal approached, floating face-to-face with him, big eyes bright and focused, expression interested, just inches away. Farley cocked his head. The sea lion mimicked him. When he raised a big hand, it did the same, lifting a flipper. He shuffled two steps to the left; it followed. A massive animal—nearly ten feet long and almost two thousand pounds, fat on salmon and pollock—it moved free of the friction and effort that haunted each of Farley's own moves, as if the glass between them were not the wall of a tank but a mirror, the animal on the other side a reflection of another version of Farley himself, a glimpse into another dimension, another possibility. Bubbles escaped its mouth, which curled into what looked like a smile.

"What are you laughing at me for? You're the asshole living in captivity."

"Am I?" it asked.

The sea lion hadn't actually spoken, of course. But that didn't mean it was wrong.

"Is that what you do here every day? Talk to the animals?"

This time the words took a woman's voice. Farley turned to find the woman from his building standing behind him. She wore a raincoat and carried a backpack and looked at him with what might be curiosity but might also be concern.

"Mostly I just listen. Occasionally I ask follow-up questions. What do *you* do here every day?"

"I work here."

He squinted at her for a beat, considering possibilities. "Lion tamer?"

"More like 'crap wrangler.' I'm a vet tech."

Farley nodded but said nothing else, leaving the three of them in a silence that began as awkward, became uncomfortable, and then threatened to turn outright painful. The woman rocked on the heels of her Nikes. Farley stood still and let the fiery pain of his muscles engulf him until his soul felt charred. The sea lion floated, waiting to see what would happen next.

"Can I give you a ride home?" she asked finally.

Farley nodded at the sea lion. "You talking to me or him?"

"You."

"You have a car?"

"No, but I know where we can catch a bus."

"What about him?"

"Can he cover his own fare?"

Farley looked at the sea lion and shrugged. For a moment its expression looked like disappointment, but then it turned to boredom, and with a flick of its tail the animal swam quickly away.

The woman set off in what Farley believed to be the wrong direction. He followed. The effort turned over the engine of pain that ran his body these days and it sprung to life with a roar.

"I know you work here," he said, turning a grunt into words. "But isn't the exit the other way?"

"I want to show you something."

They walked through the Great Northwest exhibit, threading through the crowd past the bobcat, cougar, and mountain goat exhibits. She stopped in front of the California condor cage and Farley squinted to read the plaque.

> *This critically endangered species*
> *has a wingspan of nearly ten feet*
> *and can weigh more*
> *than twenty-five pounds.*

Four or five of the big birds stood around their cage, brooding, severe, and black as soot, with pink-and-yellow heads and gray legs. Their feathers formed a sort of frill around their necks.

"They remind me of my great-aunt Margie," the woman said. "She was big and ugly and mean, and always wore this ridiculous feather boa that she thought made her look glamorous. Also, I think she ate carrion—at least that's what dinner at her house tasted like the one year she hosted Thanksgiving."

"Is this what you wanted to show me?"

"No."

With a conspiratorial grin, she walked around the side of the cage and disappeared behind it beneath an EMPLOYEES ONLY sign. He waited. After a few seconds she reappeared.

"You coming?"

He followed her around the back where the exhibit butted up against a tall metal fence all but buried by brush and the trees of the wooded area behind it. He saw a gate in the fence padlocked shut, with a barely legible NO EXIT sign zip-tied to it, faded and weather-beaten from the sun and rain. She opened the padlock, slipped it from the hasp, and opened the gate.

"The lock is broken. Has been for years. See?"

She clicked it open and closed a few times to demonstrate.

"After you," she said.

Farley stepped through the gate onto an uneven, unused path. She followed him through and closed the gate behind her. The rough path paralleled the fence for a hundred yards and then ended. They emerged from the trees behind a half-dozen dumpsters at the edge of the zoo parking lot near the bus stop.

"Sometimes I like to come and go this way to avoid the crush of the crowds at the main exit," she said. "Don't tell anyone I showed you this, but you can sneak into the zoo without paying for a ticket this way."

He stopped walking and turned to face her. "I can afford a ticket," he said sharply.

"OK. I just . . ."

"What?"

"I wanted to thank you. For saving my daughter."

"You don't owe me anything."

"OK."

"OK."

They stood there in another awkward silence, waiting for the bus.

"Hey," she said finally. "Do you want to come over for dinner tomorrow?"

13

A LONG SHELF LIFE
IS HIGHLY PRIZED

As she set the table with paper napkins, mismatched silverware, and a candle that smelled like a new car, Lissa conceded that her skills for entertaining a dinner guest had rotted on the vine. But the knowledge that, until recently, her dinner guest had been sleeping on the sidewalk gave her confidence that whatever she pulled together would be sufficiently classy. The doorbell rang just as she squeezed the lemon onto the salmon fillet.

"I'll get it," Olive said, running in from the living room. She loved to answer the door or the phone, loved to be the one to push the elevator buttons or control the TV remote, a habit she'd developed young and had yet to grow out of. Lissa put the fish in the oven, set the timer, and refilled her wineglass before following her daughter into the foyer.

Though she'd held Olive in her arms in her first minutes on Earth, a tiny squint of a life still smeared with afterbirth, never had she seen her look as small as she did greeting their neighbor. The enormous man squeezed through their doorway and into their apartment, looking uncomfortable, unsure about being there. When he backed up against the entry wall, he took up as much space as a built-in hutch. Standing with his hands clasped behind his back and something tucked under his arms that Lissa couldn't make out, she saw that he'd dressed for the occasion in a well-worn button-down, clean Carhartts, and work boots that were scuffed but clean. A huge improvement. The scars on his face glistened red and angry as if he'd scrubbed his face vigorously, and he'd combed his hair and beard and shaved his neck scruff.

He looked far more human than she'd thought possible.

"You're big," Olive said, approaching him like the lone protester standing his ground before the advancing Chinese Army tanks at Tiananmen Square.

"I know." His gruff voice sounded woefully out of place in conversation with an eight-year-old.

"Are you a giant?"

"No." He studied her for a moment. "Are you a pip-squeak?"

"No."

"Well all right then. I guess we can be friends."

Lissa saw her daughter smile and it warmed her.

"I'm Olive. That's my mom. Her name is Alissa but nobody calls her that except Grandma."

He nodded solemnly. "What do people call her?"

"Auntie Allie calls her Liss. I just call her Mom. Most people call her Lissa, so you can too." She pointed to the object tucked under his arm. "What's that?"

"It's for your mom."

He held it up for Lissa to see.

"Is that a canned ham?" she asked.

He nodded.

"Wow. OK. Thank you?"

He hung his head for a moment but recovered quickly. "Where I come from it's the next best thing to bringing a freshly killed caribou."

"Where's that?"

"Up north."

"Canada?"

"Further north."

"Well, thank you for not bringing one of *those*."

"Groceries have to be shipped in, and they're expensive, so a long shelf life is highly prized."

"It's thoughtful. Thank you." Lissa smiled. "Please come in," she said a little stupidly since he was already inside. "I just realized I don't know your name."

"It's Farley. Just Farley."

"Farley? Is that a first name or a last name?"

"Yes," he said, and pointed to the glass in her hand. "Is that wine?"

Lissa watched as he tucked into dinner with vigor. She'd made the sockeye with Dijon mustard, balsamic vinegar, and lemon, a delicate dish he ate indelicately, chasing each heaping forkful with another without pause. When he'd devoured the fish—a full pound portion—he moved on to the haricots vert, spearing five or six at a time with his fork and stuffing them into his maw. He ate quickly, as if he'd never eaten before, or not for a long time, and had a terrible hunger to fill.

Olive watched with curious glee. When he'd finished the green beans and then the rice pilaf, she pushed her plate in front of him.

"You can have mine," she said. "I don't really like salmon."

Farley looked at her, then at Lissa.

"You've got leftover mac cheese in the fridge, love. I can throw it in the microwave."

"See, Farley?" Olive said. "It's OK."

He nodded, dropped her plate on top of his own, and returned to eating. Lissa's mother would declare his behavior unspeakably rude, but she found it flattering. Olive ate like a bird—if birds ate nothing but macaroni and cheese, hot dogs, and ice cream. She rarely got to cook for anyone who appreciated a well-executed meal.

When Farley had cleared her plate too, Olive giggled.

"I guess you were hungry," she said.

"Hungry enough to eat my own combat boots. That's what we used to say in the army."

"Gross!"

"That's what army food tasted like too." He looked at Lissa. "This was delicious."

She smiled involuntarily and felt foolish doing so. Needy. She caught Olive staring at her with a big grin of her own.

"You were in the army?"

"Long time ago."

She had a million questions about why he'd been living on the street, about what he'd been through that had left those scars. She assumed a car accident—she couldn't imagine what else could cause that much damage to a man that big. It would also explain why he took the bus or walked everywhere. But now she wondered if his injuries were combat-related. Sometimes a local nonprofit brought groups of veterans to the zoo for private tours, meet and greets with the animals—a kind of therapy for their PTSD, as if petting an ocelot could erase the memories of war. Farley had the same look in his eyes she saw in theirs, as if the sight of whatever horrors they'd seen or committed had been physically burned into their vision. Though her curiosity swelled, she worried that too many questions—or even just a few—would drive him away. He'd been through something and, from what she could tell, was still fighting his way back. Or still deciding whether he wanted to. She told herself he needed kindness more than she needed her curiosity sated.

"Are you from Portland?"

"Originally. I've been away a while."

"How do you like being back?" she asked, embarrassed to be making such small talk but unable to persuade herself to stop.

"It's different. City's changing fast. More crowded. New development." He nodded her way, at her arms, the exposed flesh covered in ink, photorealistic zoo animals. "While I was gone, everyone got tattoos."

"Not me, Farley," Olive said. She rolled up her sleeves to show him her pudgy white arms.

"I see that, Pip-squeak." He turned back to Lissa. "Also the homeless problem has gotten worse."

He must have seen the awkwardness on her face.

"That was a joke," he said.

"Farley?" Olive leaned over her empty place setting to stare up at him. "Do you want to see my room?"

"Oh, love, I don't think our poor guest wants to see your bedroom," Lissa said, swallowing the panic rising in her throat like bile. She didn't know this man at all. She couldn't let him into her eight-year-old's bedroom. In fact, it suddenly felt like a mistake to have invited him into her apartment at all. He'd been sleeping on the street, and she'd seen him throw a grown man as easily as a paper airplane. If he meant them harm, what could she do to stop him?

"Do you want to, Farley?" Olive said, persisting. He shrugged.

"Sure, Pip-squeak."

Olive was on her feet, brimming with excitement, before Lissa could even react. She leaped to her own feet so abruptly that she smashed her legs against the table, rattling the plates and glasses and nearly toppling the wine bottle. She watched his face for some sign of motive but behind the scars he remained inscrutable. He hid a wince as he rose and took a moment to straighten himself out. How much pain did he live with, she wondered?

Olive reached for his hand. He recoiled like he'd been burned. Undaunted, she took his hand a second time and gave him a patient look. Her own hand was so small she could only grab his little finger.

"This way, Farley. Ready?"

When he nodded, she pulled him down the hallway like one of the tugs that towed massive barges up the Columbia River. Grabbing the chef's knife from the kitchen counter, Lissa followed, pulling out her phone in case she needed to call for help.

Olive's bedroom was barely big enough to hold the single bed, her dresser, and her toys. Farley filled it in an almost comical way.

"I feel like an elephant in a phone booth."

Olive giggled and hopped onto her bed.

"Sit with me, Farley."

She still had him by the hand. He glanced at Lissa.

"I'm not sure I should."

"It's OK, Farley. Right, Mom?"

With the knife hidden behind her back, Lissa nodded and then wondered why she had done so, wondered why she kept trusting this man she had scant reason to trust.

"It's not that." Farley's deep voice filled the tiny room like rushing water. "That little bed might splinter into toothpicks if I sit on it."

They all looked at the bed. Like every other girl her age, Olive had been wholeheartedly into Disney's *Frozen*. She'd lost interest almost as soon as Lissa bought her the matching sheets and bedspread, but they were not inexpensive, so Lissa made her keep them anyway.

"You're silly," Olive said.

She patted the bed beside her. Farley lowered himself tentatively onto Olaf's smiling, bucktoothed face. The mattress compressed beneath his weight, the springs groaned, and the slats bowed, but the bed held.

"Will you read me a book?"

Leaning against the doorframe, Lissa watched his expression change, darkening as he pondered his answer, and wondered why.

"Only if it's OK with your mom."

They both looked at her expectantly. She weighed the decision long enough to make the moment awkward.

"Mom?"

"OK. But just for a few minutes." She hoped she did not sound nervous. "Deal?"

"Deal."

"Farley?"

His expression betrayed both a happiness and profound sadness at once, a smile defeated by wet eyes that had seen something from which they had not yet recovered and might never. He nodded. Lissa slipped her phone into her pocket and smiled back at him.

Then the bed slats cracked like thunder and the box spring, mattress, and all its occupants—Olive, Farley, and Olaf—dropped through the frame to the floor.

14

DON'T WAKE HIM UP

Farley hadn't just broken the bed slats—he'd broken the ice too. As Lissa and Olive laughed with a joy that felt both genuine and unbridled, some of the awkwardness that had hung over the evening faded with it. They disassembled the bed and set the box spring and mattress flat on the floor. Farley promised to come back the next day with tools to fix it.

Despite his rough appearance, and despite his edges, Lissa saw that he was good with Olive. Gentle. In fact, she felt comfortable enough to leave them alone for a few minutes to wash the dishes while he read. She was just down the hall and could hear their voices and listened along as they worked their way through *The One and Only Ivan*. It felt good to have company over. It felt good to have Olive connecting emotionally with someone else for a change. There were no union benefits for single parents, no mandated breaks or vacations or collective bargaining agreements, and often "parenting" meant "surviving" and not much more.

"I suppose you think gorillas can't understand you," Farley read, his voice well suited for the caged silverback gorilla who lived at a mall. "Of course, you also probably think we can't walk upright. Try knuckle walking for an hour. You tell me: Which way is more fun?"

Lissa dried the last of the dishes from dinner, poured another glass of wine, and cracked the living room window. She smoked only infrequently and had made such good progress toward quitting completely since Olive asked her to a year ago that they maintained an unspoken détente—Olive knew she sneaked cigarettes but pretended not to, and Lissa kept them to a minimum. Cool air poured through the open window. It felt fresh and good. She could hear the traffic outside, the buzz of urban existence beneath the static of the rain, and she lit her cigarette and leaned out to exhale. Though the camp had been gone for more than a week, out of habit she shifted her gaze to the bus shelter. The glass had been replaced and it reflected the streetlights brightly.

A lone figure leaned against the new shelter glass, staring up at her. Lissa started when she recognized who it was. He yelled something at her. *To* her. Something lost to the ambient sounds of the city. She stuck her head out the window a little more and felt the cool, damp air on her cheeks.

"I see you, bitch," he yelled. "I *see* you. They took my dog away because of you. They took Smoke because of you. Because of *you*. I'm gonna make you pay, bitch."

Lissa mashed her cigarette out in the rain puddled on the windowsill and withdrew her head. All the sounds disappeared when she pulled the window closed. The sudden silence unsettled her. When she closed the blind, he disappeared too, gone at least from her sight. A little shaken, she took a deep breath to shake off the anxiousness and popped an Altoid to mask the smoke on her breath.

Only then did she realize that not only had the street sounds disappeared, but she could no longer hear Farley's voice either. And just like that, her anxiety turned to panic.

Her own bad judgment buckled her knees as she ran down the hall to Olive's room, grabbing her phone and the knife and punching in 911 as she ran. She burst through the open doorway in a panic, knife raised in front of her, phone to her ear, to find Farley flat on his back, occupying the full length of the mattress and then some, his legs hanging well past the edge and onto the floor. Though it did not look even remotely comfortable, he was deeply and obliviously asleep. Olive sat beside him with her back against her pillow and her book open on her lap. She put her finger to her mouth.

"Shhhhh," she said. "Don't wake him up."

They ate pistachio ice cream on the couch and watched Cartoon Network on the small TV. They laughed and giggled together like friends, Lissa thought. Or sisters. Such moments were the reward for all the sacrifice and stress of being a parent. Such moments were increasingly hard to come by. With their legs entwined beneath the afghan Lissa kept on the back of the couch, neither of them mentioned the very big, very strange man sleeping on the tiny bed on the floor of the tiny bedroom down the hall, or how very, very strange it was for him to be there at all. They didn't have to; that they both knew seemed sufficient. The shared knowledge infected their moods with a conspiratorial humor. They laughed at cartoons. They ate Farley's share of the ice cream. And every now and then, when the athletic rumble of his snores reached them even there, on the couch, they'd lock eyes and laugh some more.

After about an hour, he appeared in the hallway looking disheveled and confused. Lissa smiled to save him any embarrassment, but when Olive broke out into good-natured laughter all over again, she found herself unable to resist.

Farley did not laugh. She'd never seen him laugh and wasn't sure he even could. But he smiled, or something like a smile, and it was enough.

"Thank you for dinner. Both of you. I'll come back tomorrow and fix that bed."

"Say good night, Olive," Lissa told her.

"Good night, Olive," she said, still laughing.

Farley nodded.

"Good night," he said. "Pip-squeak."

Lissa stood behind her daughter in front of the bathroom mirror as they brushed their teeth together, a nightly ritual. Olive had an electric toothbrush, pink and white with flowers on it. It thrummed with vigor, filling her mouth with minty foam that spilled over her lips and chin like a goatee.

"Mom!" she said, locking eyes in the mirror, "I forgot," though it sounded like *Bob, I fah-gah.*

"Fah-gah what, love?"

Olive wiped her face on a towel and ran down the hall to her bedroom. She returned with one of her stuffed animals.

"I want to give this to Farley. To borrow."

"Why, love?"

"Because he's alone in his apartment and I don't want him to have to be alone. And because I think he likes this. He kept staring at it while he was reading me my story."

"OK. You can give it to him when he comes to fix the bed."

"No, Mom. I want to give it to him now. So he doesn't have to be alone tonight."

Lissa looked at her watch. He hadn't left that long ago, and really, it wasn't that late.

"OK," she said. "Let's bring it to him."

They crossed the hall and knocked on Farley's door, still giggling with carryover joy from the evening. He answered slowly, surprised, and stared at Lissa for a moment with an expression that made it clear that *his* joy had not carried over.

"What?" He sounded put out.

Lissa looked past him into his apartment and saw . . . nothing. Nothing at all, his walls bare of art or decorations, no furniture, no food or cooking utensils on the counters. Just an apartment as barren as hers had been the day the super showed it to her.

"Love what you've done with the place, man," she said, but he did not laugh.

"What do you want?"

"Olive wanted you to have this." Lissa tried not to sound hurt. When she produced the stuffed polar bear from behind her back, Farley stared at it with something like disgust. "Her name is Nora."

"What?"

"The zoo adopted a polar bear cub back in 2015." Lissa heard her voice sharpening on the hard edge of her disappointment as she spoke. "It built a whole fundraising campaign around her. Lots of merchandise. T-shirts. Hats. Stuffed animals. I brought this home from work for Olive. It's one of her favorites. She said you couldn't stop staring at it while you were reading to her."

She watched his eyes working, the dead white one and the good one both.

"I don't want it," he said.

What was wrong with him that he wouldn't accept a child's gift?

"Olive wants you to have it, Farley."

"I don't want it."

"It's OK, Farley," Olive said. He opened the door wider to look at her, realizing for the first time that she was there with her mother.

"It is?"

"You don't need to be afraid of it. It's just an ordinary bear. Like *you*."

"What do you mean, love?"

"Well, Farley is big. And he looks mean and scary. But he's not. He's not a mean bear. He's an ordinary bear."

Farley looked aggrieved. He studied them for a moment, jaw clenched tight. Then, with obvious reluctance, he took the bear but held it away from his body like a dirty diaper.

"Thanks," he said, more grunt than word. And then, more kindly: "Pip-squeak."

Deep in another room behind him, a phone began to ring. His already pained expression turned hostile.

"Good night, Farley," Lissa said, but he'd already closed the door.

15

JOHN SPENT THE MONEY ON STRIPPERS

Tired from a full night, from the effort to be social, Farley almost did not answer the phone. He could walk twenty miles on broken legs and it would exhaust him less than chatting his way through dinner with friendly neighbors. He decided to push his luck, a decision he instantly regretted.

"You always were a no-good asshole, Farley. I knew it from the first day you waddled into that rat turd of a village."

"Rebecca," he said. "What a nice surprise." Streetlights bathed the cold floor of his apartment through the curtainless window. Not without effort, he lowered himself to it.

"Before John became a preacher, when we still lived in Alabama, he worked for a company that sold things. Did you know that?"

"What things?"

"I don't know, Farley. Who gives a shit?"

Farley lay on his back, inventorying his pain with a list Rebecca was climbing rapidly. She sounded breathless and drunk as her lazy voice competed with the ambient sounds of traffic and rain through the open crack of window.

"One time he went out of state on a business trip and left me home alone. I don't think I'd ever been alone for that long before. Can you imagine that?"

She paused.

"Of course, now I'm alone all the damn time."

Her southern accent sounded like honey on a hot biscuit. Farley pictured her lips as she talked, how she bit the bottom one, the smear of lipstick like red paint on the white picket fence of her incisors, the downturn as she frowned her perpetual dissatisfaction with him and the larger world.

"He stayed at some hotel with the other men from work. The hotel was just off the highway, and it shared a parking lot with a gentlemen's club. Have you ever been to a gentlemen's club, Farley?"

An image of the Great Alaskan Bush Company came to him, the incessantly loud music, the garishly lighted stages.

"Once or twice," he admitted.

She said nothing, either ignoring his answer or waiting for a better one. Could silence be furious? Could it portray emotion?

"But just for the buffet," he clarified.

"You deserve everything that happens to you, Farley, you know that?"

"I'm exhausted, Rebecca. Is this story going somewhere?"

"After a long day meeting with clients, those men that John worked with decided to walk to the gentlemen's club for supper. Not John. His momma raised a good boy; he would never set foot inside such a place. He got room service and stayed in his hotel room watching the baseball game on TV. Later that night, when the other men stumbled back to the hotel, he could hear them laughing and carousing in the hallway like fraternity brothers, and John realized he'd missed out. Not on the dancers—those *loose* women with their hineys bared—but on something else."

Farley cracked a knuckle that echoed throughout his empty apartment, confident that no gentleman had ever gone into a club in search of a "hiney." Without getting up from the floor, he reached over and grabbed the half-empty bottle of Canadian Club whiskey and took a drink.

"What John missed out on was the shared experience. Like soldiers becoming brothers in a foxhole during a war. All of those other men— they now had a common experience that John did not share. And he knew that those men would think that *he* saw himself as better than them, and the distance between all of them and him would only grow. That would put him at a disadvantage at work."

Farley yawned, fighting off a wave of what felt like fatigue but might have been boredom. "So?"

"So the next night, when they all went back to that gentlemen's club, John went with them. They took a table by the stage. He ordered himself a drink and forced himself to watch those ladies flaunting their bits all night."

"A stunning display of self-discipline."

"Shut the fuck up, Farley," Rebecca said, unsteady with drink, "and let me finish my story."

He grunted, admonished.

"By the time they all returned to the hotel in the early hours of the morning, John was drunker than a skunk in a pickle barrel. Absolutely legless. The next morning he awoke with a bad headache, but worse than that, with a growing dread."

"Guilt."

"No. In his efforts to win over his work colleagues, he'd put several rounds of liquor on his credit card, as well as a number of lap dances too. It wasn't until later that he found out that the other men were using their corporate cards. John had been too afraid to use that account for that kind of . . . *entertainment*. So he'd put those charges on his *personal* card instead. *Our* card, Farley. Almost two thousand dollars. Can you imagine that?"

"Two grand worth of whiskey and strippers? I can try."

"John knew that I balanced the checkbook at the end of each month. He knew that I would see that credit card statement. And sure enough, when it came, I saw that charge. I ran straight to him and demanded to know what it was. Oh, I was furious, Farley. We were young, newly married, just starting out, and that kind of money was *real* money. It would take years to pay that off. But John knew that wasn't the part I was going to be most angry about. He didn't know how to tell me that he had spent a couple of thousand hard-earned dollars on something so *seedy*." She paused, and he thought he heard her pouring another drink. "Before I was a preacher's wife, I was a preacher's daughter, Farley. John might have been naive, but he wasn't dumb. I was the best thing that ever happened to him, and he knew it. He knew that lightning doesn't strike twice. And I assure you, Farley, I was lightning."

The way she said it made it easier for Farley to believe her. *Lahtnin'*.

"So?"

"That gentlemen's club was called the Lucky Lady. When I confronted John about those charges, he confessed that he'd been to the Lucky Lady, but he told me it was a casino. Not a gentlemen's club. He told me he'd lost that money gambling. 'I have a problem, Rebecca,' he said to me, 'and I need your help to beat it.' Well, I tell you, Farley, he looked so *sincere* and so *ashamed*, how could I be angry?" She took a sip. "His . . . what do you call it? His *calculus*? It was right. I was still furious about the money, but now I wanted to help him. So we found a Gamblers Anonymous group that met in the church basement and signed him up for those meetings."

"John went to Gamblers Anonymous meetings to avoid telling you that he'd spent a fortune on strippers and booze?"

"Twice a week for a whole year." She sipped whatever she was drinking. "That's love, Farley. True love."

"That's one way to see it."

"What other way is there? The lyin' nearly consumed him. John was a decent man. He hadn't sinned because he wanted to see a bunch of bare-breasted women. He'd sinned to succeed at work—to make reliable pay so we could have a happy life together."

She paused to sip. Farley noticed the sips getting closer together and her words stumbling into one another more quickly.

"Those meetings helped him find his way. Those meetings are what led him to seek advice from a preacher at that church where they met. And that advice led to John becoming a preacher himself."

"When did you find out the truth?"

"Farley," she said, disappointed. "John didn't know it, but the first thing I did when that credit card bill arrived was to call the phone number on the bill. The girl who answered told me in no uncertain terms just what it was that they did there at the Lucky Lady."

"You knew the whole time."

"Of course I knew."

"What made you call?"

"John had never gambled a red cent in his life. It just wasn't in his nature."

Having played against John in more poker games than he could count, Farley knew otherwise—he may not have been any good at gambling, but he enjoyed it—but he knew, too, that John had always kept those games a secret from his wife. A few lies weren't going to keep a Baptist preacher who drank like a fish and gambled like a shark out of heaven.

"I still don't get why you're telling me this," he said.

"Because, Farley. When John lied to me, I knew it was because he didn't want to lose me." She paused for a long time. Maybe sipping. Maybe crying. "I think that's true love, Farley. I think that's the truest thing I know. Don't you?"

He thought long and hard about how to answer that question. In the end it didn't matter because Rebecca had already hung up. He put the phone down and rolled over on his side. The stuffed bear stared disapprovingly from the dark living room. He gave it the finger.

16

I LIKE TO HIT MYSELF IN THE HEAD WITH A HAMMER

After that he couldn't sleep. Maybe because he'd napped at Lissa's. Maybe because he knew that Rebecca's call had doomed him to relive that night in Nanuqmiut again the moment he closed his eyes.

Most days his body hurt too much by nightfall to walk any more than he already had. But today he'd done laundry, cleaned himself up, and bought the ham for dinner. His legs hurt, but they could hurt more—and he wanted them to because he preferred pain to memory. The minute he stepped outside his building into the night, the rain rewarded him by magnifying the pain, tightening his scars until they burned. That's why retirees moved to Arizona, he thought—for the dry air. Certainly not for the culture.

Moving stiffly, he charted a straight line down the sidewalks and let people in his path make way, tacking and weaving and parting before him like schooled fish before a shark. Most stores had closed for the night. The few still open thrummed—Saturday night in Portland, late-night pizza, hipster donuts and whipped coffee drinks, men drinking PBR at Formica bars. It felt a world away from Nanuqmiut. Dormant even by day, at night the village rolled over on its back, the streets eerily silent most nights.

Unless they were pierced by Rebecca's screams.

Sometimes one of the locals would get blind drunk on bush hooch at a friend's house and forget where he lived, yelling and trying different doors until someone let him in and gave him a blanket and a pillow and a spot on their floor. Occasionally a Slope worker waiting for a flight would go on a bender and wander the streets like a marauding bear until the village public safety officer wrestled him into the makeshift holding tank at the community rec center. The Mexican restaurant—the world's northernmost since the one in Utqiaġvik closed—shut down around six. The combo Subway franchise and pizza counter inside the gas station closed at seven but was open just three days a week. Together, they were the full extent of village entertainment commerce. Compare that to a single block of southeast Hawthorne, on which Farley passed an artisanal butter bar, a used record store, three pot dispensaries, a creperie, a waffle window, and a holistic pet store. He knew three strip clubs he could walk to. *Gentlemen's clubs*, an echo of Rebecca's voice insisted. One served steaks the size of Volkswagens, one catered to vegan customers, and one offered illicit massages in a back room. If he wanted live music, he could find a dozen venues in this neighborhood alone. Punk. Jazz. Blues. House. Folk. Spoken word. A cappella, probably. Portland defied expectations. It defied reason. It even defied common sense. As a city, it sought boundaries to push and then complained about them once they moved too far.

Each step reminded Farley that he wasn't in the Arctic anymore, he wasn't in Alaska, he wasn't even that far north. He did not know where he was going, only that he seemed determined to walk himself there.

How long could he keep this up? How long could he do this before he ground his knees and hips to dust? How long until he'd caused himself enough pain?

A few years back, long before any of this happened, Nell had told him something about himself that he just now was beginning to think might be true.

"Some people like to hit themselves in them heads with hammers," she'd said. They'd been playing poker with Pastor John and a few other villagers in the church rec room, and after losing a week's wages and his VHS player to an on-fire Wilson Mequssuk, Farley was walking the diminutive mayor home. "I think you might be one of them people, Farley."

"Why would anyone do that?" he asked as they stopped outside her house. Nell scratched her ass and spit yellow tobacco into the snow.

"Maybe because it feels good when they stop."

But when would he stop?

And what would he do after that?

By four, even Portland had gone quiet. Everything closed but the all-night convenience stores, the streets empty but for cabs and early-shift commuters. The pain in his body had become ferocious, a need that grew. An expanding hunger. Farley had reached the threshold he'd wanted to—absolute, all-consuming pain—and then crossed it. The hurt he felt as he limped back toward home would endure.

He rounded the corner near his apartment and saw a man standing in the road, the lit tip of a cigarette glowing in his hand as he stared up at the windows of the building. Farley couldn't make him out in the dark, and the man had his back to him. But something about him felt familiar.

He limped closer, and as he approached, his alert system—dormant since the bear attack—croaked awake. The low, body-wide hum it emitted cut through his pain like a beacon in the fog.

"Hey asshole," he said.

The man spun to look at him. Farley focused his good eye, but the man wore a hood, and his features were blurred by the late hour, by the streetlights and shadows, by Farley's own exhaustion.

An off-duty bus passed between them, horn blaring, loud and fast and close. The exhaust fumes hit him and he felt the heat. When the bus passed and he could see across the street once more, the man was already half a block away and running fast. He flicked his cigarette behind him. Farley watched it arc like a red comet, sparking into a million bits of light when it hit the street.

He could walk all day. He could walk all night, even. But his days of running were forever behind him now, and he watched the man disappear into the night.

17

TELL ME WHAT'S WRONG

As Farley entered the building's brightly lit lobby, his exhaustion overtook him. He barely made it into the elevator, and as the door closed, he fell asleep on his feet, upright, like an elephant.

The bell failed to wake him. The door opened and closed. Farley, snoring, rode the car back down and lurched awake when the car stopped and the doors opened again. For a few moments he stared, confused, at the lobby. When he pieced together what had happened, he pushed the button again. This time he made it to his floor, but the fatigue threatened to crush him as he walked down the hall. Lissa's dinner. The wine. Rebecca's call, and the whiskey he'd chased it with. The weeks of wandering Portland. The months of agony in the hospital before that. The constant pain, how it was both too much and not enough for him all the damn time. Abril. John. Seeing Nirva again after so long. The racking guilt. It all washed over him like a wave pulling him under, drowning him.

He struggled to free his key from his pocket and dropped it onto the dingy carpet. It took a few tries to retrieve it, his body stiff and noncompliant, his mind shutting down.

Soon the morning light would flood his apartment. With no curtains or blinds, he fished his coveralls from his bag, lay down on the hard bedroom floor, and draped them across his face. They still reeked of sweat and kerosene. He could smell the Arctic on them and wondered if he would dream of it.

For the first time, he wished he'd bought a bed, or at least a mattress. Maybe he would do just that, a passing idea in the fractions of a second before he fell into the deepest sleep since that night in Nanuqmiut. A sleep that lasted into the next day and through it, one that lasted through that night too, a sleep that lasted nearly the entire weekend so that he did not wake at all, not even once, until a frantic banging on his door made it impossible to sleep any longer.

He got unsteadily to his feet. Pain roiled his body, rigid with disuse, the scream of damaged tendons and joints, contracting muscles protesting movement. As he made his way to the door, he fought to clear his mind. What time was it?

What *day* was it?

Though he had to piss so fiercely he feared his eyeballs might float, so fiercely he could taste urine on his tongue, he opened the door to a red-faced and teary Lissa. She wore a nightgown she held closed at the throat and duck-head slippers with bills for toes. Above them and below the hem of her nightgown, her legs were pale, muscular, smooth.

"Is she here, Farley?"

He blinked to bring the blurry world into focus.

It did not work.

He heard urgency in her voice. Anger. Something else. Fear?

"What have you done with her? Is she in there?"

"What?" The questions confused him. So did the aggression in her tone, the anxiety pulling at her features. His hand prickled as he rubbed the sleep from his eyes, and he wondered if he'd been asleep on it, groggy, still surfacing, trying to both wake up and not wet himself. "Who?"

Unsatisfied with his answers, she rushed at him without warning and tried to shove him aside, tried to squeeze past him into the apartment. Not a big woman—taller than Mayor Nell, but thin—her strength surprised him. Some people are built that way, their muscles like steel cables hidden beneath the skin.

"Olive? Olive, are you in there?" The words spilled out of her mouth, tripping over each other, her eyes frantic. Alarmed. Angry. "Olive, yell if you can hear me."

He leaned forward into the doorframe, more than filling it. Surprising them both, Lissa slapped him across a rough cheek.

"Tell me what's wrong," he said.

"She's gone, Farley. She's gone. Olive's gone."

18

DO YOU MIND PUTTING ON SOME PANTS FIRST?

She tried to shove him again. It felt like shoving a fridge. A safe. An Oldsmobile. But her determination bore enough force to move him and he backed into his apartment, stepping aside to let her in. Lissa rushed past him and ran through the empty rooms, desperately looking for any sign of her daughter.

"Where is she, Farley?" she shouted. Her panicked voice echoed like a car alarm in a parking garage. "Where is she?"

The layout mirrored her own apartment, but the starkness of the rooms disoriented her.

"Why don't you have any furniture?" She looked back into the kitchen, where he watched her sheepishly, foggy with morning, confused and alarmed, but not irritated. "What the fuck, Farley? What the fuck? Where do you sleep?"

He pointed at the smaller bedroom. Lissa looked in, hoping to see some sign of Olive—pajamas, hair scrunchie, anything—and dreading it. But she saw nothing. A huge camouflage pack. A mostly empty bottle of Canadian Club. Dirty clothes on the floor, a pair of boots big enough to use as rowboats.

Back in the kitchen, she stepped close to him—well past the zone of personal space she'd already learned he required—and pushed his chest, hard, with both hands.

"You were *in my apartment*. You were *on her bed*." The words left her mouth like throwing knives—fast, sharp, and dangerous. "I trusted you, Farley. I trusted you. I invited you into my home. I . . . I made you fucking *salmon*."

"Lissa," he said.

"I left you alone with my *daughter*."

And just like that, she'd exhausted whatever resolve she'd been gathering. As it left, her anger went with it so that only adrenaline remained. She knew that would curdle to fear and did not want to be in her body when it did.

Fighting it, she stared at Farley for a long time, trying to gauge his sincerity. He did not back away, but his expression turned pained after a minute. The cheek she'd slapped had turned red.

"Does it hurt?"

"No."

"You're wincing."

"I have to piss."

"Seriously?"

"You woke me up."

In his awkward posture, she saw Olive at Macy's after she'd drunk a cartoonishly large soda from the food court and Lissa had to put down her armful of unpurchased clothes to rush her to the public restroom on the other side of the mall. She knew he was telling the truth.

"Go," she said.

Farley moved as fast as she'd ever seen him move. As soon as he left, she grew light-headed. She leaned against the counter. Like an open-ocean swimmer, the adrenaline had kept her out in front of the waves, but they threatened to pull her under as soon as she lifted her head to take a breath. She heard him pissing from down the hall. A thunderous stream. A satisfied sigh. He returned still wearing the ratty underwear and V-neck T-shirt in which he'd answered the door.

For the first time, she realized she stood in the kitchen of a man she barely knew—a man she'd thought homeless, a man she'd seriously thought might have kidnapped Olive—and they were both in their underwear.

Self-conscious in spite of herself, she pulled her robe more tightly closed. Below his briefs she could see the scars on his legs, thick lines of raised and shining skin crisscrossed like stitching, a topographical map of intertwined rivers and roads, and she realized they ran all the way from his face to his feet.

She did not know why, but she no longer suspected him. A feeling. Instinct. Something else. Maybe she just needed a friend. A confidant. Someone.

Anyone.

How thin the lines are, how fragile our control over our worlds and ourselves, how much of it is just pretending in the first place. With her back against the cabinets, she slid down to the floor and sat, hard, on the linoleum.

"Tell me what happened, Lissa."

She told Farley how she'd woken up with her alarm and gone to wake Olive for school. How she'd found her bedroom empty, the drawers open, some clothes gone, her backpack too.

"Could she have left on her own? Run away?"

"No," she said, adamant. "Why would she?"

He waited.

"You saw her, Farley. She's a pretty happy kid."

"Was the door to the apartment locked?"

"Yes."

"Are you positive?"

She closed her eyes and thought. Olive loved to fiddle with the locks, loved to push buttons and twist knobs and answer phones, and always had. Lissa would turn on the radio to find it tuned to static, volume blasting, or scorch toast because the settings had been slid to high. Most nights she had a bedtime routine—the lights, the locks, make the coffee and set the timer—but last night she'd had a couple glasses of wine and had fallen asleep in front of the TV well into the night. When she'd woken to late-night infomercials, her neck stiff and her bladder full, she'd forced herself to get off the couch and go to bed.

She'd been so tired. Had she checked the door? She couldn't say for certain.

"No," she said. "I'm not."

"Then who might have taken her? I mean, besides me?"

She met his eyes and started to speak, but the words turned to sobs before they'd even left her lips. "I'm sorry," she said. "I'm sorry." They heaved out in broken bits, her breath hitched, the muscles of her face too busy to be bothered with forming syllables. "When I woke up and she was gone, I panicked. All I could think about was you lying there with her the other night, in her bed. How much she liked you. How I didn't really know you at all."

He stared impassively but did not say anything.

"I didn't really think," she said, the breath coming in fits and spurts, her voice unsteady, irregular, bent and warped and elongated by the sobbing. "I didn't think you . . ." She swallowed hard and set her jaw. "I just . . . I freaked out."

Farley nodded, absolving her, but she could still see his discomfort even through her tears. Women's tears are like fire—some men do everything they can to put out the flames, some back away out of fear of getting burned, and some are just arsonists. He just stood his ground, waiting for hers to run their course.

Lissa looked around for a tissue or a dishcloth or anything to wipe her eyes with but saw nothing.

"I'm scared," she said.

He nodded again. "Have you eaten yet?"

"What? No, I—"

"Call the police. They won't do anything yet but take your statement, but it's a start. Then let's go across the hall to your place. I'll cook you breakfast, and we'll figure this out together."

"My place?"

"I don't have any food." He looked around the void of his apartment as if noticing the emptiness for the first time. "Or plates. Or pans to cook in. You've got to shore yourself up for what's ahead, and you can't do that on an empty stomach."

"What's ahead?" she asked, drawn and quartered by fear.

"The waiting."

"Waiting? No, Farley. I have to go look for her."

"We will."

"She's out there somewhere. I need to find her."

"We *will*."

"We're wasting time." Though it did not quite reach the level of a shout, either in volume or vehemence, the sound of her voice surprised her. Frantic. Afraid. Overwhelmed.

Farley nodded, the calmness of his response a crutch for her to lean on.

"It's a big city. We don't know how long she's been gone. Running around the streets like a pair of headless chickens is unlikely to be the best way to go about this," he said. "Cops first. Then food. Then we'll make a plan. OK?"

She steeled herself, giving in, letting him lead her. Not just because he sounded sure but because she *wanted* to be led.

"OK," she said, or tried to, outflanked by another phalanx of sobs. They drew the word out in a way that made her think she was a long way from done with tears. She shimmied her way back to her feet using the cabinet and counter for support.

"I'm scared, Farley."

"I know."

He watched her with a concern she would not have thought him capable of. That concern felt like a ray of sunlight she wanted to crawl into, and she realized she wanted to be held. Needed to be. Just for a moment. It had been so long since she'd touched another human besides her daughter. She needed to know other people were real, that she wasn't completely alone.

"Will you hug me?"

He looked deeply uncomfortable with the idea.

"Please?"

Though he still looked unsure, he nodded and opened his arms, his wingspan wide enough to take flight. Instead of stepping into them, Lissa leaned back and looked him in the eyes.

"Farley?"

"What?"

"Do you mind putting on some pants first?"

19

"F-A-R-L-E-Y."

Farley made breakfast while Lissa talked to the cops. She watched him out of the corner of her eye, how he seemed to marvel at the fragility of the eggs as he broke them into a bowl. Six. Eight. The entire dozen. Eggs were nearly six bucks at Trader Joe's; she couldn't eat more than three. And that was when her stomach wasn't turned inside out. Could he eat nine? Probably—and a loaf of bread. A side of bacon. The whole pig. Why was she pinching pennies when her daughter was missing? Was this what the world did to you?

The cops arrived an hour after she called. Uniforms. Stern glares. They spoke in sober voices and wrote everything down on small paper pads. But they weren't taking Olive's disappearance seriously. That's what Farley had told her as they'd stood by the window and watched the cruiser pull up outside the building.

"How can you tell?"

"The uniforms." A few floors below them, two officers conferred with each other on the sidewalk before coming inside. "They'd have sent detectives, not beat cops."

"How do you know that?"

"My job."

"You were a cop?" She heard the disbelief in her voice, how it carried an edge of accusation. She hoped it didn't sound as sharp to him.

"No. I did internal investigations for one of the big oil companies up on the North Slope."

"What do you investigate at an oil company?"

"Land rights stuff. Environmentalist issues. A lot of sexual assault."

"Sexual assault?"

"A drill site is basically a few dozen roughnecks living in barracks in some of the most remote, isolated places on the planet, far from civilization. Most are men. One or two are women. Bad shit happens."

"That's because they're human. I work with animals. Animals are inherently better."

Farley's expression said he fundamentally disagreed with her premise, but he let it go.

"These uniforms won't ask any questions that will help them find Olive," he said. "They're just here to placate you. They won't take it seriously for another day at least."

"A *day*?"

"She'll be home by then," he said. "The cops are just creating a paper trail to cover any legal stuff that comes out of this." He squinted his good eye. "We'll make a plan to get her back after they leave."

"I'll *make* them take it seriously." She'd believed it when she said it. But within minutes of their arrival, she knew Farley was right. They entered without urgency, spoke with the calming tones of a Sunday school teacher, and treated her like a child who'd lost a favorite doll—not a mother who'd lost an actual child.

"I know you want to believe that your daughter was kidnapped, but it's statistically unlikely that anyone took her," said the female officer, her ponytail so tight it left her eyes misshapen, temples taut as drumskins. "Kids go missing all the time and turn up again. They wander off to find candy or a video game. They follow a dog on the street and get lost. Or they hide somewhere to worry their parents. It's a form of manipulation."

"Manipulation? She's eight years old."

"Yes, ma'am. It's to scare you."

"Why would she do that?"

"So you treat them nicer when they come home. Extra ice cream. More TV. Like that."

"Extra ice cream?" Lissa said, trying for a conciliatory tone even though she wanted to grab the woman by her tactical vest and shake her into action. She had the Boy Scout gene, her father always said, a need to follow the rules and walk on the paths. Teacher's pet.

"Cake. Sweets. Kids love sweets."

A loud, metallic sound echoed through the kitchen, startling Lissa and the cops. They all looked up at Farley, who stood on the other side of the counter holding the lid to the canned ham he'd just opened. A gelatinous seal hung from its edges like a ring of moist stalactites.

"You don't have kids," he said. It was not a question.

The police studied him for the first time, this scarred giant slicing meat with Lissa's chef's knife and lowering it in a hot frying pan, where it sizzled like static on a radio. She saw the expression on the male officer's face change and knew he thought he'd solved the case.

"Sir? You're the father?"

"No."

"Mother's boyfriend?"

"No."

"Your relationship to the girl is what exactly?" The male cop had cut his hair in the high-and-tight style they must teach at the academy—half the cops Lissa saw around town had the same cut—but the crown shone through from the hair gel he'd used. *Product*, the girl who cut Lissa's hair called it. He had tight freckles that looked like ants on his face, the kind of glare meant to intimidate. She knew the look well. What had she expected when she'd called the police? Matlock? Kojak? Columbo?

"Farley lives across the hall."

High-and-Tight looked at Lady Cop, who put her pencil to her notebook.

"Farley . . . ?"

Without looking up, he folded the slurry of eggs around the skillet. "F-a-r-l-e-y," he said.

"Sir? Is that your first name or last name?"

"My name is just Farley."

"Sir..."

"Am I a suspect?" he asked.

The way High-and-Tight readjusted in his seat, Lissa could tell he was fighting to retain his cool. He put his own notepad into the pocket of his tactical vest and leaned forward in his chair, elbows on his thighs, to stare at Farley. His pants rode up over his socks, exposing an expanse of smoothly shaved skin the color of a sliced pear. She figured him for a cyclist—the lean build, the shaved legs.

Typical Portland.

"Do you have kids of your own, Mr. Farley?"

"I used to."

"You did?" Lissa said.

Farley nodded. They all stared across the counter, waiting for him to elaborate, but he did not.

"Where'd you get those scars?" High-and-Tight asked, his tone moving a measurable amount toward the hostile end of the spectrum.

"The secret to good eggs is to add the salt ten minutes before you cook them," Farley said. "You can put that in your notebook if you want. It's more useful than asking me about my scars, which have nothing to do with her daughter going missing. If you're not going to help, at least stop wasting our fucking time."

Farley seemed unafraid of the cops, unintimidated. Lissa wondered why that surprised her. Maybe because of how he lived. Sleeping in the camp. The unfurnished apartment. Or because of his scars and the hint of trauma—she assumed he'd want to avoid interaction with the police. Hell, even *she* felt intimidated, and she had nothing to hide. She'd called them, she'd asked for their help, but in their presence she still felt a kind of deference or an assumed guilt. As if she feared drawing their attention *too* closely lest they find some infraction or violation she'd committed and trundle her away to the station in cuffs. Their uniforms created that involuntary reaction, she knew, the same way her stomach dropped when she passed a police car while driving. She knew, too, that it was precisely the point of the uniforms. But Farley seemed immune. Maybe because of his history with uniforms in the army, or because of his history as an investigator. Or maybe simply because of his size. What could harm someone that big? The pit in her gut grew watching the cops' reactions as Farley scooped a pile of ham and eggs onto a plate and slid it across the counter for her.

"I'm telling you I know who took my daughter," Lissa said. "The Asshole. A drugged-up, homeless guy. Farley saved Olive from him last week."

Lady Cop turned back to her, interested. High-and-Tight kept his eyes on Farley, his posture unchanged.

"Ma'am? Tell me about this . . ." Lady Cop consulted her notes. "Drugged-up, homeless guy."

Lissa told them about the incident at the camp. She didn't mention that Farley had been a resident there and downplayed his actions to protect him.

"The dog was vicious, and that asshole had a bat. A metal baseball bat. Olive fell into the street and almost got run over. Farley must have been walking by—right, Farley?—and he grabbed her before she could get hurt."

"Is that right, sir? You just happened to be walking by?"

"Something like that."

"Then what happened?"

"I dealt with the situation so she could get her daughter home safely."

High-and-Tight did not take his eyes off Farley. "What does that mean, exactly? You 'dealt with the situation'?"

"I called you," Lissa said so he did not have to answer. "The police. I called that night. I'd been calling for weeks, ever since the camp first appeared. Those people were awful. I know how that sounds—'those people'—but they were dirty and rude and aggressive. Some of them did drugs in public. One of them kept shitting in the street. Another one flashed his dick at me. At Olive. Who knows what that man would have done to us? Or his dog? I don't know if they arrested him, but they took his dog away."

The cops stared at her in that unnerving way that cops will stare at you.

"How do you know that, ma'am?"

"He told me," she said, hearing herself snarl and fighting to keep her voice leashed. "He's been back since then, standing outside the building. Watching me. Threatening me."

"He has?" Farley asked.

Lissa met his eyes and saw the concern. She nodded.

"Can you describe this man?" High-and-Tight asked.

"He's got tattoos on his face, and sores. Mean eyes. Broken teeth."

"He calls himself The Ferryman," Farley said.

"The Ferryman?" Lissa said, noting that the name got the cops' attention. "What the fuck? I mean, what the actual fuck? What a psycho."

"How do you know that, Mr. Farley?" High-and-Tight asked. Lissa heard the accusation in his tone and saw that Farley did too.

"Look," she said, drawing their attention back to her. "I'm a Democrat. A liberal. A progressive. I supported the plastic bag ban, the plastic straw ban. I support all the right causes. All the good causes. I know I'm not supposed to be unkind to people, and I know how serious addiction can be. I'm not trying to make light of it. But after watching these people acting like animals outside my building for so long, I started to think of them as monsters."

She looked at Farley. He nodded his reassurance.

"I just don't know what they're capable of. And now one of them took my daughter and I'm scared. I'm scared to *death*."

"Ma'am—" High-and-Tight started, but Lissa cut him off.

"I called you. The police. A bunch of times. You can check your dispatch records or whatever. I don't mean to be rude. But you didn't come. No one did. I reported the homeless camp and all the disgusting behavior and drug use, and nobody seemed to care. And then when something bad happened, you weren't there. Farley was. He saved us. That's more than *you've* done. So if you please, I'd very much like you to help me find my daughter, because she's just a kid and she's missing and that meth-head asshole took her and I'm terrified of what he'll do to her."

The cops stood in unison, as smoothly as if the action had been choreographed. Like dancers. Lissa would bet that Lady Cop led.

"I'm sure she'll turn up, ma'am," she said. "We'll check back in with you tomorrow. In the meantime, maybe lock your doors and call us when she comes home."

20

WHAT DO I DO NOW?

After the police left, Farley watched Lissa fill the space they had occupied with panic. To still her trembling, he convinced her to eat some eggs, but she said they'd gone cold. He convinced her to take a shower to warm up, a small gift of privacy, and did the breakfast dishes while he waited. When she had not returned after a while, he stood outside the bathroom door and heard her crying over the fan and running water.

A few minutes later, she came out with her wet hair slicked back, her skin goose-bumped. She went straight to the window, opened it, and lit a cigarette. He didn't know she smoked and didn't know where she produced it from, but he sure as hell didn't blame her.

"What do I do now?" She exhaled a plume of blue smoke.

"Sit." He pointed at the couch. "There."

Though he knew she'd meant "What do I do *about Olive*," he recognized a greater need for guidance in the mechanics of how to fill time when each minute feels worse than the one before it. He handed her a mug of coffee. "Drink this."

"I should be out there looking," she said, sounding both sincere and unconvinced.

Farley understood. Her maternal instinct to find her daughter, to do something, anything, would be running on all cylinders. But Portland was a big city with a lot of places to hide a little girl, and she wouldn't even know where to start. Fear was a great motivator. But it could also debilitate you—she'd just spin her wheels out there, losing traction to her desperation.

He took the blanket from the back of the couch, a knit afghan in colors that might have been in fashion forty years earlier, and laid it across her lap. Easing himself down in the armchair opposite, still suspicious of her furniture after what he'd done to the bed, he looked at her hard.

"The cops don't believe you," he said. "I do."

"But . . . ?"

"But. Let's talk it through. Are you sure it was him? That Ferryman asshole?"

"Who else could it be?"

"That's what I'm asking."

"What do you want to know?"

"Tell me about Olive's father."

She returned his hard look. "What about him?"

"Is he in her life? Could he have done this?"

"As far as Olive is concerned, her father is just a story I tell," she said. "A fairy tale."

"So tell it to *me*."

"Why?"

"To rule him out."

"It's not him."

Farley leaned in as best he could with the limitations of his broken body and tried to soften his expression.

"Convince me," he said.

21

YOU OPENED THIS
CAN OF WORMS

"I knew him my whole life. But we didn't start dating until my senior year of high school."

"What was he like?"

"I don't know. He was . . . cool. Artistic. He had long, shaggy blond hair. A goatee."

"He *sounds* cool." Farley smiled—a joke. Lissa didn't much feel like joking but knew he wanted to keep her calm, keep her from panicking, so she smiled too, a low-watt bulb, a rusted filament.

"Goatees were cool back then," she said.

"No, they weren't."

"You're gonna love this, then. His name was Stace. He read poetry. Talked about art. That made him seem worldly and sophisticated. Especially in Sandy, Oregon." It embarrassed her now to remember her pathetic jackrabbit heart, how she felt *chosen* when he'd pull up outside her parents' house in the old Toyota Land Cruiser he'd fixed up in shop class. Sad Cinderella. Most boys in her runt of a town wore flannels and drove pickup trucks and grew up to become men who wore flannels and drove pickup trucks. But Stace quoted Lorca. After dating a string of casual boyfriends who quoted Zeppelin and crushed beer cans against their foreheads, it felt like entering the Age of Enlightenment. "I fell for him hard, but it turned out I was only falling for an act," she said.

"I don't know why it didn't occur to me that someone so outwardly bohemian and cool could be just as much of an asshole on the inside as the rest of them."

Farley said nothing but looked like he knew what it felt like when your heart creates a blind spot big enough to drive a truck into.

"By the time I finally figured it out, I was seven months pregnant. A little scared, or at least nervous. Until graduation night, when he told me he was still going away to college in the fall, to Evergreen, even with the baby coming. He hadn't even told his parents I was pregnant."

Farley got up to refill her coffee. She lit another cigarette while he was gone.

"That was not one of my finer moments," she said, mumbling with the butt between her lips and remembering how her older sister had comforted her outside the school auditorium, how she'd fixed Lissa's tear-streaked makeup but had been unable to do anything about the visible bulge in her graduation gown. Her sister had seen through Stace right from the start.

"If you ever see any signs of that baby taking after her pretentious piece-of-shit father, burn it at the stake," Allie said, trying to make her laugh but not entirely joking.

"What kind of signs?"

"I don't know, Liss. Smoking clove cigarettes? Reciting Rimbaud?"

"It's pronounced like 'Rambo,' not 'Rim-bod.'"

Allie lowered her eyeliner pencil and gave her a sad look. "The infection has spread, Doctor. I'm afraid it's already too late."

"What am I going to do, Al?"

"You're not going to do anything, Liss. *We* are. That's what big sisters do. I'm with you every step of the way."

And she had been.

Until she wasn't.

Farley put her mug on the table, startling her. Maybe seeing something in her expression, he took his seat again without a word and gave her a moment to recover.

"I had Olive over the summer," she said finally. "Stace and I tried to make it work when he went to Olympia, but *it* had never been much to begin with. I think that he was surrounded by so many other people at college who were all experiencing their freedom for the first time that he started to resent me and the baby-shaped cage limiting his own. By Christmas he'd stopped coming home on the weekends. By spring he almost stopped calling entirely."

She took a sip of the coffee.

"I thought I'd be heartbroken, but I was actually relieved. We met to officially break up and agreed that I would raise Olive, since I'd been doing that more or less on my own anyway." No courts, no lawyers. No paperwork. Just a handshake agreement hashed out over coffee. Even now, she remembered the conversation almost word for word, remembered how it felt to realize he was capable of just walking away from her and their child completely.

"It couldn't have been easy," Farley said. "Raising a child on your own."

"No. But it was better for her not to have her father in her life."

A distance came into his eyes. Lissa watched it expand as if he'd been caught in an undertow that pulled him farther and farther away from the shore. She let the next wave take her too, going under as she remembered that time in her life, the blur of it, how she'd moved through the world deprived of sleep, deprived of solitude, deprived of any human touch that did not also involve baby powder or rash ointments. But she also remembered how driven she'd been, some previously dormant maternal instinct possessing her to make something more of herself than the "teen mother" legacy already claimed by a number of her Sandy High School classmates. Despite her exhaustion, she'd worked part-time, took out massive student loans, enrolled in night school, studied when she should have been asleep, and within a few years, she'd earned her associate's degree in veterinary technology from Portland Community College.

"I wasn't entirely alone," she said, her voice snapping Farley back into focus. "My parents and my sister helped. A lot. I couldn't have done it without them."

"Are they still around?"

She shook her head. *No.*

"I'm sorry."

"Allie lives in New York now. Married a guy she met at Coachella."

"What about Olive's father? Stace?"

Lissa considered her answer. She'd never told anyone the story before and didn't think she ever would.

"My vet tech program offered me an internship at the zoo," she said. "Mostly grunt work. But I rotated around different animal habitats each day based on needs and assignments. I liked working with the elephants best. Did you know that when a female gives birth to a calf, the entire herd works to protect it so the mother can get some rest? Humans don't do that. We make it almost impossible for women to raise a child while holding down a job. Like we're punishing them. And we don't do shit to protect our children either. We couldn't even bother to pass gun laws after some nutjob shot up a kindergarten. Somehow we've managed to erase a few million years of natural instinct and distinguish ourselves by being worse than the species we keep in cages. Great work, humanity."

She took a sip of her coffee, aware it was growing cold.

"Elephants were the reason I became a vet tech in the first place. In the late nineties, a handler at the zoo abused one of the Asian elephants. A female named Rose-Tu. He beat and stabbed her with a bull hook so badly that they found more than a hundred and seventy-five lacerations on her body. The zoo fired him immediately, and a court charged him. But he almost walked free because the district attorney didn't want to press charges. Apparently, the law said it wasn't a crime unless they could prove that the elephant felt pain, and he didn't think he could do that. What kind of vapid asshole can look at an elephant, or any animal, really, and think for even a second that they don't feel pain?"

Though she'd been just a kid at the time, the incident had stuck with her and led to her decision to find a job that let her help animals. The first time she met Rose-Tu after she began her internship, she'd burst into tears like a fool. The other interns stared at her with a kind of embarrassed pity, but the big elephant studied her with what she chose to believe was *understanding*. Or at least a kind of recognition.

"Not long after I started working at the zoo, Stace showed up on my doorstep one night. He looked completely different. Older. Beaten down. He told me that letting me and Olive go had been the biggest mistake of his life. He wanted to be a part of our lives. Both of us."

Farley raised an eyebrow.

"I know," she snapped. She knew she sounded defensive; she *was*. The intelligent part of her—the reasonable part, the one she wished made all the decisions—knew exactly who Stace was. But that part had atrophied from disuse while she used other muscles fighting for survival as a single mother.

"Look," she said. "It wasn't like that. I saw an opportunity. Not for a sweep-me-off-my-feet romance. Not even for True Love. But for something more primal than that. Something simpler. I saw someone to take turns making peanut butter and cream cheese sandwiches for Olive. I saw someone to share the burden of childcare and transportation. I saw someone to field a few of the ten million questions a four-year-old can muster in an hour."

Lissa didn't think she'd ever felt as vulnerable as she had that night. When he stood in her doorway and asked her to take him back, something in her collapsed, a dam breaking, her resolve drowned.

"Take me back," Stace said, putting his arms around her.

"OK," she said, relenting in spite of herself. "But this time we're using rubbers."

Almost immediately, her traitorous conscience had tried to shame her. To humiliate her. But shame wouldn't help with potty training. She'd disappointed herself, but disappointment wouldn't sit up all night with a feverish child. Shame and disappointment could go fuck each other and see how hard it is to raise a baby in this world.

Farley cleared his throat, measured but obviously growing impatient at her talk of elephants and exes.

"You opened this can of worms," she said, and he nodded.

"At first he was solicitous. Moody. He didn't know the first goddamned thing about parenting. But at least he made an effort to try to win me over. Pretty quickly, though, I started to understand that he had a problem with drugs. He'd go out nights and come home late, stumble around in the dark. I found a soiled pair of underwear in the kitchen trash. When I asked him about it, he said he'd gotten so high he'd shit himself. The dumbass didn't even have the self-awareness to be embarrassed by it."

She shook her head, the disbelief lingering even so many years later.

"I wanted an adult to co-parent with. Instead I got another baby to raise." She took a deep breath. "And then it got worse."

"Worse how?"

"I can't believe I'm telling you this," she said. "I barely know you." She looked at Farley, but he said nothing to argue the point or reassure her. He barely knew her either and would offer no false platitudes. "I knew it was never going to be more than a relationship of convenience. At least for me. But it turned out that even that was too much to hope for. Almost overnight, he became belligerent. He was always mad, always yelling, insulting my looks, my cooking, berating me for how much time I spent with Olive. What kind of weak man is jealous of his own daughter? Then I started to notice things missing from the apartment. Grocery money. Jewelry. My grandmother's pewter."

Though the memories were clear in her mind, the images vivid, it felt like they'd happened to someone else.

"My getting back together with him alienated my family," she said. "They pulled away. Cut me off, hoping I'd make the right choice. I didn't."

"You weren't in it for love. Why'd you stay?"

"I wish I knew, Farley. Maybe pride. Maybe fear. I took an econ class in school—we studied the 'sunk-cost fallacy.' Maybe it was that. It doesn't matter now. I ended up having less help with Olive than before, plus all the chaos of having a drug addict in the house. Want to know how bad it got? One night I had to call my sister to borrow money for food until my next paycheck because Stace had pissed it away on drugs. She just tore into me. I couldn't believe it, couldn't believe the things she said about me. Not because they were hurtful. Because they were true."

"Get rid of him, Liss," Allie told her point blank, done with the bullshit. "You're better than this." Lissa promised she would, promised she was. Her sister gave her the money but could barely look at her. She felt as guilty and as shameful as if *she* were the addict—and in a way, she was.

"I summoned my fiercest maternal instincts and confronted him," she told Farley. "Said I didn't care how drunk or high he got or how many times he shit himself, but if he ever stole food from our daughter's mouth again, I would leave him. I would call the police. I would take him to court and make sure he never saw her again."

"Good for you."

"Good for me? You know what he did? You know what that fucker did?"

Farley nodded.

"He punched me in the mouth."

She closed her eyes, let her heart settle a bit.

"For a few nights I slept on the couch. I was pissed at him, and he knew it. He felt guilty. I know he did. I don't think he even knew he was capable of sinking that low." She opened her eyes again, looked up at the ceiling, and took a deep breath. "But I guess my bruises lasted longer than my resolve because by the weekend, I was back in our bed."

When he hit her that first time, he'd crossed some Rubicon. After that, he had no trouble following the tracks he'd left back to the other side. More insults. More yelling. A few slaps. Then pinches hard enough to leave blood blisters. A punch to the belly that left her vomiting. One night he threw her into a coffee table hard enough to splinter the glass. She cleaned it up shard by tiny shard while Olive wailed, doing to her heart what had happened to the table.

"I always thought of myself as a strong woman," Lissa said, lighting another cigarette. "But I made excuses—not for *his* behavior. For my own. For letting him stay. For putting Olive at risk."

Her coffee had gone entirely cold, and a film had settled on the surface. She stared into it for a moment and then dropped her half-smoked American Spirit into it.

"Not long after that, I got called to the elephant enclosure at work to help clean some skin abrasions Rose-Tu had suffered. There was a whole team of us—veterinarians, trainers, vet techs—but for some reason,

Rose-Tu looked into my eyes and just stared at me. Like she was seeing deep inside me. Seeing who I was."

Despite elephants' massive size, their eyes are comparatively small—just half an inch bigger than humans'—but infinitely more expressive. In Rose-Tu's eyes, Lissa saw herself not as she *was* but as she wanted to be. A strong, defiant mother. A thick-skinned woman with the strength to crush those who stand in her way. The world had beaten her down, bent her, but it had not broken her. Not yet.

"Most zoos were phasing out the use of bullhooks," she said. "It was a whole big thing with the Association of Zoos and Aquariums, with all the animal rights groups involved. The Oregon Zoo had already stopped using them after the trial, but it still kept some on hand in case of an emergency."

She looked at Farley, held his eyes to make sure he understood.

"I swallowed my pride and asked my parents to watch Olive overnight. They were so thrilled to see her that they drove into the city to pick her up. As soon as they left, I packed all of Stace's stuff into trash bags and lined them up against the wall outside our apartment. Then I poured myself a glass of wine and waited." Again she saw the memories clearly, in high resolution and perfect focus, but felt removed from them, as if it had been another woman pushed to the edge, another mother desperate to protect her daughter. Not her. What she had done was so out of character for her that even now, even afterward, it did not seem possible. "He came home late. Drunk. Reeking of whiskey, sweat, cigarette smoke. Reeking of malice. He saw the bags in the hallway and just went apeshit, yelling, banging on the door. He didn't try to convince me to let him stay, didn't try to apologize. He just started threatening me."

She closed her eyes.

"I started swinging that hook the minute he stepped into the apartment. I didn't stop until I was sure he'd gotten the message." When she opened them again, she saw Farley had not looked away. She searched his face for judgment but saw none. "I didn't stop until he was gone," she said.

She lit another cigarette and smoked it quietly for a few drags.

"That was the last time I saw him. A few years later, Allie called from New York to tell me that she'd seen on Facebook that Stace had been killed in a car accident. A DUI. Killed two other people too. I know how it sounds to say this, but I'm glad he's dead, because now I never have to worry about him coming back into Olive's life, that lousy piece of shit."

22

GIVE ME YOUR PHONE

A silence settled over them. Lissa could hear her own heart beating, and maybe Farley's too. She could hear the city outside the window, the traffic, the rain, and knew that Olive was out there somewhere. They both sat with the silence for a while. And then Farley leaned forward in his chair.

"You could have just told me that. That he was dead."

"I know I could have. But I needed you to know, Farley."

"About him?"

"About *me*. That I have no trouble looking Rose-Tu in the eyes. Not anymore. That I'm stronger than I look—stronger than you think. And that I'll do whatever I have to do to get my daughter back."

"Give me your phone," he said. She handed him her iPhone, and he punched a number into it. Somewhere in his pocket she heard his own phone's muffled ringtone.

"Now you have my number." He handed it back to her. "Call me right away if you hear from The Ferryman."

"Where are you going?"

"I'm going to find him. I'm going to bring Olive home. And I'm going to make him pay."

She looked at him as he stood in the open doorway, filling it with his bulk, this scarred and damaged guardian angel who kept trying to save them.

"Why are you doing this?" she asked. "Why are you helping?"

"Why am I helping you find your missing daughter?"

"Yes. You don't have to do this. You barely know us."

"I know everything I have to."

"What if he . . ." Lissa started and faltered.

"No," Farley said, adamant. "The Ferryman may be a piece of shit, but he's also a coward. He's going to want money. This is about ransom, that's all."

He closed the door behind him, hoping like hell he was right.

PART THREE

23

ARE YOU A FUCKING COP?

The army had taught Farley a lot of things that had so far proven less than useful after his discharge. He could dig a hole like nobody's business, for example, but found the need for military holes dramatically outpaced the need for civilian ones. Though it *had* also taught him a few things that helped him land work as an investigator at the oil company—which, he had to admit, had been a pretty good job. His single greatest asset had not been any particular skills but his size. He looked like a brute. His appearance alone often sufficed to intimidate, coax, or frighten perps into compliance or confession. And if appearances sometimes *weren't* enough, well, he could do that too.

While the job had required some investigative legwork, most of it had been done by teams of lawyers in distant offices at corporate headquarters, far from the dirt and sweat of the drill sites. In his role, Farley had served more as a boots-on-the-ground liaison between the suits and the roughnecks. Some of the job had been menial—serving papers, babysitting the visiting corporate emissaries—and some had been more physical in nature. A few times a year, he got sent into one of the villages to collar a roughneck who'd drunk too much bush moonshine and gotten violent with a couple of underaged Native girls.

If The Ferryman wanted ransom for Olive, he would make that known somehow. Until then, Farley would work the problem and try to find him through other means. Most investigations didn't require any Sherlock Holmes–level skill. You just had to ask questions, listen to the answers, and have a pretty good sense of when people were lying to you. He was no detective, no private eye, and nobody would write books about his powers of deduction, but he was big and stubborn and he could be mean as hell. And now that he'd promised Lissa he'd find her daughter, he planned to crack heads at every homeless camp in Portland until someone told him where to find The Asshole.

His own daughter had vanished right in front of him, and he'd been unable to save her. Saving Olive wouldn't bring Abril back, but it might bring back some of the parts of him that he'd lost with her that night. If nothing else, he would make The Asshole pay for what he'd done. He could be in any one of dozens of camps around the city, but if he had Olive, he would avoid them and the missions and shelters too. More likely he'd be holed up alone somewhere. The woods. A motel. He might even have left town if he had the means. He could be anywhere. Without knowing what resources he had, Farley didn't bother to speculate—he knew the prick lived on the streets but not much else. During his own time at the camp, Farley had kept his interactions to a minimum. Better to wear his hair shirt in the smoldering solitude of self-hatred. The only person he'd engaged with at all had been Wayne. Farley hadn't seen him since the camp got rousted and hoped he'd landed somewhere safe.

He'd seen other homeless camps in a dozen locations on his walks around the city, some entrenched, semipermanent, others nomadic, appearing and disappearing between evening and dawn. Determined but with no real plan, he set out on foot to the nearest one. People in the camps knew each other. He figured someone would know where The Asshole had gone. If Wayne's PO and social worker could find *him* every couple of weeks, that meant it was possible.

Though his legs hurt, he'd built up strength over the weeks of walking, and he tested them with as brisk a pace as he could manage. For the first time, he'd left his pack and cane behind. The pack would only slow him down, and nobody's afraid of a man with a cane. Anyway, he might need both hands for what lay ahead of him.

A light mist fell as he approached the first camp. It sat on an empty lot where a house had been razed to make room for new construction. An empty lot was a unicorn in Portland. Driven by Californians and the growth in the region's tech infrastructure—the Silicon Forest—the real estate market had caught fire. Anyone who'd been to Seattle in the last two decades could see the future plain as day. Panicked locals had been plastering stickers on FOR SALE signs all over town, a map of the West Coast with the slogan "Oregon is above California." Clever, but not clever enough to stop the storm. As soon as this lot cleared escrow or whatever legal skirmish had stalled it, some shithead would build a pair of narrow duplexes with a charging station for Teslas and cash in. In the meantime, a dozen campers were squatting on the property, some in the foundation, some where the backyard used to be. Beer cans, food bags, and broken glass littered the foundation slab, its walls spray-painted with graffiti but somehow still less of an eyesore than most of the new construction around.

Some of the campers sat in the morning drizzle, smoking lazily and drinking coffee out of paper cups. Farley's arrival didn't seem to alarm anyone—a reminder that he looked like he belonged with them. The camp itself had not yet taken root or spread like the one he'd been part of. Just a dozen residents or so, with a transient feel. He milled around checking out tents and shopping carts and looking for anything familiar.

"Anyone know The Ferryman?" He did not direct the question at anyone in particular, just asked it out loud. Some shook their heads. Most ignored him.

He walked two more miles before he reached the next camp, which had taken over a neighborhood park at the confluence of two small urban streams. The rivers provided campers water for bathing and drinking, and the public restrooms gave a measure of privacy. At the other end of the park, the playground equipment sat unused. The neighbors would not bring their kids to play among the occupying invaders, and in this more suburban neighborhood far from the heart of downtown, they had other options.

"Anyone know The Ferryman?" Farley asked as he poked among the tents and tarps. Everyone he asked shook their heads. *No.*

"How about Wayne? Older guy? Talks to himself?"

"You a cop?" The voice came from behind him. He turned to find a man sprawled on a piece of cardboard under an improvised rain fly made out of what looked like a shower curtain salvaged from someone's trash. The clear plastic curtain was yellowed with age and use, decorated with faded sunflowers. The man squinted up at him, eyes heavy with medically induced weight.

"You know The Ferryman?"

"I know Go Fuck Yourself. Are you looking for him too?"

"Good one," Farley said. He limped over to the man and, without pause, kicked him in the ribs, swallowing the pain that burned up his leg like fire.

"What the fuck?"

The man tried to get to his knees. Farley stepped on one of his hands and put all his weight on that foot.

"Jesus Christ!"

Farley could hear the pain in his voice, could feel the bones threatening to yield beneath his boot.

"Jesus Fucking Christ!"

"How about now? *Now* do you know The Ferryman?"

No more than twenty-five, acned still, greasy hair, the kind of mustache that seems aspirational at best, he wore a black sweatshirt and black jeans burdened with dirt and sweat and sloughed-off skin. Though he stared defiantly, his face revealed his agony, the quivering bottom lip. "None of your fucking business, cop."

"I don't know what drugs you're on," Farley said. "But you're going to need more of them." He twisted his heel until the man cried out, a wordless squawk, the sound stolen by the pain.

"OK! OK! Jesus Christ, yes, I know him."

"Was that so hard?"

"Fuck you."

"Where can I find him?"

"Why? What do you want with him?"

"None of your fucking business," Farley said, leaning on his heel.

"Fuck! Last time I saw him, he'd set up camp on the Springwater, north of Oaks Bottom."

"When?"

"I don't know. Couple days, maybe."

Farley lifted his foot. The man immediately yanked his hand away and cradled it with the other like he was trapping a live bird against his chest.

"Are you a fucking cop?" He flinched a little out of fear of retribution.

"Do I look like a cop?"

"Honestly? You look like an asshole."

Farley nodded. "Fair enough," he said.

24

THE KIND OF NAME
YOU GIVE A POODLE

Farley followed the Springwater Corridor north along the Willamette River atop a steeply sloping bluff roped with ivy and brush. The multiuse trail ran some twenty miles along a former railway from the community of Boring to the heart of Portland. As it neared the downtown area, it meandered through the neighborhoods of Southeast Portland and paralleled the river before crossing it into the city, whose amateur skyline beckoned from the western bank. As he walked past the Oaks Bottom Wildlife Refuge, he watched for tents or tarps. The refuge itself—a tangle of brush-covered wetlands the city had turned into a 140-acre park—provided a home for migratory birds, small herds of deer, and a few coyotes that sometimes wandered up the hill to the highway that marked its eastern border. Increasingly it also provided cover for homeless camps.

Though he checked each outpost he passed for anyone familiar, he recognized no one, and no one had seen The Ferryman. The camp he'd slept in had a few dozen residents. In the five or six he'd already trolled through, he had yet to encounter a single person he recognized. How many safety nets had to fail for a city this small to generate a homeless population so large?

Development of the Springwater Corridor began as a hard-fought community effort to secure rights of way and funding and pave the pedestrians-and-bicycles-only path. Upon its completion, it became, briefly, a triumph for commuters who traveled from the suburbs to the city by bicycle, a traffic-free safe haven for joggers and walkers, and a model for urban planning. But that triumph proved short-lived. The community jewel quickly devolved into a kind of homeless highway, a lawless stretch of fringe Portland. Inaccessible to cars, hidden from roads, the corridor functioned as a kind of DMZ, difficult for police to patrol, a wasteland that existed both within city limits and apart from them. Wherever The Ferryman had taken Olive, he probably would have used the path to move her. She had only been gone five or six hours at most, and Farley was betting that the trail remained fresh enough that someone had seen something.

Just north of the refuge, he saw a thin line of dark smoke rising from the steep bank beneath the trail. When he reached the smoke, he peered downslope and saw two tents near the water patched with duct tape and streaked with dirt and rain. He tried to scoot down the bank to approach them but only made it about a quarter of the way before his damaged leg protested against the steep and unsteady hillside. Unable to reach them on foot, he instead grabbed a fistful of stones from the bank. One by one, he lobbed them down the hill at the tents like grenades. The first two missed entirely and skittered down the slope toward the river. The third caught one of the tents square on and bounced off the taut fabric like a trampoline.

Now that he had the range, Farley chose a bigger stone. It hit in almost the exact same spot, collapsing the tent, revealing two men sitting on either side of a barrel stove. They looked up the hill and spotted him, and he waved. With the remaining stones he'd gathered, he trained his aim on them. They yelled as the stones pelted them like rain, but Farley couldn't make out their words as they moved, bobbing and weaving and crying out when one of the stones made contact. After a few moments, they began searching for stones of their own. But Farley had gravity on his side; those that reached him atop the slope had no momentum left. He sidestepped them neatly and continued his bombing campaign.

One of the men finally grabbed a two-by-four from the pile of junk next to the tent and began the long climb up the bank. His friend followed behind. Farley turned and began his own slow way back to the path, wanting to greet them on level ground.

His legs throbbed and stung like hornets had built a nest beneath the skin and were burrowing into the muscle. The men's shouts turned to threats, and he heard them more clearly as they scurried up the bank behind him. They had more ground to cover than he did, but were moving a lot faster too. He knew it would be close. His body ached, vengeful for what he asked of it. Their voices grew louder as they approached. He did not look back, focused on keeping his footing on the unsteady slope as he shuffled uphill at an angle in his solemn effort to reach the path. Now it was a race.

Even before his injuries, before the bears rearranged his physiology, Farley had been a Clydesdale. Not a racehorse. Nobody would ever bet on him to be first across the line. But breathing hard, he reached the pavement, pulled himself up to level ground, and turned to find the first of the men right on his heels. Younger than Farley, maybe in his twenties, with a scraggly beard and facial tattoos, he crested the hillside onto the trail and wound up to swing the two-by-four. Farley caught it as it began its downward arc, stopping it cold. The man's face revealed his shock; clearly, he'd expected a different outcome. It seemed clear too that from a distance, he'd misjudged Farley's size. Now, face-to-face, he recognized his error. Without much effort, Farley twisted the stud from the man's grip and swung it like a battering ram. It hit him square in the chest, knocking him not just off his feet but off the path entirely, sending him rolling down the slope. Limbs flying at frantic and awkward angles, he passed his friend, who was moving up the hill at a slower pace—he'd just reached the top of the slope but now looked like he might be reconsidering.

Farley didn't give him the chance. Grabbing him by his sweatshirt, he pulled the man onto the path and held him tight. The man squirmed but could not break his grip.

"Relax," Farley said.

"Fuck you. *You* relax."

"I *am* relaxed."

"You don't look relaxed."

"I'm just trying to catch my breath."

"That's 'cause you're a fat piece of shit."

"Don't be a dick."

"What the fuck do you want?"

"I'm looking for The Ferryman."

"Who?"

"Oh, you're the first asshole I've met in this town who doesn't know The Ferryman?"

"I don't know where he is."

"I don't believe you."

"Are you a cop?"

"Why do people keep asking me that? Do I look like a cop?"

"I don't know *what* you look like."

"That's the first thing you've said that I believe."

Something in the man's expression changed, a tumbler moving. In Farley's experience, that's how interrogations worked. Questions were like keys you insert into a lock—find the right one to depress the tumbler pins, and the lock opens. He relaxed his grip.

"I'm not going to hurt you."

"I don't believe *you*. You threw Bobby off the cliff."

"Don't be dramatic." Farley looked down the riverbank toward the water. "It's not a cliff. And he tried to brain me with a two-by-four."

"You were throwing rocks at us," the man said, sounding defeated.

"I just wanted your attention."

"Well, you fucking have it."

"What's your name?"

"Chad."

"Chad? Seriously?"

"What about it?"

"It sounds like something you'd name a prep-school boy. Did you play lacrosse?"

"Now who's being a dick?" Chad looked genuinely hurt. "What's *your* name?"

"Farley."

"Farley? Fucking Farley? That sounds like something you name a poodle."

Farley smiled. "Where's The Ferryman?"

"What do you want him for?"

"He took something. I want it back."

"You don't want to fuck with The Ferryman. That dude's crazy."

Farley was still holding him by the collar of his sweatshirt. He grabbed Chad's belt with his other hand and lifted him off the ground. Not high—just high enough to make it seem like he could lift him overhead as easily as a morning stretch before coffee. The truth was that the effort did not come easily, nor did it come without pain. But he knew that the pain would show as anger, and he saw the fear it engendered in Chad's face.

"Take it easy," Chad said. "Jesus."

Farley let go of his shirt and belt, and he collapsed onto the path like a flower closing at dusk. He took a few breaths, calming himself.

"The Ferryman's a prick," he said finally. "Most of us out here kind of look out for each other. Not him. That ass bag has no boundaries. He's got fucking problems."

"Who doesn't?"

Chad looked at him, considering the question. "Is Bobby alive?"

Farley looked down the slope and saw the other man pulling himself out of the river. "How do you two know each other?"

Chad pulled his legs in front of him and wrapped his arms around them like a sulking child. "We were roommates at prep school."

Farley laughed.

"Hey, what did he take from you? The Ferryman?"

"A little girl."

"Fuck." Chad drew the word out—*fuuuuuuck*—but did not seem surprised. From downslope, they heard Bobby yelling his name, and both peered over the edge and waved at him. Bobby flipped Farley the bird.

"Where do I find him?"

Chad looked at Farley. "On the water," he said after a while. "A liveaboard. An old sailboat, painted black. No masts. There's a pirate's flag at the back of the boat. It's Flex's boat, but he's crashing there. I don't think Flex is happy about it, but he's as afraid of that psycho as everyone else."

"Flex?"

"It's his boat. They call him the Pirate."

"Where's it anchored?"

"Just off Ross Island. In the channel. There's a fleet."

"A fleet?"

"A bunch of homeless boats. They tie up together. You can't miss it."

Without another word, Farley began walking south along the path, the way he'd come.

"Hey, Bobby's going to be pissed," Chad yelled after him, but he did not stop or look back.

Portland life revolved around two rivers: the Willamette, which bisected it, and the Columbia, which connected it to the rest of the state, from the coast to the high desert. Critical to fishing, recreation, transportation, and cargo, the rivers comprised no small part of Portland's cultural identity too, and thousands of people lived in sanctioned floathouse communities on the northern and southern edges of town. With the river playing such an integral role in Portland life, it should not have surprised anyone when the homelessness crisis found its way to the water as well.

Boats are expensive to buy and maintain. They're also expensive to dispose of. The flesh and bones and blood of boats—oils, fluids, solvents, wiring, fiberglass, bottom paint—pose environmental issues, making hulls and fittings difficult or impossible to recycle. Unwanted boats must be hauled to appropriate facilities for dismantling and disposal. This leaves unscrupulous owners who are unwilling to pay for decommissioning with two choices for their unwanted boats: scuttle them—drill holes in the hulls and sink them without ceremony, like mariners of yore did—or abandon them in empty fields, parking lots, or tied to public docks. The first option created navigational hazards and added to the river's existing environmental ailments; the second created toxic, unwieldy garbage.

But some creative thinker saw the abandoned boats not as a nuisance but as an opportunity. He realized that amid skyrocketing housing costs and community uproar about homeless camps, he could get his hands on an old boat big enough to live aboard for nothing, or next to it. It might not be fancy. It might not even run. But it came with a sleeping berth, a galley with a table, even a deck.

The idea proved to be an elegant solution. Like many elegant solutions, it spread quickly, and within a few years, the Willamette was home to what locals unofficially called "The Hobo Armada," an admiralty of ratty scows anchored in a jurisdictional void just off the river's banks. As on land, where a homeless camp could appear and take over a park, block, or entire neighborhood in just a few days, the floating camps grew quickly, anchoring in groups, rafting together. Their occupants lashed ramshackle docks to their transoms, piled their decks with stolen bikes and grills and lawn furniture, and created entire communities on the water. Portland Police, Multnomah County Sheriffs, Oregon State Troopers, even the Coast Guard passed the buck on enforcement authority, and the Hobo Armada of Portland, Oregon, grew.

If you kidnapped a girl and wanted to hide her far from prying eyes—somewhere she was unlikely to be found—you could do worse than a boat anchored in the river, Farley figured as he backtracked along the Springwater. By his best guess, he'd covered five or six miles since breakfast. He'd not eaten anything since, and his hunger made him mean.

Meaner.

Boats dotted the Willamette as far as he could see, upstream and down, hog lines of salmon and sturgeon fishermen, Jet Skis buzzing like mosquitoes, a dozen identical sails of rented Sunfish dipping and bowing to each other in the breeze. He watched a rowing scull unzip the river with its long, quiet wake—probably a college team from Lewis & Clark. Near Ross Island he could see the fleet Chad had told him about anchored a couple of hundred yards from the bank in the channel.

To reach it he would need a boat of his own. His best chance at finding one was the floathouse community at the channel's southern reach. Procuring one might pose a challenge, but he'd figure it out—not exactly a plan, but that didn't worry him. He'd never been much for planning, preferring instinct or ingenuity, or just brute force.

To reach the floathouses, he had to cut through Oaks Amusement Park, a small, sad facsimile of a fun park nevertheless beloved by the community. During the season you could hear the screams and laughter of children on the rides from the Springwater, but this late in the year, the park was closed. Farley heard only traffic from the nearby bridge, rain hitting pavement, his heavy breathing.

He'd brought Abril to the park for her fifth or sixth birthday. Jet-lagged from the flights, thrown off-balance by being back in Portland, and over-scrutinized by Nirva, he'd expected the day to be another Classic Farley Disaster. But as he walked along the chain-link fence that separated the rides and games from the parking lot, he remembered her joy. How she'd cheered from his lap on the Cosmic Crash bumper cars, the way she'd laughed as she rocketed down the giant pink slide fifteen times in a row.

He didn't have many happy memories of her—or many memories at all—but this one lifted him up, a bright kite in the overcast sky. Almost immediately, more recent memories cut the string, and his happiness floated away. As he stood alone in the rainy parking lot, pain and grief amplified by his hunger welled up inside him. Deep in his chest, his heart kicked into overdrive as the memories became physical, and he struggled to breathe as his vision blurred, struggled to swallow. The past turned to pain in the present, and he threw up in his mouth.

It tasted like cotton candy.

Farley turned and leaned against the fence, eyes closed, waiting for the misery to pass. When it did, he straightened up, opened his eyes, and turned back around. His vision remained hazy, but he saw three men standing in front of him—overwhelmed by his panic attack, his early warning system had failed.

One of the men leered at him.

One of them scowled.

The third hit him with something hard. His legs folded beneath him, and he blacked out before he even hit the ground.

25

A HEAVY SONOFABITCH

Farley briefly regained consciousness three times. The first time, he found himself face down on the wet pavement, fielding relentless kicks to his ribs by what felt like the Bolivian national soccer team. "How does a shepherd keep track of his sheep?" Wayne had asked him once. "Count the legs and divide by four." Before he could even try to count, he took a boot to the groin and lost consciousness again.

The next time, he woke curled on his side like an apostrophe. When he opened his eyes, his vision remained hazy, like looking through frosted glass. He could make out vague figures, shouting voices, motion, but failed to parse any of it. The figures did not move in any natural way that he could make sense of. The effort of trying overwhelmed his system, and he blacked out once more.

The third time, he came to on his back. The good news? Nobody was kicking him. The bad? He could not move, his arms and legs bound, his face covered. He felt motion, an odd weightlessness, as if he were floating through space.

He heard voices—female voices—talking in short bursts. Commands.

"Hold the front end."

"Don't drop him."

"Watch the door!"

"Get him inside."

"Heavy sonofabitch."

"Seriously."

Agony roiled his body, waves of nausea and fatigue. He thought he could smell fried food, sweat. Lysol. Perfume. None of it made sense. Then something changed, maybe gravity itself. He spun upside down in a chaos of motion and pain, and just like that, Farley was out again.

26

A BIG FLIGHTLESS BIRD

He came to one last time, slowly rising from the bottom of a dark ocean toward the surface and the light. What is pain? Pain is the ocean he fell into, the sea into which he'd been pushed. Pain was the water he swallowed, the currents that carried him. Pain was the creatures that called that dark sea home, crabs that reached up from their rotten beds to pinch at his tired feet, toothy fish that nibbled his flesh, eels that entered through his pores and ribboned their way through his veins. Pain was the jellyfish whose sting embraced him, the whale that swallowed him whole.

It did not feel like weightlessness anymore. Instead he felt as if the pressure of the depths at which he'd been sunk pressed against him with deadly strength, compressing his organs, crushing his bones. If he moved too quickly, he feared the bends. So he did not move—not immediately. He did not even open his eyes.

Starting at his feet, he initiated a methodical system check that ran the length of his ravaged and hideous body straight to his throbbing head. He wiggled his toes—check. He stretched his legs, igniting the now familiar fire along the fall lines of his scars—check. When he took a deep breath and inflated his lungs to their capacity, he discovered his abdomen and torso in possession of a new and unfamiliar pain—if he could see, he knew he'd find bruises to match—but his lungs still worked, which meant no broken ribs or significant internal damage.

So . . . check?

Pleased to find that he'd regained use of his arms, which lay unbound and unrestricted at his sides, he lifted them tentatively overhead, like a referee calling a field goal. Check. They worked, but they hurt like hell.

Legs and toes, arms and elbows, the TV commercial from his childhood went. *Check, check, and check.*

He opened his eyes. The darkness failed to disappear.

Assured that his body remained more or less intact, Farley turned his attention to assessing his situation. He'd awakened seated, slumped against a wall. Beneath him was a limp mattress or pad of some kind. He patted for the edges and found a cold, hard floor beneath it.

From another room he could hear muffled voices. Yelling, but not angry. Short bursts of words. Commands. Shouts. Cheers. Beneath them he heard a steady, irregular rumbling, like machinery. Like thunder. The surface-on-surface roar rose and subsided in waves and crescendos but never ceased entirely, punctuated regularly by high-pitched squeaking. Like sneakers on a basketball court, maybe. The sound annoyed him, at the same time familiar and unrecognizable. Over it all he heard music. Aggressive, guitar-driven punk. Music with momentum.

Using the wall for leverage, he struggled to his feet. His head exploded, and a wave of nausea flushed through him, like he'd opened a jar of pain and swallowed it whole. Breathing deeply to stave it off, he rested against the wall. As he did, his eyes adjusted to the darkness. About ten feet away, he saw a crack of light under a doorway. After another minute he could make out more of the room around him—a supply closet, maybe. Shelves of cleaning products, paper towels, cans of paint. "Lemme ask you something," Wayne had said one night, greeting Farley upon his return to camp. "What's red and smells like blue paint?" Wayne's jokes tended not to be thinkers. But much to his surprise, he'd not been able to guess the answer, simple and obvious at once and yet just beyond reach.

Red paint.

Pushing away from the wall tentatively, he pitched and yawed as he fought for a balance stubbornly slow to return. From a shelf he grabbed a paint can by the wire handle, a makeshift weapon. Something to swing. Weaving slowly in the darkness like he'd drunk too much whiskey, he reached for the handle to see if the door was locked. As soon as he touched it, his cell phone rang, the vibration against his leg from inside one of the cargo pockets of his fatigues startling him.

He fumbled it to his ear. "Lissa?" he said. "Did Olive come home?"

But it was not Lissa's voice that greeted him.

"Farley, you fat fuck. You fat, useless fuck. I've not had a decent night's sleep in months, and it's all your fault, you chicken-fried turd of a man."

"Now's not a good time." It hurt him to speak.

"Oh? Is that right? Is that fucking right, Farley? Is it not a good time for you?"

"Not really."

"Is your husband of eighteen years dead? Did you find the man that was your heart's very beat, marry him, and move to the North Fucking Pole with him because you had the absolute certainty that you would spend eternity together? And if he was right, the afterlife too? Only to watch that man get eaten by a goddamned *bear* right before your very eyes? Do you want me to wait for that, Farley? Would that be a better fucking time, Farley?"

Sometimes Rebecca seemed to have forgotten that he'd lost a daughter too. Sometimes he wanted to ask her, ask if she'd forgotten that he'd been mauled that night, his body undone, the course of his own life changed as inalterably as her own. But to what end? She blamed him because she needed to blame someone—how else could she hope to live with the consequences of that night? He blamed himself for the exact same reason, so he said nothing and shuffled back across the room to reclaim his spot on the mattress.

"What am I supposed to do, Farley? I'm a middle-aged widow with no experience in the world. John's the only man I ever dated. The only man I've ever slept with, Farley. The only man I've ever *fucked*." She paused, not for effect but to take another sip of whatever she was drinking at that particular moment. "He's the only man I've ever loved. I haven't been on a date since high school, and that was with John. Do you know where he took me?"

"A gentlemen's club?"

"Fuck you, Farley. To an amusement park. Did anyone ever love you enough in your whole miserable life to take you to an amusement park?"

"As a matter of fact," he began, but she cut him off.

"We rode the Ferris wheel and the roller coaster and the . . . what's it called? The teacups. They had a petting zoo. I got to feed the baby goats and the lambs and those big flightless birds."

"Ostriches."

"No."

"Emus?"

"Fuck you, Farley. You remind me of them, you know that? That's what you look like. A big goddamned flightless bird."

His phone said it was twelve thirty, eight thirty in Nanuqmiut—either she'd been up all night drinking or she'd begun the day with it. Or maybe she'd left the village, left the Arctic entirely, and gone back to Alabama. Farley waited while she took another sip of her drink with something that was not patience. Maybe penance. Maybe resolve.

"We ate funnel cakes and cotton candy, and John played that game where you throw the baseballs at the old-timey milk jugs. 'I'm gonna win you a prize, Rebecca,' he said. 'You start picking out what you want and let me just do my thing.'" She did a remarkable impression of her late husband's voice, dropping to an effective baritone, capturing his syntax and timbre, bringing him to life in the dark closet for just a moment. "And you know what, Farley? He won. He fucking won. It took him twenty minutes, and probably fifty dollars, but he just kept tossing those baseballs like Satchel Paige in the Negro Leagues until he knocked those milk jugs over."

She took another sip.

"Maybe he didn't even win. Maybe the boy behind the counter just took pity on him. I don't know. I don't remember."

Another sip.

"I got to pick out a prize. A stuffed animal. A big one. The size of a toddler. There was a whole shelf of animals to choose from. Every goddamned animal under the sun, just like Noah's ark. And you know what I chose, Farley? Do you know what I chose?"

He knew.

"A goddamned bear," she said. "A polar bear."

Sip.

"I chose it because it seemed so . . . erotic."

"You mean 'exotic.'"

"Fuck you, Farley, you fat fuck, don't tell me what I mean."

A beat passed.

Then another.

"You're right. I meant exotic."

After that, she was quiet for a long pause. When she spoke again, her voice had changed; the aggression gone, the fear returned.

"Do you think it's possible that I'm responsible for what happened to John that night because I chose that bear? Did I make that happen? Is that . . . *fate*? Like time folding over on itself or something? What if I'd chosen a . . . a . . . a . . . *seal*? Or a toucan? Or a . . . a . . . a puppy dog? Would what happened to John still have happened?"

"Rebecca, I—"

"That's what I think sometimes."

She took another sip, a long one. When she spoke again, the meanness had returned to her voice, and Farley found it almost comforting.

"But you know what I tell myself when I feel that way? When it gets to me? I tell myself, 'Of course you're not responsible, Rebecca. Of course it's not your fault. You may not be blameless in this life—you don't go the places you've been without getting a little dirty—but you. Did. Not. Make. This. Happen. Because you know who did? That shit-for-brains, rat-fucking peckerhead Farley. And you're never gonna stop blaming him for taking your John away.'"

A long moment passed in which neither of them said anything. He could not hear her anymore, not her drinking or crying or even her breathing. The silence drew on and on until he checked the phone to make sure the call remained connected.

"Farley," she said finally, her voice subdued.

"What?"

"Are you . . . OK?"

It didn't matter that she'd never asked him that before. It only mattered that he did not know what to tell her. What could he say? That he thought he was getting better, but that he might be getting worse? That sometimes he could barely breathe because of the pain, but that he welcomed it because the pain in his body helped him cope with the much worse one in his heart? That he'd made a friend and lost her all in the same weekend, and maybe that was his fault too, and that maybe it would be better to never care about anyone anymore ever again because he never wanted to lose anyone else or be responsible for anyone else?

In the end it didn't matter because before he could tell her anything, the door to the supply closet opened, and he hung up the phone.

27

TODAY'S THE DAY
I WASH MY HAIR

Alone with her fear in the minutes after Farley left, Lissa lit her third straight American Spirit in a row and tried like hell to calm herself. The lit end of the butt burned down to ashes. Her lungs ached. Her eyes burned. But still she found no reason to be calm. Though Farley had just left an hour ago, she reached for her phone to check for messages and instead found herself dialing her sister's number. It had been a few months since they'd talked last, their relationship good but not great. Not what it once had been. Lissa blamed herself. Sometimes she wondered if it would have happened anyway—both of them getting older, Allie moving away, their lives gathering momentum in unlike vectors—but her decisions had eroded the foundation and made it more difficult to weather those natural changes. And as the phone rang, she realized just how much she missed her sister.

"Hey, bitch," Allie said. "Can't chat now, I'm getting my cooch waxed." Their familiar greeting, an old in-joke that went back years. Lissa didn't remember how it had begun, exactly, but in their childhood they'd watched enough television together to recognize recurring patterns in the portrayal of female social behavior—patterns that could only have been written by men. Single men. They had co-opted the idea for their own ruthless humor, and sometimes carried it to near extremes. "How 'bout you, sister? It's still pretty early there—are you at work?"

"I'm staying home all day," she said weakly. "Today's the day I wash my hair."

"What's wrong, Liss?" All the jokiness had gone out of her sister's voice, replaced by genuine concern.

"That obvious?"

"Yes."

Lissa could hear ambient noise spilling through the phone. Other voices. Tinny music.

"Where are you?" she asked.

"Nail salon. We've got a fundraiser tonight and I wanted to get my tootsies done."

Tootsies? Lissa couldn't tell if her sister was being sincere or still playing their game. In fact, it occurred to her that she didn't actually know all that much about her life or her world or about who she was becoming as an adult. A fundraiser for what?

"Can you talk, Al?"

"I can be home in less than an hour. I'll call you then."

Still clutching an unfinished cigarette, Lissa left the window and wandered down the hall to Olive's room, stopping on the way to toss it into the open toilet bowl, where it went out with a hiss. Olive's dresser drawers were still open, the folded clothes within a rumpled mess where they'd been rifled through, thinned out by the few missing items. He'd taken clean clothes when he took her. That meant he planned to keep her for a while—but it also meant that he planned to look after her, right? You wouldn't bring clean clothes if you . . . Unable to see the thought through to completion, Lissa straightened the clothes and shut the drawers. The mattress lay on the floor, the busted frame still where Farley had leaned it neatly against the wall. Jittery from the smokes and the stress, she sat down hard on the mattress. She looked around the room and saw how small it really was, how crowded it felt. The entire apartment felt small, and yet it had been the extent of Olive's world outside of school and daycare. Growing up in Sandy, Lissa and Allie had endless outdoor space, woods to roam, the river to swim in. Why had she only seen the shortcomings—the lack of culture, the finite pool of people, the limitations of the rural sensibility? She couldn't get out of there fast enough. But now she saw that raising a child in the city had been a mistake.

Her parents had always been out in the yard of their home, landscaping, gardening, sipping lemonade on lawn chairs. She remembered her father buying a tray of pachysandra to plant behind a retaining wall he'd built in the backyard of their raised ranch, hoping the ground cover would fill the twenty-by-twenty slope and shore up the soil against erosion. But within a few years, the invasive plant had taken over the entire yard, choking out native and established plants and encroaching on his prized lawn. Sitting on Olive's mattress in her tiny room, Lissa recognized that her fear was like that too. That if she didn't fight it constantly, pulling it out by the roots, it would choke the life out of her.

Her phone rang and she answered it immediately without looking at the screen.

"Farley?"

"Who's Farley?" her sister asked, and just like that, Lissa began to sob.

Allie stayed quiet. After a minute Lissa wiped her tears on the Frozen bedspread and told her about Olive being taken. She'd thought telling someone might help, but as she recounted the events of the last few weeks that led up to it—the homeless camp, the incident at the bus stop, Farley's arrival in their lives—Lissa felt even worse. Hearing it out loud made it more real, and she imagined how it must sound to her sister. As if not just her parenting skills but her common sense was no longer even up for debate. She told her about the police visit that morning.

"Jesus Christ, Liss," Allie said.

"I know. I *know*."

"You trust this guy? Farley?"

"What choice do I have, Al?"

"I don't know, Liss," she said, a coolness to her voice that hadn't been there before.

"What?"

"It's just . . . I don't know."

"Just say it, Allie."

Her sister sat on her thought for a few moments, either letting it form or wondering if she should say it aloud. Though she had just two years on her, it sometimes felt like an entire generation. Though Lissa had a baby, Allie had gotten her life together sooner, faster, more smoothly, transitioning more seamlessly from childhood to adulthood without drama. Becoming a teen mother forced you kicking and screaming into parenthood at the same time that it denied you all the formative experience you needed to become a functioning adult.

"It's just that you don't have the best track record with men," Allie said.

Without getting up from Olive's mattress, Lissa found and lit another cigarette. She knew she'd never get the smell out of the room and that Olive would be furious with her, but at least that would mean that Olive was home. She'd deal with her anger when she had to.

"That's not what this is. Farley's just a neighbor. A friend."

"What about the guy who took her?"

"He's homeless, Al. I told you. An addict. A creep."

"Come on, Lissa. People don't just walk into other people's apartments and steal their children. There's got to be more to the story than that."

"Al . . ."

"I mean, for Christ's sake, Lissa. You don't know where your daughter is. Your only real friend is some scary sad sack who lives next door? But who also sleeps on the street sometimes? You let this man into your home? Around your daughter? Seriously? How is this your life? How did you let something like this happen?"

"I didn't *let* anything happen, Allie."

"You have to admit, Liss. You have a history of making pretty bad decisions."

Though the urge to fight roiled her from within, Lissa grew very quiet. She looked at the cigarette in her hand and saw it shaking, the ashes falling onto the comforter like snow. Every muscle in her body had gone tight.

"You're right," she said calmly. "I have made bad decisions in the past. But the only bad decision I made this time was calling *you* and expecting sympathy. Or help. Or anything other than blame." She hung up before Allie could respond.

The anger coursing through her blood at that moment felt better than the fear had, or the self-pity. Anger motivated her, at least. No way she was going to sit around all day waiting for Farley or The Ferryman to call—she would get out there herself, beat the streets, cruise every homeless camp in the city if she had to, whatever it took to find Olive and protect her and to hurt the man who had taken her.

28

MEET THE STUMPTOWN SAVIORS

Blinded by the sudden light pouring through the doorway, Farley raised a hand to block it. Noise rushed in through the open door with it, the pumping music, the voices, the machine roar. Again he waited for his eyes to adjust, his pupils constricting so aggressively he could almost hear them.

When he lowered his hand, a solitary figure stood silhouetted against the light. Joined to the shadow where it gripped the doorframe, it did not look human—not exactly, the head too big and round, the arms and legs misshapen. Confused, Farley got to his feet with some effort. Friend or foe, he didn't know, but he lifted his paint can and readied himself to fight.

"Easy there, big guy." A woman's voice. "Good to see you back on your feet. We were kind of freaking out."

"Where am I?"

"I bet you've got a banger of a headache. Come on out, I'll get you some Advil."

The silhouette detached itself from the doorframe and glided backward with a ghostly, fluid movement that Farley failed to make sense of until he followed it through the doorway into the light and saw the roller skates. She also wore black knee socks with scuffed black pads on her knees and elbows, tomato-red tights under tiny black shorts, and a matching red tank top. Brilliantly colored tattoos covered much of the pale skin of her arms, and a fringe of blue hair hung from a black helmet, framing her face, which was painted with black-and-white makeup into a Día de los Muertos mask.

"Welcome to roller derby practice," she said, rolling slowly backward and spreading her arms like wings.

They were in a cavernous hangar with bleachers at one end surrounding a rink with a banked track circuit. Ten women in uniforms similar to hers raced counterclockwise around the track, yelling to one another. As he watched, the noises he'd heard from the closet coalesced: the wheels on the wooden track, the squeak of foot brakes, loud music over the PA.

"I think I used to skate here when I was a kid," he said.

"Me too!" she said. "But that was probably over in the main rink. That's in another building across the way. This is the annex. The park rents it out to derby teams. We get it Mondays and Wednesdays—shit days, because it's midday and most of us have to take time off from work to practice around our lunch hours—but we're the newest team, so."

"Roller derby? Wasn't that a seventies thing?"

"Maybe *you're* a seventies thing." She gave him a look. "We don't even have a name yet. Most of the girls skated with other teams but some are just getting started too. Hey, we're trying a few names out. Which do you like better? Derby Dames, Rip City Rollers, or the P-Town Posse?"

Vegas was Sin City, Chicago the Windy City, New York the Big Apple. Boston was Beantown, though nobody in Boston called it that. But Portland? It had a seemingly endless list of nicknames, as if it contained so many multitudes that no single one could fit it right. Or maybe because its personality changed so quickly that none stuck for long. Rose City, Rip City, P-Town, Little Beirut. PDX, for its airport code; Bridgetown, for the thirteen bridges spanning the Willamette; Stumptown, which dated back to the mid-1800s, when developers cleared land at a greedy pace that reduced the forest to tree stumps.

Farley felt like one of those felled trees, like the rest had fallen directly on him. "You said something about Advil?"

"Sorry, right. There's a bathroom over there. Advil and Band-Aids on the shelves."

Inside the small bathroom, Farley pulled the string for the light and winced involuntarily at his reflection in the broken mirror. Dried blood caked in his hair and one ear, around his swollen lips, and all over the front of his shirt. Painfully he lifted his shirt and saw the bruises already forming, his abdomen and ribs yellowing. He swallowed a fistful of Kirkland ibuprofen and stuck his head in the sink to clean himself up as best he could. A lost cause.

The woman waited just outside the door.

"We haven't formally met," she said, sticking out a hand. "Lady MacDeath."

He took her hand and shook it. "Farley."

"Are you hungry, Farley?"

Rolling slowly so he could follow, she made her way to the snack bar and ordered two soft pretzels with cheese and a corn dog from the elderly woman behind the counter. She gave him the corn dog to eat while they waited for the pretzels. Farley swallowed it nearly whole. Olive needed him, and Lissa was counting on him, but he felt justified taking a few minutes to nurse his wounds and eat a late lunch after getting his unconscious ass kicked.

They sat in the front row of the bleachers and watched her teammates skate around the track. Moving rhythmically, they gathered speed—a school of fish, a flock of birds, a murmuration of swallows. Not synchronized. Not choreographed. But as one. A hive. Farley felt the breeze as they passed, heard the whir of their wheels on the maple boards, felt the energy of their determination. Many of the women were inked, and they all wore garish tights and socks, tank tops, sports bras. Some wore death mask makeup like Lady MacDeath; others wore war paint. One looked like a psychedelic Ziggy Stardust.

"Want to tell me how I ended up at the roller derby?" he asked between bites.

"Some of us skate to practice together from downtown. We take the Springwater, and we skate as a pack for safety. It's full of degenerates. No offense."

"None taken. At least there wasn't until you said that."

"When we rolled into the parking lot here at the rink, we saw you on the ground with three guys kicking the shit out of you." She studied him for a moment. "Not for nothing, Farley, but it looks like maybe that wasn't the first time that's happened to you."

He nodded.

"You owe them money or something?"

"It's not like that."

"What's it like?"

"The three guys. What happened to them?"

"We did our thing."

"Your thing?"

She nodded at the track. Farley saw two women with starred helmets break away from the pack as they reached the opposite end of the circuit. Pulling ahead, they bent at the waist, pumping their legs methodically, passing where he sat like fleet ghosts. Already they began to close ground between them and the back of the pack they'd left behind. The group passed him again—the gathering breeze, the smell of sweat and perfume and Bengay—and then the first of the starred skaters caught up to it. As she worked her way through the crowd, she weaved among them, the opposing skaters shifting position to block her passage, bumping her, cutting her off. She pulled alongside two of her own teammates and shouted something. They each grabbed one of her hands and skated ahead. She dropped back between them, like loading a slingshot, and as they headed into a turn, they launched her forward at an alarming rate of speed. As the pack approached his side of the loop again, an opposing skater moved to block her, but one of her teammates swooped in and caught her with a vicious hip check that knocked her legs out from under her. In a flurry of arms and legs, she crashed into the wall with a sickening thud.

"As you can see," she said, "we're not exactly defenseless little maidens."

He nodded approvingly. "These guys—what did they look like?"

"Fucking losers. I can only describe their backs because they ran away pretty damn fast."

"Can you tell me anything about them?"

"I don't know if this helps, but one of them was soaking wet."

Bobby.

"You carried me inside?"

"That, my friend, was not easy. We have a spine board in case any of the girls gets hurt. It took six of us, but we got you on it and rolled you inside like pallbearers."

The flashes of consciousness he'd experienced began to make sense. The movement. The figures. The sounds.

"Not to complain," he said. "But . . . did you drop me?"

"Sorry." She winced, but he could see a smile buried beneath it. "One of the Jammers is a doctor at OHSU. She checked out your wounds and said you'd be OK, so we decided to let you sleep it off."

"She's a doctor?"

"Ob-gyn." She looked at him, trying to read his face. "What, you think derby girls are just punks and sluts?"

"No, I—"

"I'm just messing with you, Farley." She smiled again.

Two of her teammates rolled up, holding water bottles and towels, their face paint smeared with sweat, skin flush with exertion.

"Farley, meet Pain Eyre and Skate Hipburn. They were with me when we found you."

"Thanks for the rescue," he said.

"Don't worry about it." Shorter than either of her friends, and stockier, Skate Hipburn had a brightness to her eyes that felt honest and good—like a child's, not yet made cynical by the aggregate misery of life on Earth. "Honestly, we kind of enjoyed it. This city is full of douchebags. It felt pretty good to rough a few of them up."

Pain Eyre—tall and slender and serious, despite her clothing and face paint and the wheels strapped to her feet—nodded at Farley. "You should get that head looked at. I don't think it's serious, but I bet it hurts."

He nodded. Though the ibuprofen had helped his headache subside, the motion gave it a second wind. "You're the doctor?"

"Yes."

"I've had worse." He watched the familiar way they fell silent, the awkward and expected acknowledgment of his scars, his dead eye, the noticeable limp. At that moment he thought of Abril, how she might have grown up to be smart and strong and interesting like these women. How she might have joined a roller derby team or become a doctoral student or a doctor. How many other opportunities had she missed out on?

He would not let the same thing happen to Olive. He got to his feet.

"I appreciate what you did for me," he said. "But there's someplace I really need to be."

"Come back Friday night," Skate Hipburn said. "We've got our first bout. Just a scrimmage, but we need to fill the bleachers with paying customers to get the park to let us keep using the rink. Bring some friends."

"My friends couldn't fill your bleachers. They couldn't even fill your skates."

"Then help us pick a name. We can't compete without one, and none of us can agree on one."

Farley thought for a minute. "How about the Stumptown Saviors?"

Lady MacDeath accompanied him to the door, rolling alongside as he took one tentative step after another, testing the effects of all the ground he'd covered that morning and the beating he'd taken on his wrecked legs. A clock over the big double doors to the hangar said it was almost one. Farley looked outside. A light rain fell on the parking lot.

"So, what's your story, Farley? Really?"

He told her about Olive and The Ferryman, about the black-hulled boat and his day so far. How it had led him to their parking lot and their supply closet.

"Motherfucker," she said. "I've seen that scow. We paddle right by it at dragon boat practice."

She thought for a moment.

"Why *you*, Farley? Are you some kind of private eye?"

"No. That little girl and her mother—they're friends."

"Thought you didn't have friends."

"They might be the only ones."

"How do you plan to get out to that scow?"

"Find a boat. That's what I was heading to do when I got jumped."

"Wait here." She skated back inside the hangar and returned a few minutes later in street clothes, her face still painted, blue hair up in double pigtails. Farley saw she'd traded her skates for Rollerblades.

"One of my professors lives in a floathouse at the head of the channel," she said. "I watch it for him sometimes when he goes out of town to conferences or whatever. I take care of his stupid cat. That asshole's got a boat. It's nothing fancy, but it will get you where you're going."

She threw her backpack over her shoulders.

"Come on," she said. "I'll show you."

29

THE LAUREATE
OF AMERICAN LOWLIFE

The largest in a cluster of four islands a few miles southeast of downtown Portland, Ross Island was beautiful on the surface—wooded and hemmed with sandy beaches, home to both bald eagle and osprey rookeries—but ugly beneath, owned mainly by a sand and gravel company that for decades had been mining it out of existence. Piece by piece by piece, the company carved away the island's gravel heart, dumping it into barges, floating it to the river's east bank, and hauling it away in trucks. The contrast of industry and nature created dissonance. No longer a circle, the island had become just the outline of one, its center now a lagoon. Many years ago, the gravel company's owner bequeathed some forty-five acres of the island to the city for use as a nature preserve, but plans remained stalled over an unresolved debate about who should be responsible for the environmental cleanup of the toxic fill used in the mining operation. A lesson, Farley thought, about gifts.

As they approached the floathouse community, he could see the hobo fleet anchored near the northern end of Holgate Slough, the long channel between the island and the east bank. The floathouses sat at the southern end. Each home occupied its own float, anchored to the river bottom, and the homes ranged from tidy craftsmans with the riparian equivalent of curb appeal to more exotic designs, including an architecturally stunning contemporary built to mimic the shape of a breaking wave.

"Must be nice living in one of these," he said.

"I don't know. It's a lifestyle choice."

"What's not to like?"

"You get seasick on the toilet."

They cut through the residents' parking lot and took the long gangplank down to the docks. This time of year, before the heavy rain began in earnest, the low river level meant a steep descent. Lady MacDeath went first, holding the railing to check her speed and dragging the toe of one of her Rollerblades as a brake. Farley followed behind, watching the rooster tail of rainwater her wheels threw.

Her professor's floathouse was a utilitarian foursquare lacking any charm that sat a few docks from the northern terminus.

"This is it," she said, wheeling around his waterfront picnic table with a flourish. "Professor Bag-o-Dicks."

Farley raised an eyebrow.

"Dr. Marko Bogadek, professor of Balkan literature at Reed. I'm a doctoral student there. He's Croatian by way of New Jersey. A real twofer if you ask me. Everyone calls him Bag-O-Dicks, and honestly, it suits him. He's sleeping with half his students."

She saw his expression and made a face.

"Hell no. Gross."

She rolled over to a fiberglass rowing boat chained to the end of the dock and unlocked it.

"Case in point: the combination to his lock is eight-sixteen-twenty. Bukowski's birthday."

Farley raised another eyebrow.

"*Charles* Bukowski? The laureate of American lowlife?"

"Sorry."

"You seriously don't know Bukowski?" She looked at him hard, unbothered by the light rain that fell on her blue hair. "Well, that might make you one of the good guys, Farley."

She slid the chains through the boat's rails and dropped them on the wooden deck, stood up, and rolled over to him. The dock swayed beneath them.

"It was nice to meet you, Farley. Good luck out there."

"Thank you." He reached out a hand. She looked at it for a moment. "What are you going to do to the guy who took her if you find him?"

"I don't know," he said.

When she put her arms around him and hugged him tightly, it caught him off guard and nearly off-balance. He could feel her strength, the athleticism, and though his bruised torso exploded in pain, it felt good to touch someone again with affection rather than violence. It felt good to be touched.

Twice in one day, he thought.

Then he thought of Olive and tensed. She felt it and let go, rolling backward a foot or so, watching him.

"You're doing a really good thing," she said.

Farley nodded his thanks and, with some effort, lowered himself into the boat. It sunk more deeply into the water under his weight but did not tip. She handed him the oars from the dock, and he seated them into the locks.

It had been a long time since he'd rowed a boat, and it took a few strokes to coordinate himself. Once his muscles remembered and he could pull a straight line, he looked over his shoulder to find the scow, aligned the bow toward it, and leaned into the effort in earnest.

Lady MacDeath waved from the dock.

"Go get her, Farley. Bring that girl home to her mother."

The rowboat felt inconsequential beneath him, a thin layer of salvation between him and the river. It didn't feel like much, but it wasn't much different from how most people sailed through life, a wafer-thin shell the only thing keeping them from tragedy. And sometimes, he knew, that wasn't enough.

The cheaply built boat had two square ends, visible threads of the inexpensive fiberglass weave, the seat just an untreated pine plank. Someone had stenciled a quote on the inside of the hull in black paint:

"How inappropriate to call this planet Earth when it is clearly Ocean." — Arthur C. Clarke

Farley had no quarrel with the quote, but painting it on a cheap rowboat docked on an inland freshwater river felt like a lot of hype. Lady MacDeath might be right about Professor Bag-o-Dicks. He knew the boat had a specific name—johnboat, maybe, or punt—but didn't know it, knew only that mariners classified boats like a taxonomy of animal species. You couldn't call a sailboat a sailboat. You had to say schooner, yawl, ketch, or sloop, with some vague differentiator—the placement or height of a mast—all that distinguished them. A rowboat might be a wherry, a skerry, a skiff, or a dory. All drift boats were rowboats, but not all rowboats were drift boats. Sailors spoke in a secret-handshake language: port and starboard, fore and aft. Why not left and right, front and back? Ropes were *lines*, kitchens *galleys*, bathrooms *heads*, walls *bulkheads*. Never mind how they pronounced things—gunwales were *gunnels*, forecastles were *fokesulls*, boatswains were *bosuns*—like a semester-abroad student coming home from France and ordering *charcuterie* at a fucking Applebee's.

Pretentious bullshit, he thought. *It's a goddamned boat.*

The current favored him as he rowed, pulling him north toward the river mouth. The misery of rowing with a broken body did not hesitate to make itself known. With each stroke, his shoulders were a conflagration, a wildfire that spread through his torso and legs.

Route 99E ran high above the river on the eastern bank, and even from the water, he caught a stench of exhaust from the traffic that roared along it. Though he could hear the passing cars, he could also hear his oars feathering water, the wood squeaking in their locks, his own labored breathing, and it gave him a focus he would need once he boarded the black-hulled scow.

As he approached the anchored fleet, he craned to look over his shoulder at the boat Chad had identified. He could see that it had once been beautiful, with fine lines and open space on the deck. But with her mast and sails gone, she'd been reduced to a barge. Trash littered the open cockpit, bags of it, milk crates stuffed with various treasures molding in the steady rain.

His best option was to approach and board silently, retaining the element of surprise. He pulled alongside the ass end—the *stern*—to keep himself out of sight of the cabin windows—fucking *portholes*—and shipped the oars as he approached, letting his momentum and the current carry him to the boat. He tied the rowboat to a cleat, grabbed the stern rail, and hoisted himself aboard as gently as he could.

Which, he had to concede, was not particularly gentle—the boat dipped beneath his weight, bowing and rising again, pitching and yawing as if at an invisible wake. His body protested his efforts, the maneuver better suited to someone more svelte than he was. Water slapped against the hull.

The Jolly Roger flag flew from a rusting plow stake zip-tied to the rail. Farley cut the ties with his pocketknife and gripped the stake tightly. The wet metal felt cool against his hands.

Moving as quickly as he dared—or could—he crossed the cockpit. The cabin sat belowdecks, the entry a saloon-style door hinged on both sides with a center latch. He paused at the door and took a deep breath to steady himself.

Hoping to break it open and catch anyone in the cabin off guard, he lifted his good leg and stomped the door as hard as he could, using the plow stake for balance and putting all his considerable weight behind it. But years of rainwater and moisture and rot had weakened the thin wooden door. His foot tore through it with almost no resistance. Thrown off-balance, he crashed through the frame and fell headfirst down the steps into the boat's cabin.

30

TO THE HOTELS

Lissa called for a cab to pick her up at the apartment but found herself at a loss when the dispatcher asked her destination.

"I don't have one," she said.
"You don't have a destination?"
"No."
"Then what do you need a cab for?"
"I need a ride. I'm just not sure where."
"Ma'am. We're not a joyride service."
"Can't I pay by the hour? Or by the mile or something?"
"Hold the line."

The dispatcher mumbled something to someone else. She could hear muffled scuffling, a few different voices. He came back on the line and cleared his throat.

"My cousin Freddie drives for a black car service," he said. "His shift's just ending. He got nothing better to do, says he'll drive you around for a while."

She stood under her apartment awning, boring holes in the bus shelter with her stare as rain fell on the sidewalk where the camp used to be. After a few minutes, an immaculate old Lincoln pulled to the curb. The window rolled down, and an elderly man leaned out.

"Miss, you the one needs the ride?"

"Yes."

He leaped out of the door, pulled on his derby hat, and held open the back door for her. She saw his three-piece suit and recognized it of a certain vintage, like the car and the man himself.

"You can't smoke in here, miss," he said. "I'm sorry."

Lissa nodded and shotgunned the last drag of her cigarette, stamping it out in a puddle before she climbed in.

"I need a tour of the city," she told the driver when he'd taken his seat again.

"Usual highlights?"

"No. Just the homeless camps."

"Just the homeless camps?"

She nodded.

"I been driving this car for thirty years," he said. "And if that ain't a first."

"I'm looking for someone."

"Who's that, miss?"

"My daughter."

He eyed her in the rearview mirror. "Beg your pardon, but you don't look old enough to have a daughter living on the streets."

"She's not. She doesn't. She lives with me." Lissa bit her lip, the pain a shield to keep the tears at bay. "Someone took her and I'm trying to find him."

"Someone took her?"

"Yes."

"Like, he took her *from you*?"

She nodded and bit her lip harder. Freddie turned around to face her, his skinny arm resting on the back of the car's front seat.

"Forgive my saying so, miss, but you don't need a taxi. You need the police." He stressed the first syllable, making the O long. *PO-leece*.

"I already called them."

He nodded.

"They were no help."

He nodded again.

"Mmm-hmmmm," he said and started the car. "Police is useless in this city."

Freddie knew where many camps were because people who drive for a living know where to find just about everything in a city. The long days of circling the same blocks, tracing the same routes, you naturally start to recognize patterns—and conversely, changes in them. When a few tents pop up on a corner, you notice, he said. He drove carefully and methodically. Maybe that was what distinguished him from a cabbie. That and the suit. Slowly he'd pull up at each camp, rolling slowly along the curb while Lissa studied the campers through the tinted windows, straining for any sign of The Ferryman or Olive. The action felt familiar to her after the weeks of taxonomy at the camp outside her apartment. The campers stared back at the black limo, and she wondered what they made of it. A businessman looking for a wayward child? A rock star seeking lyrical inspiration? A billionaire in search of some desperate poor to hunt as game on his sprawling riverfront property?

Camp after camp, she saw no sign of them and recognized no one. How could a city as small as Portland have so many homeless people? How could the city allow this to continue?

"There's so many," she said.

"Lots of camps, miss. My cousin works for the city. People there say it's a crisis."

"I thought your cousin was the dispatcher?"

"Different cousin, miss."

This particular camp in the heart of downtown was particularly bad, and the campers themselves were in various states of filth and disarray.

"Some of these people desperately need help," she said.

"Mmm-hmmm," Freddie agreed.

"Not all of them deserve it."

"Mmm-hmmm."

Every few minutes she checked her phone to make sure it was still on and that she still had bars and battery, looking for messages and hoping both that she'd get one and that she wouldn't. She hoped Farley was having better luck with his own investigation.

After casing their seventh or eighth camp, an increasingly desperate Lissa began to wonder about the futility of her task. Freddie only knew about the big camps established on the city streets, not the ones that took root in the parks and along the Springwater Corridor, up on Mount Tabor and Powell Butte. Olive could be in any of those too, and since they weren't visible from the road, she thought it more likely that The Ferryman would have taken her there.

"Maybe he ain't in a camp at all, miss."

"He's homeless."

"Homeless ain't a permanent condition, miss. Maybe he got a hotel room or something. Someplace to hide out like. My cousin works at one out by the airport. You wouldn't believe the things he sees there, miss."

"Can you take me to those?"

"Those what, miss?"

"The hotels."

"Which ones?"

"All of them."

Freddie put the car in park and turned around again, arm on the seat back. "Miss, it's your dime. I'll drive you all day if you want. But let's talk it through together. How's that gonna work? You aiming to knock on every door of every hotel room in Portland? Maybe ask at the front desk if they seen your daughter?"

Lissa answered him with tears. He had a point, and she knew it. But at the thought of stopping, the creeping ground cover of fear started to choke her from within.

"I got a better idea," Freddie said.

She sniffled and wiped her eyes on her sleeve.

"How 'bout you let me buy you some lunch?"

31

IT'S A LITTLE EARLY FOR DINNER, ISN'T IT?

Upside down with his foot caught in the door, Farley hung like a bat with his head at the bottom of the stairs. He peered into the dim cabin. The walls—*bulkheads*—were wood-paneled. Like the deck, garbage littered the counters and floors, a noble collection of takeout containers, crumpled paper bags, empty beer cans, vodka bottles, and burnt tinfoil. More trash filled the built-in bunk beds. A small galley station held a dormitory fridge and shallow steel sink, and a pan on a small butane stove filled the cabin with wisps of steam.

It smelled like beef stew.

Tinny music poured out of a transistor radio, some kind of Latin beat. Bossa nova, maybe. Salsa. Fado. A narrow door opened at the far end of the cabin, and a man high-stepped over the threshold, dancing with his eyes closed, an imaginary partner in his arms. Despite the claustrophobic quarters and tight floor space, he danced with abandon, in complete surrender to the music, to the dance steps, to his nonexistent companion.

From Farley's disadvantaged position, it looked like he was dancing on the ceiling.

"Dance like nobody's watching," Farley said as the man spun his invisible partner. He opened his eyes and shrieked with a shrillness that could clear birds from trees and strip paint from shingles. Looking around the cabin in an obvious, frantic panic, he grabbed the nearest object—the pan on the stove—and hurled it at Farley, who instinctively raised his arms to protect his face. Or lowered them, being upside down. The pan collided with his forearms and spilled its contents on his chest and face as it fell to the floor.

Definitely beef stew. And not yet hot, thankfully.

"Fuck," the man said. "Fuck! That was my dinner!"

Farley knew it was still just early afternoon despite everything he'd been through already. Some days are like that, sprawling and unstructured, stuffed full until bursting.

"Little early for dinner, isn't it?"

The man stared at him from across the narrow cabin with the bluest eyes he'd ever seen. He wore orange Grundéns rain gear, stained black in places with what looked like tar, and had gathered his long white hair in a ragged, thinning ponytail.

"I was hungry," he said finally, sounding defensive. "Who are you?"

"Santa Claus. I couldn't find the chimney on your boat."

"Fuck off."

"Are you Flex?"

"You look disappointed."

Farley shrugged and felt the stairs digging into his back. "Someone told me you were a pirate."

"You were expecting a parrot and a patch?"

"I'm not sure *what* I was expecting."

"If you're here for my treasure, you picked the wrong boat."

"I'm looking for The Ferryman."

"That piece of shit? He's not here. And he's not welcome here. If that garbage human ever comes back here, I'll . . . I'll . . ." He paused, unsure how to finish his threat.

"Throw hot soup at him?" Farley suggested.

Flex looked embarrassed. "It was lukewarm at best."

Farley's instinct told him Flex was a man in possession of a gentle nature, not one well suited to threats or violence. That can make you a target. Get you taken advantage of. Whatever crimes The Ferryman would end up being guilty of, he didn't think Flex was an accomplice. If anything, he was another victim.

"That guy's a full diaper," Flex said, turning off the music. "I let him stay for a couple of days, and he completely trashed the place."

"When did he leave?"

"Yesterday."

"Know where he went?"

"Why? What do you want with him?"

"He took something that I very much want back."

Flex nodded, unsurprised. "Try the mission on Grand. He eats there sometimes. Hangs out there before dinner. Mostly he goes to sell drugs to other guys in line."

"What about Wayne? Do you know Wayne?"

"*Insane* Wayne?"

Farley nodded, a defiance of physics in his inverse position that he suspected looked as odd as it felt.

"Is he involved in this too?"

"No. He's just a friend."

"Wayne goes there sometimes too. Or the food pantry on West Burnside, at the bottom of the bridge. They don't sleep there, they just go for two squares. Maybe a shower." He leaned against the counter. "Living on the boat works for me. I like the quiet. I like being alone. But Wayne and The Ferryman? They like the camps because they like being around other people. Just for different reasons."

Though the blood had been rushing to his head for a good few minutes and he could feel its effects, Farley thought about what he'd said.

"Other people make Wayne feel safer."

"That's right," Flex said.

"What about The Ferryman?"

"For him they're just prey."

Flex went through the forward cabin and climbed out the bow hatch onto the deck. From there he circled around to the aft cabin door and, with a little effort, managed to free Farley's foot, releasing him. He slid down the steps and got to his feet. Even hunched he could not stand comfortably belowdecks.

"You look like someone stuck a salmon in a sardine can," Flex said, sounding genuinely amused. He pointed to a narrow cabin door with a flashlight on a string hanging from the handle. "The head's in there if you want to clean up. You'll need the flashlight. There's no electrical."

"Why is it called 'the head,' anyway?" Farley asked as he limped across the cabin, scraping one shoulder against the ceiling. "Why can't you just say 'bathroom'?"

"The bow's the only part of a sailboat that's always downwind. In the old days, if you had to go, you went off the 'head' of the ship. That way the wind would take care of the smell, and the water rushing by would flush it away."

Farley hadn't expected a sincere answer. "But why does *everything* on a boat have a different name than on land?"

"Most of it is utilitarian. Port and starboard instead of left and right—those names refer to fixed points, regardless of which direction you're facing, so there's no confusion. But some of it, well . . . Maybe it's just protecting traditions that might otherwise get forgotten."

Flashlight in hand, Farley squeezed into the tiny stall, banging both elbows repeatedly while washing beef stew from his face and studiously avoiding his reflection in the hazy mirror. The sink operated by a foot pump. From the way the water smelled out of the tap, and the oily film it left on his face, he figured Flex had jerry-rigged it to pump river water.

Maybe you couldn't blame the floating homeless for dumping their sewage into the river when the city had done the same thing for most of the last century. The Willamette of his childhood had been full of industrial chemicals, creosote, and unchecked amounts of human waste. When they were kids, Farley and his friends used to dare each other to swim in it, the only prize being a week of itchy skin and burning eyes. After the feds designated it a Superfund mega-site in thirteen locations, the city mounted a $1.5 billion "Big Pipe" project to eliminate most of the sewage flow, but on rainy days the new system could not keep up, and residents were warned not to make contact with the water. *Thank God it never rains in Portland,* Farley thought as he slouched over the sink and scrubbed stew from his hair.

He emerged to find Flex at the stove making a fresh pot. Farley had eaten his share of the prepackaged "meals ready to eat" in the army and thought he'd recognized the metallic taste of the weaponized stew.

"MRE, right?" he asked.

"Freeze-dried," Flex confirmed. "They sell fancy ones at the camping place for twenty bucks, but I get these at the army navy surplus for three."

"We used to divide them into two categories. 'Meals reluctant to exit' and 'massive rectal expulsion.'"

"You were in the army?"

Farley nodded. "You?"

"No. I don't have the temperament for it."

"For what?"

"For killing."

"In my experience, that's not what being in the army is about."

"OK," Flex said, stirring the stew in the pot with one of the disposable wooden chopsticks stacked like cordwood on the counter in their paper wrappers with red kanji characters. "What's it about?"

"In my experience, being in the army is mostly about putting up with shit. You get real good at it, and you're a goddamned expert by the time you get out. After the army, you can put up with almost anything if you have to."

"In *my* experience, that's the same thing civilian life is about."

Farley considered that he might be right.

"How'd you end up homeless?"

"I'm *not* homeless," he said defensively. He stared into his warming stew for a few moments. "Do you read, Farley?"

"Not much, no."

"In *The Sun Also Rises*, Hemingway wrote that going bankrupt happens two ways: gradually, and then suddenly. Losing your home? Losing everything? It's like that. I used to fish commercially out of Newport. Dungies. Salmon. Had my own boat, my own crew. But fishing's not what it used to be, yeah? A couple of bad hauls and you're in the hole. Some of your crew jumps to a boat that's catching fish instead of water sets. So you have to hire new guys, greenhorns who maybe don't know what they're doing. Then a cylinder goes in the engine, and you go into debt to pay for it."

He stirred the stew with a chopstick.

"Boat fuel ain't cheap. And the fish? Well, they don't always cooperate. The next thing you know, your boat's on the hard and so are you. You've got a lifetime of experience, but no other captain will hire you because you're too old or because they don't want you to know their secret spots, or both. I loved Newport but I had to leave because it's a lot harder to be homeless in a small coastal tourist town than it is in a city. It's a lot harder to blend in when you're sleeping behind one of the few businesses in town. There's no support. No infrastructure. I hitchhiked to Portland and bounced around the shelters and missions for a while, trying to make something work. Slept on the streets." He looked at Farley. "Did you know they call it 'sleeping rough' in the UK? Sounds much nicer than 'sleeping on the streets,' right? But it's the same degrading bullshit."

He exhaled, remembering those nights, maybe.

"I was homeless for a long time," he said. "Many years. But not anymore. *This* is my home."

Farley nodded. "Well, sorry about your door," he said. Flex looked up from the stove and stared at him for a long time, as if trying to decide something.

"It's a hatch," he said finally.

32

WELCOME TO THE ROACH COACH, JACKASS

Letting the current do most of the work as he rowed downriver, once Farley cleared the northern tip of Ross Island, he hugged the river's east bank. First, he passed beneath the Ross Island Bridge, which carried traffic on Route 26 from the Oregon Coast all the way east to the Idaho border, and then the new Tilikum Crossing, a cable bridge the metro area's regional transit authority had built to carry its MAX light rail, streetcar, and buses. The bridge allowed cyclists and pedestrians on its wide lanes, but no other private or commercial vehicles. It had not been built the last time he'd been in Portland, and the first time he saw it lit up at night, it had impressed him. The bridge was funded as a public art project, and its two hundred lights were linked to water sensors that triggered changes in color and motion to reflect the river temperature, tide direction, water speed, and depth. In all the years he'd lived in the Arctic, he couldn't remember seeing even a single bridge—if you wanted to cross a river, you took a boat or waited for winter. But Portland had taken stock of its dozen bridges across a single river and thought, "Let's build one more, and let's make it beautiful."

Just north of the new bridge, he saw the familiar big red letters on the side marking the Oregon Museum of Science and Industry. For a moment he considered calling Lissa once he reached it, but she would have called him if she'd heard from The Ferryman. He would wait until he had something tangible to report. Instead he let his mind wander to distract him from the brute agony of his body as he rowed toward OMSI in the rain.

The museum had purchased the USS *Blueback*, the navy's last non-nuclear submarine, prior to its decommissioning and docked it in the river as an exhibit. More than two hundred feet long, the submarine was half-submerged, her sleek dorsal spine and conning tower rising out of the Willamette in front of him like a giant snub-nosed dolphin.

He slid Professor Bag-o-Dicks's boat alongside the *Blueback* and lashed it to a cleat. Tired and sore from the hard row, he pulled himself onto the dock with relief and stretched his back and neck, happy to be back on land. His first few tentative steps felt like learning to walk again. Knees like broken glass, the shards ground together with each step and cut into the tendons and muscles, scraping skin. Every inch ached. His head felt defeated.

But he was alive. And until that changed, nothing would stop him from finding Olive.

Dragging his left foot more than he would have liked, he lurched along the sidewalk toward 99E and the mission as the daylight began to wither. The Portland of his childhood had been blue-collar, rough-edged, not the gentrified paradise it had become. The heart of the southeast industrial district felt more like the city he remembered than all the other miles he'd walked since his return. All these years later, he still had a clear memory of a day he'd spent riding around this part of town with a barrel-chested boyfriend of his mother's. His mother worked—school nurse, a job ill-suited to her non-nurturing, unsympathetic nature—so when Farley himself got sick, she needed someone to watch him. She refused to leave him home alone, fearing he might burn the house down or run up the long-distance bill or any of a dozen other imagined catastrophic possibilities that plagued her. Sometimes she'd hire a babysitter. Sometimes the elderly neighbors took him in for the day. But this particular day, all her usual suspects were unavailable, so Farley went to work with "Mommy's friend Bill."

Bill came around the house sometimes, mostly at night. Farley's interactions with him were limited by design. "Bill's here to look at the furnace for me," she'd say, tucking him into bed. "It's not easy for a single mother. I need you to stay in bed so you don't disturb him while he works." He rode shotgun in Bill's truck as they made the rounds all morning, meeting with warehouse foremen, contractors, construction workers. Farley didn't know what he did, exactly, and didn't care. Bill mostly ignored him, leaving him to stew on the bench seat of his hot truck.

When he got hungry, he asked to go to McDonald's. Instead, Bill took him to a reflective silver box truck parked outside a warehouse. The truck had refrigerated drawers lined with prewrapped sandwiches, bags of chips, sun-warmed bottles of Coke. Men in hard hats and work vests drank coffee out of Styrofoam cups, eyeing Farley over their cigarettes while they waited in line. He chose an egg salad on white when his turn came up.

"Get a hot dog, kid," Bill said.

"I want egg salad."

"Get a hot dog."

"I don't want a hot dog."

"Suit yourself, kid."

The vendor handed him a warm sandwich in a thin film of plastic with divots from someone's fingers in the soggy bread. The warm egg salad tasted like it had been mixed with wallpaper paste. Two hours later, Farley turned his insides out in an alley behind the post office.

"I told you to get a hot dog," Bill said.

"I didn't want a hot dog."

"If there's one smidgen of knowledge I can impart to you on this day when your mutha saddled me with the burden of haulin' your dumb ass around town, let it be this: do not order a mayonnaise sandwich from a wetback selling food out of a truck parked in the sun."

He shook his head sadly, watching with an amusement that bordered on glee as Farley decorated the brick wall with yellow chunks.

"Welcome to the Roach Coach, jackass."

Despite the memory, Farley remained hungry. It didn't help that he could still smell the beef stew on his shirt. When he passed a pod of food carts tucked behind a chain-link fence in the parking lot of a shuttered gas station, he stopped for food—whatever lay ahead, he would need his strength. Though the dozen trucks offered artisanal gastronomical takes on everything from beef tongue tacos and Salvadoran pupusas to bulgogi and vegan sushi—whatever the fuck that was—Farley settled for a carnitas burrito and ate it as he walked. The cart pods might be one of the changing city's few innovations he appreciated.

At Southeast Grand, which doubled as 99E in this part of the city, he turned north toward the mission. He'd seen people queueing down the block, waiting for meals or for rooms to turn over. As he approached, he saw the dinner line had already begun to form. He studied the faces but did not recognize anyone—at the same time, he recognized *all* of them, the expressions of detachment borne from desperation, from hunger, from shame, the exhaustion of the relentless hustle for shelter and food. He recognized the defiant pride that kept them alive despite the constant fear living on the streets forced upon them. He saw, too, how that detachment might be perceived as menace to outsiders with a comfortable life and a place to call home. They carried well-worn backpacks, tote bags, garbage bags, even five-gallon buckets filled with their most critical belongings. Maybe he had an apartment, maybe he had some money in the bank, but how different was he, really? Everything he owned fit in a single bag, and all his tethers to the world had been severed.

Still, he drew suspicious stares as he walked straight to the front of the line. He heard grumbling. A few comments. Finally, someone called him out.

"No cutting, asshole."

The small man had white hair that looked like a horse had been chewing on it. He wore tortoiseshell glasses with black electrical tape on the temples. In another life—one in which he'd gotten a few better breaks—he'd be the kind of man who spent a measurable portion of time writing letters to editors or demanding to see people's managers, Farley thought.

"The line starts at the back." Other voices nodded their assent, seconding the motion now that a leader had declared himself.

"I'm not here for a handout," Farley said.

"Is that what you think this is?"

"That's not what I meant."

"What *did* you mean?"

"I'm not here for the food or looking for a bed or a shower."

The man appraised Farley closely, his damp clothes, the mud on his fatigues, the bloodstains. The beef stew.

"You might reconsider the shower."

A few people laughed.

"Let's start again," Farley said. "I'm looking for someone."

"Who?"

"The Ferryman."

"That prick?" the man said, but Farley noticed that the chorus of other voices had stopped. The name had a chilling effect. "What do you want with him?"

"You know him."

"So what? Everyone knows him."

"I need to find him. He took something that doesn't belong to him."

"That piece of shit has probably taken something from everyone in this line. If it's not bolted down and he finds it, it goes in his cart. He sells anything he can at the pawns for a few bucks for drug money."

"Will I find him here?"

"Maybe not today. But if you wait a few days, he'll show up sooner or later."

Farley thought for a minute.

"Who's in charge here? Who runs this place?"

"You want Isaiah."

He thanked the man, approached the door to the mission, and knocked. A woman appeared after a minute. She pointed first at the CLOSED sign taped to the glass, then to her watch. She held up four fingers. *We open at four.*

Farley shook his head. "I'm not here for food. I'm looking for Isaiah."

She studied him through the glass. After a moment she fiddled with the locks and opened the door a crack, keeping it chained.

"What do you want?" She had an African accent of some kind. Mild. Nigerian, maybe.

"Someone said Isaiah might be able to help me. Is he here?"

"That is all we do here. We help people. People in need. People in crisis."

"I don't need that kind of help."

"What kind of help do you need?" Though her voice remained measured, her eyes had already appraised him. Farley could tell she was making a list of his flaws.

"I'm looking for two people. The Ferryman and Wayne."

"Why?"

"Different reasons."

"Should I get a pen?"

"I mean, I'm looking for The Ferryman for a different reason than Wayne."

"Are you going to tell me or are you going to stand there wasting my time?"

"Is Isaiah here?"

"Why do you want Isaiah? Let me guess. Different reasons?"

Farley paused and took a deep breath. The conversation had gone off the rails before he even began it. He'd learned not to reveal too much about an investigation until he knew all the players and where their sympathies lay, but he had to show some of his cards if he wanted this woman to let him in the door.

"The Ferryman took something he should not have," he said. "I'm trying to get it back safely for the person it belongs to."

Her expression changed, but she did not open the door. "And Wayne? Do you mean *Insane* Wayne?"

"I want to check in on him. See if he needs anything. He's . . . a friend."

She closed the door and fiddled with the locks once more before opening it wide enough for Farley to enter. She closed it quickly behind him and locked it again before looking him up and down. Finally, she stuck out her hand.

"Sister Isaiah," she said. "I run this place."

"*Sister* Isaiah? You're a nun?"

"No, I'm a sister. There's a difference."

"There is?"

She rolled her eyes.

"Follow me," she said. "I have things to do."

33

DINNER AND A SHOW

Freddie pulled the car into a downtown alley so narrow he had to slide across the front seat and exit on the passenger side. Lissa thought it odd until she realized he'd done it so he'd have enough room to open her door for her.

"Miss," he said, pulling on his hat. "Care to follow me if you please?"

He led her down the alley to a screen door in the brick wall, which he held open for her. She stepped inside and saw they were in a busy restaurant kitchen. Staff in hairnets and whites hustled over counters and stoves, the heat and smell oppressive, the noise uncomfortable. Hat in hand, Freddie cut a confident path across the kitchen to a swinging double door. Lissa followed him into a gorgeous dining room. Arching stained glass ceilings. Dark, heavily oiled wood. She recognized it immediately as Huber's. Set off the street in the Railway Exchange Building, the Portland institution had been serving meals since the 1870s and had thrived during Prohibition as a speakeasy. Lissa had first learned about it from a movie she saw with Keanu Reeves and River Phoenix. Freddie waved to the hostess, a fiftysomething woman in tomato-red heels and a black dress two sizes too small, and led Lissa to a table at the back. The hostess returned the wave vigorously.

"She's my cousin," he said.

"Big family."

"And how, miss."

Almost immediately a waiter appeared. He wore a black vest over an immaculate white shirt with ribbed armbands and looked suspiciously like Freddie.

"Freddie."

"Walter."

"Miss," Walter said.

"Cousins?" she asked.

"Brothers," they said in unison. "Twins."

"We'll have the house specialty, Walter," Freddie said. "Both of us. But make hers Spanish." His brother nodded and shuffled away.

"The house specialty?"

"This place is famous for its turkey, miss. They make more than three hundred pounds of it every day. Nothing like it."

"And what's Spanish?"

"Spanish coffee." He leaned across the table and whistled. "Dinner and a show, miss. You'll see."

Lissa felt restless. Anxious. She jiggled her leg a hundred miles an hour beneath the table, checked her phone, moved her water glass and the salt and pepper shakers around the table endlessly. A different waiter appeared, younger, swarthier, carrying a tray filled with bottles of liquor and a steaming carafe of coffee. He set the tray down on the table and traced a half of a lime around the rim of a glass mug. He dipped the glass in sugar and then, with a flourish, raised a bottle of 151 rum so the stream leaped into it from several feet above like a waterfall. He repeated the pour with triple sec and then struck a long wooden match and touched it to the glass. As flame shot into the air, he swirled the mug so the alcohol mixed and the heat melted the sugar on the rim. He poured in some Kahlúa and coffee, added a generous dollop of fresh whipped cream, and hit it all with a handful of dusted nutmeg.

The man bowed. Freddie clapped and handed him a five-dollar bill. The man produced a second glass mug filled with plain black coffee for Freddie. They both stared at Lissa expectantly. She looked from one to the other until Freddie nodded at the drink.

"Miss?"

"Oh!" She took a tentative sip and gave them a thumbs-up. "Delicious."

"I'm not in the habit of ordering for women, miss, but considering the day you're having, I thought you might be in need of a drink." Freddie lifted his own coffee to his nose and took a long, deep sniff as the waiter gathered his liquor and left. "I'd have one myself, but I'm still driving. Maybe I'll fix one for myself when I finally get home, but it won't be near so fancy as that one."

Walter reappeared with two plates, each saddled with a pile of turkey and mashed potatoes in a gravy bath, cranberry sauce, broccoli. He set them down, nodded again at his brother, and left. She'd always loved Thanksgiving dinner, but for some reason it had never occurred to her to eat it any other day of the year. Now she smelled the sage in the stuffing and knew she was starving. Maybe Freddie was onto something. Maybe food would calm her down some.

He tucked his cloth napkin into his shirt collar like a bib and picked up his fork and knife.

"So," he said. "Tell me 'bout your little girl."

34

PUNY LITTLE LIVES

Though tiny—he'd be surprised if she broke five feet—Sister Isaiah carried herself with a presence that belied her size. She walked with purpose and no wasted effort. Despite their disparity of height, Farley found himself lagging. She had dark skin and wore a brightly colored headscarf in her hair, a flannel shirt, ripped jeans, and sneakers.

"What's the difference? Between a sister and a nun?"

"Is that what you came here to learn?"

"No. But we could make it a twofer."

Sister Isaiah had almost reached the end of the hall. When she stopped and turned to face him, she saw his limp and seemed to understand why he lagged so far behind.

"Nuns take a solemn vow and live cloistered in a convent. Sisters take a simple vow and live and work in the community."

"No habits?"

"No habits."

"Not even smoking?"

She finally broke a smile. Interrogation takes different forms.

"That's a vice. Not a habit."

"Are you allowed vices?"

"What's your name?"

"Farley."

"Mr. Farley, have you ever known a religious person without vices?" He heard Pastor John's voice in his head, felt it like a cramp in his leg. Sister Isaiah must have seen it on his face. "Come with me, Farley," she said.

A handful of men worked in an industrial kitchen, preparing meals for the dinner rush. The kitchen had seen better days. So had the men. Mission regulars worked part-time as a means of getting back on their feet, Sister Isaiah told him.

"It gives them experience, a little pocket change, and the satisfaction of doing good in the world." She looked at the crew. "Right, gentlemen?"

"Sure thing, Sister," said a man standing over a large steaming pot. Nearly Farley's height but half his weight, he had skin the texture of corduroy and a voice like an ashtray. "It's good to have a purpose." Like the others, he wore a white apron, plastic gloves, and a shower cap.

"Mr. Farley, meet Ranger Rick. Rick's been around this mission longer than anyone. Even me."

"Why do they call you Ranger Rick?"

Rick smiled a wide, easy smile. "I've lived in Forest Park for years, man."

Farley had heard stories about people living in the large urban forest that covered an eight-mile stretch of hillside overlooking the Willamette. Six times the size of New York's Central Park, with more than five thousand acres of woodland, the park offered plenty of places to hide. The city prohibited camping within its boundaries, but some years back, a man and his daughter were found living entirely off-grid in a semipermanent encampment.

"There's a few of us who stay there on the regular," Rick said. "A lot of newbies try to camp there like they're the first ones who ever thought of it, but it's hard, man. It's a long walk in and out. So you gotta be self-sufficient. And there are lots of lookie-loos that hike and run and mountain bike and walk their dogs in there, so you gotta be invisible too. The cops sweep it all the time now. Most people don't last long in there."

"Except you?"

"That's right, man. That's why they call me Ranger Rick."

"Behind his back, they call him *Stranger* Rick," another man said, "because he's so fucking weird." Short and round enough to be the same height lying down or standing up, he stood over a tray of sandwich bread, and as he talked, he swiped a liberal gob of mayo on each one. Rick laughed.

"We're all fucking strange," said another man washing dishes in a big steel sink, half under his breath. He looked up at Farley and briefly made eye contact before lowering his head to his task once more.

"Yes, you are, Edge," Sister Isaiah said. "Every last one of you—and I find it endearing."

Farley watched him for a moment, but he did not look up again.

"Who are you, man?" Rick asked Farley, pulling his attention away. "Are you working here now too?"

"No," Farley said. "Just passing through."

"We all are, man. The world spins and spins and spins, and we all just spend our puny little lives looking for something to hold on to tightly enough to not get spun off."

The sandwich maker pointed aggressively. "See what I mean?" he said. "Stranger Rick."

But Rick just smiled, undaunted and sincere. "That's what this place is, man. Sister Isaiah helps us get back on our feet."

"The Lord helps those who help themselves," she said.

"Maybe he can help me—I'm looking for someone," Farley said, but Sister Isaiah shook her head.

The other men waited expectantly. Admonished, he said nothing else, and after a beat they all went back to their work.

"Well, I hope you find him, man," Rick said.

Sister Isaiah's office looked like it might double as a broom closet. Not just because of its diminutive size but because of the supplies heaped in crates and tubs and piled on every surface. She had a small bookshelf stacked two and even three rows deep, half a dozen paper coffee cups on her desk.

"Close the door," she said as Farley squished himself inside the room.

She took a Zippo lighter from a drawer, climbed onto the folding chair behind her desk, and opened a small window. Then she pulled a tightly rolled joint from under her headscarf, lit it, and took a long toke. She held one finger up to Farley.

Wait.

After a pause she exhaled out the window.

"Like I said. You ever know a religious person who didn't have a vice?" She offered him the joint, but he waved it away.

"Medicinal?"

She shrugged, raised her eyebrows.

"The church is OK with it?"

"The church might not be, but I think the Lord is. I gave up sex and material belongings for him. At the very least, I think he would look the other way."

She pointed to the other chair, and Farley sat across the desk from her. It felt good to get off his feet, but he could not afford the rest. He had to keep moving.

Sister Isaiah took another pull and held it. When she'd exhaled out the window and waved the smoke away with her hand, she stubbed the joint out on the sill, pinched off the end, and tucked it back under her headscarf.

"I'm sure I reek of it, but it's safer than keeping it in my desk." She took her seat. "So. Mr. Farley. If you don't mind my saying, you look like you're having a rough day. And I say that as a woman whose job it is to look after people who have had very rough days."

"I've had worse."

"I believe you." She studied him again. "What do you know about Wayne?"

"He told me about his kids. About the voices he hears. I'd like to do what I can to help him. But The Ferryman is my priority right now."

"OK, what do you know about *him*?"

"Not a lot. I know he deals. For all I know, he's an addict too, which is a dangerous combination. And I know he's an asshole with a stupid fucking street name."

She smiled and tried to hide it. "His given name—the one his mother gave him—is Asher. Do you know what it means?"

"Dangerous piece of shit?"

She flashed him a look, not amused. "It's Hebrew for 'happy' or 'blessed.'"

"So?"

"So, it might do you good to remember that he's a man, just like you. A man who had a mother. A man who has faced his own challenges in this cruel and difficult world. A man who has his own scars."

"You don't really expect me to feel sorry for him."

"Why not?"

"I haven't told you what he took yet." He thought for a moment. "Why does he call himself The Ferryman?"

"People choose their street names for a variety of reasons. Some want to stay hidden, and it suits them when those who seek them ask for them by a different name. Some, like Asher, want to intimidate or impress. Are you familiar with Greek mythology?"

"Someone told me I looked like a Minotaur once."

Sister Isaiah closed her eyes and muttered something silent. Maybe a prayer for patience.

"Charon, the ferryman, delivered the souls of the newly departed to Hades—hell—upon their deaths," she said.

"He chose it to intimidate people."

She shrugged again.

"Does he stay here?"

"No. This mission exists solely to provide a safe shelter and meals for people who need them. Certain requirements need to be met before we allow you to stay here to ensure we're able to provide that safety. Asher does not meet those requirements. Asher *will* not meet them."

"Because he deals?"

"Because he deals. Because he has threatened some of the others.

Because he has a dog, or he did, and we're unable to provide rooms to people with dogs. It's a city regulation."

"Do you know where I can find him?"

"Sometimes he comes here for meals. I cannot predict if he will come, or when."

"If he doesn't sleep here, do you know where he does sleep?"

"I know he prefers the camps."

"He won't be in a camp."

"Why's that?"

"He'll be someplace he can hide something."

"Something?" Her expression darkened. Farley understood.

"You think I'm a competing dealer who lost some supply to him."

"It would not be the first time."

"The *something* he took is actually *someone*. A little girl. He kidnapped my neighbor's daughter."

Sister Isaiah caught her breath. Her expression changed again, and she waited for him to explain.

"He was staying in a camp across the street from her apartment. She got crosswise of him one day, an accident. It scared her. She called the cops, and the cops rousted the camp. Maybe they booked him. I don't know. But he says she got his dog taken away, and he's pissed."

"I heard about that." She closed her eyes. "They put his dog in the pound, and it tried to bite someone there. A mandatory kill after that. They put it down."

She drummed a thin finger on her desk blotter.

"That was the camp on Southeast Salmon that they swept a week or so ago?"

"Yes."

She opened a drawer and pawed through files until she found the folder she wanted. Pulling it out, she took a photo from it and tossed it onto the desk in front of him. Farley leaned in and saw a photo of The Ferryman and his dog at the campsite, the dog curled on the ground, The Ferryman in his filthy sweatshirt.

"Smoke," she said.

"No thank you."

"The dog's name was Smoke. It caused some problems for him over the years. They were very protective of each other, but it's against regulations at all the usual places. Sometimes he'd tie the dog up outside. It would scare anyone who walked by. But he loved that dog. And that dog might have been the only thing in this world that loved him back."

"That doesn't make it right."

"No, Mr. Farley, it does not." She crossed her arms and studied him. "You never told me how you got involved with this. Why it falls to you to find this little girl."

"Because I know what it's like to lose a daughter, and no one deserves that."

"How long were you living on the street?"

"Who says I was?"

Sister Isaiah took a second photo from the folder and tossed it on top of the other one. Farley saw himself sitting on an overturned plastic bucket, watching Wayne eat a cup of instant soup. Though he'd had months to get used to the scars, his own appearance still shocked him. A trick of the brain, maybe, or a failure, how it held on to an image of his face and body that was no longer accurate and never would be again. Aging was like that too, or losing your hair. The brain chooses a point in time to develop its self-impression and is forever frozen after that. The photograph showed him as others might see him. Comically large. Rough around the edges, as if he'd been cut with pinking shears. The scars enveloping his face. The milky eye.

"When social workers visit the camps, they try to take pictures of the residents to help us track the population," she said. "It helps the city coordinate with all the nonprofits for the safety net. And sometimes someone will come looking for somebody—a family member off their meds, an estranged parent or child—and it's helpful to track them down."

"It's not what you think."

"It's OK to ask for help."

"That's why I'm here. Help me find The Ferryman. Asher. Help me find this girl."

She stared at him across the desk, hard.

"What are you going to do to him when you find him?"

He knew a challenge when he heard one.

"Whatever I have to," he said.

Sister Isaiah closed her eyes and lay her head back for a few moments, as if weighing her options.

"We see a lot of troubled people come through here," she said finally. "Some have just been victims of bad luck. Some are victims of far worse things. There's so much mental illness and drug addiction that it's difficult for a rational human brain to grasp. That's why I smoke, I think. The Lord wants me to help these people, all of them. And I try. I really do. But . . ."

She looked hesitant to finish her thought.

"Some desperately want to be helped. Some struggle to admit they need help. Some need more help than they're aware of—more help than I can give. And some? Well, some are just *beyond* help."

She crossed herself and raised her eyes to the ceiling, or to something beyond it, asking her God to deliver forgiveness, or patience, or maybe another joint. Then she seemed to settle on the answer, retrieved the stub from her headscarf, and tucked it between her lips. Farley took the lighter from her desk and lit it for her.

"Which is The Ferryman?" he asked.

She snapped her head to glare at him, coughing out her response in a fit of small clouds like smoke signals.

"That's not the question."

"What's the question?"

"The question is, which are *you*?"

35

THE LORD *STILL* WORKS IN MYSTERIOUS WAYS

Sister Isaiah led Farley past the communal showers and spartan overnight rooms—simple furnishings, vinyl-covered mattresses, plastic tubs to stow belongings—to the back of the building, where she stopped and eyed him appraisingly.

"Wait here," she said. She disappeared into an adjoining room and returned a few minutes later holding a gaudy, brilliantly patterned Hawaiian shirt the size of a beach towel. "It's the only clean thing we have in your size."

She held a hand out expectantly. When Farley unbuttoned his shirt and handed it to her, she balled it up and tossed it in a trash barrel. As he buttoned the new one—bright yellow, green parrots and palm trees, some kind of red tropical drink in tall glasses—she saw his scars but did not mention them.

"How do I look?"

"Like a fever dream. Like Jimmy Buffett's vomit. Like Jesus hates you." She pursed her lips. "But now you can spill whatever you want on yourself, and no one will notice."

"It was stew."

She crossed her arms.

"Thank you," he said. Sister Isaiah nodded curtly and opened the back door of the building, which led to a parking lot the mission shared with a Salvation Army distribution center. Dumpsters, loading docks, wheeled bins. She held the door for him as he stepped outside and saw the afternoon yielding to evening, the overcast sky gone prematurely dark.

"I'm sorry I can't help you more, but I will pray for that mother to get her daughter back unharmed."

He nodded.

"And remember, Mr. Farley, the Lord works in mysterious ways." She closed the door. Behind it, the dishwasher, Edge, sat smoking a cigarette on the loading dock. He still wore his work apron over a Motörhead T-shirt, and a lilac wool beanie big enough to hide a full head of long hair, dreadlocks, or even a large cat.

"Why do they call you Edge?"

"Why do you think?" he said without looking up.

Farley thought for a minute. "Because you live on the edge of society? Because you like knives? Because of your winning personality?"

The man smiled.

"Because my name is George Edgeworthy." He exhaled a puff of smoke that hung between them in the still air. "That name looked OK on the side of my van when I ran my own finish carpentry business, but it sounds ridiculous on the street. 'Edge' gives an air of danger and mystery that helps keep me safe."

Gradually, Farley thought, *and then suddenly.*

"What happened to the carpentry business?"

He took a drag from his cigarette. "Can I give you some unsolicited advice?"

"OK."

"Asking someone on the street how they ended up there is like asking someone in prison what they're in for. Or like asking someone their salary. It's rude."

"I didn't know."

"I don't mind," he said. "It's not complicated. It's a problem that compounds itself."

"How so?"

"You live paycheck to paycheck. You've got a job, an apartment, a car. Then your car breaks and you can't get to the job anymore so you can't pay the rent. Or your rent goes up and you can't pay for the car anymore. Or you lose your job and have to sell the car to pay for the apartment."

He took a long, slow drag from his cigarette.

"For me it was my tools."

"Your tools?"

"I had to sell them to pay the rent. But then I had no way to earn the next month. When you can't pay the rent anymore, you're out on the street. And you know that all you need is a job—anything at all, flipping burgers, washing cars; all you need is a break—but no one will hire you because you've got no place to shower, no clean clothes. You spend so much time and energy just trying to eat, trying to stay alive. Trying not to get beat up or assaulted by some of the psychos living on the streets. Trying not to get arrested for trespassing because you fell asleep in a doorway to get out of the rain just for an hour because you've been on your feet for twelve hours. It becomes almost impossible to do anything except stay alive." He inspected the burning end of his American Spirit. "And after a while, you start to wonder if you even want to anymore."

"The Earth is always spinning," Farley said. "Lose your grip for a second and you get spun off. Ranger Rick was right."

"Ranger Rick," Edge said, looking at him sidelong. "What about you? You look like maybe you've lost your own grip once or twice."

Farley considered what he'd said. About how close we are to exactly that, all of us. About the pressure bearing down on us and how little it takes to undo everything you've worked for. How all you have to do is slip. He thought about Nirva, about John and Rebecca, how the world had changed them all, transforming each of them into someone entirely new. Different. Worse. A mother who was now childless. A sudden widow. He thought about Lissa. About Wayne. About Flex. Maybe The Ferryman's story wasn't all that different—maybe he'd been somebody too. A husband or a dad. A son. Maybe the world had been unkind to him in ways that bent him and broke him.

But then he pictured Olive, that innocent little pip-squeak, and the anger filled him again. Getting broken by the world was one thing. Doing it to someone else was another thing entirely. Something for which there was no excuse. Something for which he would allow no mercy.

"Do you know The Ferryman?"

Edge snapped his head up to meet his eyes.

"What do you want with him?"

Farley saw the fear in his expression. He put his hands in his pockets and found that he'd absentmindedly pocketed Sister Isaiah's Zippo.

"I want to retrieve something that doesn't belong to him."

"He won't give it back. Not without a fight."

Farley nodded. "I'm counting on it."

Edge flicked his cigarette butt into the parking lot and exhaled a formless bank of smoke that smelled like death itself.

"That works for me," he said. "Let's go."

36

ARE YOU ONE OF THOSE TRAIN GUYS?

They headed north and west, back toward the river, where train tracks ran like arteries through the city. They picked up the tracks and followed them through the industrial district, which seemed to be in the midst of a faltering attempt at development. They walked past new microbreweries, coffee roasters, pot dispensaries, and gastropubs, all of which presented themselves with a forced hipness—if not an embrace of the neighborhood's industrial bona fides, then a concession to them, at least—that seemed designed to both assimilate with and soften the neighborhood's nature. But you can't gentrify train tracks, and as they ran through the gravel and puddles and rebar skeletons of the busted cement barriers, they remained littered with graffiti and trash.

Edge nimbly picked his way from tie to tie, and Farley followed, laboring to keep his footing on the loose gravel. He could feel the miles he'd covered in his muscles and bones. His own natural stride would skip every other tie, but his injuries shortened it. Each awkward step took a kinetic effort to readjust his gait that exhausted him. He watched the ground as he walked, an unfamiliar action in itself. The level of concentration it required confused him. Hadn't he been walking his entire life? How had it suddenly become so difficult?

"In other countries, those ties are called sleepers."

Farley looked up to see Edge had stopped ahead to wait for him.

"The railroad has its own language," he said.

"Like boats."

"Both the ties and the overall mass of the ballast are necessary to hold the tracks in place."

"Ballast?"

"Crushed rock. It creates an elastic base and holds the sleepers in place. Every time a train passes, its centripetal force and vibration shift the tracks ever so slightly. If those tiny shifts go unchecked, the train derails."

Edge resumed walking, more slowly this time.

"Crews used to roam the tracks to maintain them. They carried heavy lining bars with one end chiseled to dig into the gravel beneath the rail and fit against it. The crew faced the rail, working the bar into the ballast, and stepped forward, lifting up on the bar to lever the track." He demonstrated the motion with an invisible bar, took a knee alongside the rail and pointed to a spike. "They were called gandy dancers. They used spike mauls to drive these, tamper bars to move the ballast, and rail dogs to carry rails."

Farley imagined a crew of men in synchronous movement shifting the track, imagined the lives of itinerant railroad workers in the maw of the last century.

"Hard work, lousy money," Edge said. "Most of the work was done by immigrants and Black men."

"How come?"

"How come? What do you mean, how come? Because nobody else would hire them. Chinese. Mexicans. Irish. Italians. Eastern Europeans. Even Native Americans."

Farley wondered how Professor Edgeworthy planned to conclude this particular lecture.

"Ever hear any of the railway folk songs?"

"No."

"I bet you have." Edge took a deep breath and, in a surprisingly sweet voice, began to sing.

Up and down this road I go
Skippin' and dodging a 44
Hey man won't you line 'em . . .
Hey man won't you line 'em . . .

For a moment he looked vaguely embarrassed by his song. Then he smiled. "The crews used the songs to sync their movements," he said. "One man led the song—he was the caller. A good caller could inspire his crew like a preacher. The work became a kind of dance. Jimmie Rodgers incorporated them into his songs years later, which kind of brought them into the public consciousness."

"Jimmie Rodgers?"

"The Singing Brakeman. The father of country music. You don't know him? His old man worked a railroad section in Mississippi and used to bring him to work as a boy."

Bukowski. Rodgers. Farley was beginning to think he'd managed to get through life without learning a goddamned thing.

"Are you just a railroad nut?" he asked. "One of those train guys?"

"Train guys?"

"Those guys who chase trains. They take pictures of them, make long videotapes of them steaming along tracks. They know the different engines and car types and all the train routes around the country."

"Videotapes? How old are you, Farley?"

"How old are *you*, Jimmie Rodgers?"

Edge laughed.

"No. I'm not a train guy."

"So, why are you telling me all this?"

"Because the Black gandy crews became famous for the songs they sang as they worked. Those songs weren't just to help them sync their rhythm—they used them as a kind of code to send messages that the foreman or other workers couldn't understand. That way they were able to function as an entire kind of separate, fringe society, invisible in plain sight."

Farley looked at him for a few moments, considering.

"You're telling me the same thing happens with the homeless."

"With the camps."

"How?"

"At the missions and pantries. That's where word spreads about where the next camp is going to be. People leave messages there."

"How?"

"Takeout menus."

"Takeout menus?"

"Someone pins a takeout menu from a local restaurant to the bulletin board to let the others know what neighborhood they're going to set up camp in. It's how everybody knows where to go. It's how we find each other."

"So, the next big campsite. That's where I'll find The Ferryman?"

"No. He's off the grid now."

"You said you'd bring me to him."

"Not exactly."

"Then what, exactly?"

"The city is a living thing, right? The streets are like the neural pathways that transmit information from its brain to its extremities and vice versa. Which means you can find all of its knowledge there, on the streets. If you know how to interpret the data."

"So where are we going?"

"To someone who knows how to interpret the data," Edge said. It looked like he wanted to say something else.

"Spit it out."

"You look like a guy who can handle himself. But I'm not sure you know what you're getting into with The Ferryman."

"He and I have already met."

"On a good day he's an asshole. On a bad day . . ." Edge looked along the length of tracks behind them. "Ever since he lost his dog, he's been on a tear. Everyone's talking about it on the streets. He tried to get it back—went to the pound a bunch of times, pleaded his case—but I guess it bit someone, a volunteer or someone who worked there. They decided the dog was beyond rehabilitation. Couldn't be reformed. So they put it down. He snapped after that. He loved that dog."

"He took a little girl from her mother. That's not a one-for-one exchange."

"No," Edge said. In the short response, Farley heard something else. "But?"

"Look. I'm not saying it's right. Because it's not. It's obviously not. But he didn't have anything else. Not a thing in the world. Just that dog. He came up hard. Not like me. I came up easy, man, and when I fell, it was my own damn fault. That's the case for a lot of us. But not him. I've heard stories. About his childhood. His . . . circumstances. He grew up with addicts. The things they did to him?"

He spit in the dirt and spread it around with the toe of his foot.

"The world looks different to him than it does to the rest of us. People mean something else to him than they do to you and me. He doesn't recognize himself as part of society because society failed him. Society *made* him. It's his enemy."

He took out a cigarette and lit it.

"He didn't just fall. He got thrown over the edge. Over and over and over. And in his whole miserable life, that dog might just be the only thing that ever loved him."

"He kidnapped a girl. I'm going to get her back to her mother."

"And then what? What will you do to The Ferryman?"

Farley stopped short, a sudden movement that took more effort than walking, and looked Edge in the eyes.

"The same thing they did to his dog," he said. "Put him down."

37

EVERYONE HAS A PLAN UNTIL THEY GET PUNCHED IN THE FACE

Near Water Avenue they left the tracks and made their way north. Built under the eastern side of the bridge from which it took its name, the Burnside Skatepark occupied a plot of land once known as "Hobo Camp" for the groups of homeless who gathered there to sleep out of the frequent rains.

Skateboarders flocked there for the same reason—a dry lot in a wet city is prime real estate. Begging leftover cement from a construction crew building the nearby highway on-ramp, some of the more enterprising skaters mounted a guerilla development project of their own, and before long, Portland had its first skate park. The city fought it at first but eventually allowed the sanctioned but unsupported park to continue. Thirty years later, the gritty park survives. Skaters maintain it themselves and police it the same way locals govern the wave breaks on Oahu's North Shore. Farley had never been on a skateboard in his life, but he liked the story. A grassroots effort outwitting bureaucracy. It gave him hope. The only other thing he knew about the park was that you could find skaters there no matter the time of day. Long ago, home on leave one night, he stumbled out of a Burnside bar he'd just closed to find a van parked so that its headlights illuminated the park. A lone skater worked the cement ramps and bowls. He looked immune to the laws of gravity, rolling around the obstacles, gathering and dispersing speed, launching himself into the night. Gravity always won, but that lucky bastard had figured out a way to confound it longer than the rest of us.

Since then, lights had been installed on tall poles set around the periphery of the park. Edge let him catch his breath while they watched a pack of skaters flow through the ramps like a flash flood in a culvert, their shadows doing different tricks in every direction around them. All boys, mostly in their teens, they ran the cruel gamut of puberty. Farley remembered how two classmates the same age could look like different species entirely, one a hairless and undeveloped tenor, the other a brutish and mustachioed baritone. His own sophomore year had been a kind of Rubicon that some of his friends crossed, distancing themselves in sudden and unexpected ways from the others, puberty creating an inequality that destroyed lifelong friendships. He saw the signs of it in the group of skaters—but he saw, too, that one of them was much older and looked street-hardened and mean.

"That's Skelly," Edge said.

"He the guy we're looking for?"

"Yes."

"How come?"

"He'll know something."

"Then let's talk to him."

"Hold on," Edge said. "He won't just give it up. The Ferryman's a total psycho, but Skelly's just a prick. If you want something from him, he'll want something in exchange. That's how the street works."

"What do you suggest?"

"No idea," Edge said, but his expression said otherwise.

"I'll get him to talk."

"How?"

"I've got a plan."

"OK. Want to let me in on it?"

"No."

Edge looked worried. "Mike Tyson said that everyone has a plan until they get punched in the face."

Farley nodded and yelled to the skaters, who looked his way and rolled over as a group. Tattooed, long-haired, acned, they skidded to a stop in formation and smirked. He knew they were going for menace, but they looked like a flock of annoying birds shitting on your deck that you could frighten off with a broom. Wheels to wheels, they wouldn't stand a chance against a roller derby team.

The one called Skelly rolled to the front of the pack, a lanky, shirtless man in baggy khakis rolled up at the ankles. The day remained warm for September, even in the damp darkness, but not take-your-shirt-off warm. Farley knew that the world contained shirt men and no-shirt men—some who wore T-shirts into the ocean or pool, others who stripped off their tops without provocation as if in constitutional opposition to them—but with Skelly it felt like an affectation. Prison tattoos covered his hairless, bony chest and stomach. He wore his hair in an extreme mullet. Farley's generation had called the business-in-the-front, party-in-the-rear style "hockey hair." He didn't know when or why the name had changed. This being Portland, he also didn't know whether Skelly's was ironic or sincere, or what the difference was. The sides were cut high over the ears, with racing stripes, and black, heavy-gauge piercings distended his ear lobes like Silly Putty.

"Edge, you little pussy," Skelly said. "I'm surprised to see you show your face around here."

He spoke derisively with an unexpectedly high-pitched voice, and Edge struggled to meet his eyes. Skelly turned to study Farley.

"Who's this big ugly fucker, Edge? Your bodyguard?"

The younger skaters snickered. Skelly seemed to feed off their energy, and confident in his shadow, they deferred to him as if to Fagin.

"I'm looking for The Ferryman." Farley watched Skelly's eyes narrow in response. The skinny man carried not so much as an ounce of visible body fat—he knew the type, all core muscles, wiry and taut as steel cables, and made a note not to underestimate him.

"What for?"

"He took something that doesn't belong to him. I want it back."

Skelly appraised him with a new interest.

"What's it worth?"

"It's priceless."

"No, dumbass. What's it worth to *me*?" Skelly spit at the ground as the other skaters tittered and sneered in their formation behind him. "Better be enough to cover Edge's debt too."

"Edge's debt?"

"*He* owes *me*. And *he's* been avoiding *me* like a chickenshit. *You* want something from *me*, *you* gotta pay for it, but *you* gotta pay enough to cover *him* too." He accentuated the pronouns in a singsong manner, his voice some kind of addled back-alley street patois. "Or *we* gonna fuck you *both*."

Edge looked embarrassed, and Farley wondered if he'd been set up.

"So, I'll ask again," Skelly said. "What's it's worth *to me*?"

Farley shrugged.

"I guess it depends on what you know."

Skelly's mouth dropped open like a tailgate, full of metal, and he stared, gape-mouthed. Incredulous. He had crooked teeth, a bent ear, scars like a Glasgow smile.

"What I know? Nothing happens on these streets that I don't know about. I'm all-knowing. All-*seeing*. I have eyes *everywhere*."

The skaters cheered and testified like a preacher's congregation.

"Besides," Skelly said. "The Ferryman is a close personal friend."

"But you'd sell him out?"

"For the right price." He laughed and looked back at his pack, who all laughed along despite the implications of his words.

Skelly dropped his skateboard to the ground with a fast, fluid motion and pinned it with one foot. He shoved off with the other, quickly closing the distance between him and Farley. When he reached him, he snapped his board up by the tail, caught it, and stepped close enough so that their bodies almost touched. He tilted his neck to meet Farley's eyes and pointed a long finger adorned with a bulbous chrome skull ring into his face.

"I'll ask you one more time, dumbass. What's it worth to you?"

Farley could smell the sweat, the body odor, the stink of old pot.

"You tell me," he said.

"Money. Drugs. Maybe a cut of whatever The Ferryman took, if it's so fucking priceless to you."

"No, *dumbass*," Farley said. "I meant, *you* tell *me* where I can find him and *I* won't embarrass *you* in front of *your* little friends."

Edge exhaled loud enough for Farley to hear it. Skelly's expression shifted from menace to disbelief, from disbelief to fury. He turned to face his pack of skater minions.

"Fuck this guy, right?"

The teen choir raised their voices in a joyous frenzy.

"Let's show him who owns this park!" Skelly yelled.

Cheering, shouting, roaring, they lifted their skateboards high over their heads like weapons.

"Let's fuck him up," Skelly yelled.

When he turned around, Farley punched him in the face as hard as he could.

38

WHERE ARE YOUR PEOPLE AT?

Lissa unburdened herself of the entire story as they ate, laying even her most embarrassing fears and guilt on the table between them beside her cell phone. Freddie listened intently and nodded a bunch, giving the occasional "Mmm-hmmm" and asking clarifying questions. When they finished their turkey, he ordered two slices of pumpkin pie. Lissa rarely ate dessert, but he promised a full stomach would better prepare her for whatever lay ahead.

"This whole thing is terrible, miss." He dabbed his chin with his napkin, which he then untucked, folded, and placed on the table beside his plate. "Can I ask, though? Where are your people?"

"My people?"

"Your family. Your community." He pronounced *community* delicately, giving each syllable its due.

"I don't really have one."

"You go to a church, miss?"

She shook her head. *No.*

"What about this gentleman out looking for your little girl? He's your people, then?"

"Farley? I guess so. I barely know him, though. We just kind of crossed paths."

Freddie nodded again. Then he raised his hand and signaled to the hostess. She put down the menus she was stacking and clacked her way over, her towering heels slipping and sliding on the tile floor.

"Rosaree," he said. "This is my new friend Lissa. Some homeless drug addict kidnapped her beautiful little daughter right from out of her home in the middle of the night."

His cousin raised her hands to her face in dismay. Her nails were painted the same color as her shoes and matched the leather booths and stools of the restaurant.

"We been out looking for her all day," Freddie said.

Rosaree wore a number of rings, all polished to a sheen, and her teeth were big and white. She put a hand on Lissa's arm.

"Where are your people at, girl?" she asked.

"She ain't got no people, Rosaree."

Now Rosaree looked at her in shock, her eyes gone wide beneath their dark lashes. She grabbed Lissa and pulled her to her feet with an uncanny strength, despite being off-balance on her spike heels. Putting her hands on Lissa's shoulders, she looked her square in the eyes.

"Your little girl?" she said. "She gonna be OK. I just know it." Then she wrapped her arms around Lissa, squeezing her against her ample bosom in a long, tight hug that Lissa hoped never ended.

"We your people today, miss," Freddie said.

39

I FIXED IT FOR YOU

Having found occasion to punch a few faces over the years, Farley had learned a universal truth: upon being punched in the face, men invariably respond in a predictable way. Some punch back; some try like hell not to show any reaction at all; and some cry like a baby. A very small subset of outliers responds with an incredulous, sputtering rage and threats of legal action—a rarity. The exception that proves the rule.

He'd expected Skelly to be the type who punched back. He was wrong.

Skelly's eyes widened, irises like black olives in white cocktail bowls. Blood streamed out between his tattooed fingers as he cupped his face with his hands.

"Motherfucker! Motherfucker! Ow, ow, ow, ow, ow."

"Tyson was right."

"It was supposed to be a metaphor, Farley," Edge said.

"Goddamnit. God*damn*it. My nose is broke. My fucking nose is broke!" Skelly danced around, his hands muffling his words, though not enough to disguise the fact that they were being delivered at least two octaves higher than usual. The nasal whine was only partly attributable to his busted nose. "I think you broke it."

Farley grabbed him by the neck and pulled him near, looking closely at his nose.

"I definitely broke it," he said.

"It fucking hurts!"

"That's the idea, asshole." He looked at the other skaters. Having abruptly paused their advance in the face of their leader's rapid incapacitation, they now looked less sure of their commitment. "Who's next?" Trading meaningful glances among themselves, they hopped on their boards without even a word and skated back to the other side of the park.

"You little fuckers," Skelly yelled. "Cowards."

Farley grabbed him by the ear. Twisting painfully, he led him to a bench where he sat moaning, blood covering his hands and chest.

"Where do I find The Ferryman?"

"Downtown." Skelly spoke through his fingers, looking forlorn. "There's a crash pad in Chinatown that some of us know about. He stays there sometimes. He's been there a couple of days. He put a padlock on the door so nobody else can use it."

"Has he ever done that before? Locked other people out like that?"

"No."

"He tell you why? He tell you what he's got in there?"

"No."

Farley nodded. "Give me the address."

Skelly gave him a street and number in Old Town, across the river. Farley wrote it in his notebook.

"We're done here. Go play with your little friends if they still want to play with you."

Edge cleared his throat. He still seemed anxious.

"Whatever Edge's debt to you was?" He pointed his pen at Skelly. "It's settled. Right?"

"Fuck."

"Right?"

Skelly scowled. Deliberately, Farley put the pen in his shirt pocket and took a step toward him.

"OK, OK. What about my nose?"

"What about it?"

"You broke it. It's fucking broke."

Farley leaned in close and studied the nose. Without warning he grabbed it and twisted it back into place. Skelly shrieked. The squeal rent the air, scattering pigeons and drawing disgusted stares from the other skaters across the park.

"I fixed it for you," he said, and let him go.

They did not talk as they crossed the Burnside Bridge. Edge seemed a little shaken, and the traffic made it difficult to hear. Farley felt optimistic about finding Olive—after pissing away the better part of the day, he'd made progress. Each stop had brought him closer to The Asshole, and now he could practically smell him.

At the west end of the bridge, another line of people waited outside another mission. High above them, an antlered neon deer leaped across the neon outline of the state on a sign welcoming people to Portland. The sign had changed hands a number of times since it was built in the forties and had advertised everything from White Satin sugar to White Stag sportswear to Made in Oregon retail gifts. Eventually the city bought and restored the iconic sign, and now it welcomed westbound drivers not just to the city itself, but to Old Town, the original urban core—and, like Manhattan's Bowery or San Francisco's Tenderloin, long since known as Portland's skid row. Farley thought it ironic not just that the famous sign towered over the homeless district, but that the monthly electric bill to keep the neon tubes juiced could probably feed most of the people queued up beneath it.

"This is where I get off," Edge said. "I've been as much use to you as I can."

Farley squinted at him, trying for a read.

"You seem troubled."

"I'm a little worried about the backlash."

"Skelly?"

"He's gonna be pissed, and he's got to be pissed at someone."

"Just stay off his radar."

"It's a small world, the streets."

"Skelly's not the hard man everyone seems to think he is. Hell, he's not even the hard man *he* thinks he is. He's just a bully."

Edge looked skeptical.

"If he gives you shit, just hit him in the nose. I already loosened it for you. What did you owe him?"

"Does it matter?"

"I guess not."

"I need to do better," Edge said. He looked at the line of people, the sleeping bags and camp mats and tents and shopping carts, the garbage bags full of their belongings. "All of this? It's getting old."

Farley nodded.

Edge bit his lip, unsure whether to say what he was thinking. "Listen," he said. "The Ferryman? He's not like Skelly. He's not just a bully. It's not just a front with him. The Ferryman's the real thing. There are stories about the things he's done. What he's capable of."

"Do you think he'd hurt the girl?"

Edge looked away, thinking. Measuring. "I don't know," he said finally. "I don't think so. But he took her, so who knows? All I'm saying is, he's violent and unpredictable. Promise me you won't take him lightly."

Farley nodded again. They shook hands, and as Edge took his place in the darkness at the end of the long line, he turned and headed into the heart of Old Town.

40

YOU GOTTA BUY
A DRINK, HONEY

The Willamette divided the city vertically. Burnside divided it horizontally. West of the river, it ran straight through the center of Old Town, proudly continuing the long tradition of disappointing tourists. To the north, an ornate archway marked the entrance to Chinatown, but anyone expecting the thriving Asian district experience of other cities was in for a surprise. Though the street signs bore Cantonese translations, and a few Chinese-owned businesses remained, you had to work pretty hard to find yourself some dim sum within its boundaries. The link to Portland's rich Asian heritage had become almost entirely historical, and in the intervening years, Chinatown had been overrun by drugs, crime, and homelessness. Local business owners drawn by affordable rents found themselves in chronic battle with society's backside. Shopkeepers arrived early each morning to chase away the drunks who'd slept in their doorways and hose off the sidewalks; panhandlers harassed customers and tourists; addicts broke windows and rifled through parked cars.

The situation south of Burnside was not much better. There, at least, some long-standing Portland businesses continued to thrive: a celebrated donut shop, a 120-year-old oyster bar, a few drag bars and nightclubs.

Old Town still made the news a few nights a week. Stabbings, shootings, fights after the bars closed and spilled an incoming tide of furious drunks into the streets. The district had become the theater for the long-running existential battle for the soul of the city. What did Portland want to be? A safe, efficiently run, tourist-friendly destination that supported local businesses? Or the progressive Pacific Northwest bastion with the mantra "Keep Portland Weird"? The war began long before Farley had left for the Arctic. He hadn't been back long before he saw that the fighting on the ground had only escalated.

He found the address Skelly had provided without difficulty. It belonged to an old fourplex with two units upstairs and down, and a fire escape overlooking a dumpster. The back of the building shared an alley with a bar. He stood in the street in the faltering twilight and looked up at the second floor, assessing the situation. Someone had nailed boards over the windows. Graffiti covered not just the boards but the brick walls and the dumpster too. Weeds grew out of the old window boxes, and the doors had been boarded over and wrapped with yellow police tape. He wondered whether the building had been a crime scene or just declared unsafe for human dwelling. Or both.

From the street he could see no sign of anyone coming and going, or even how they would get in. He'd been on his feet all day. He'd covered a lot of miles. Now his body was turning on him. His throat burned, dry as a bone, the only part of him still dry. He needed a bathroom. He wanted a drink. So, he walked around to the other side of the building across from the apartment and went into the bar, hoping to catch his breath and steady himself for what lay ahead and to check in on the phone with Lissa.

The bartender, a heroically buxom blond, waved from the other end of the long, polished walnut counter.

"Bathroom?" he asked.

"Customers only. You gotta buy a drink, honey."

He threw a twenty on the bar. "Need to get rid of the last one first."

She laughed and pointed down the hall.

The mirror inside the poorly lit john had been cracked repeatedly, the silver faded, but he could still see well enough to startle himself. Each time he'd seen his own reflection that day, he'd seen a steady and significant degradation, as if he'd been walking not through Portland but through time, inching inexorably closer to his demise. He'd never been much to look at—and the bears had not helped—but Christ on a popsicle stick, as his mother used to say. He washed his hands in the sink, wet down his hair, and tried to comb it into shape with his fingers. Somehow that made it worse.

The Ferryman wouldn't give a shit, he thought, returning to the empty bar.

"What can I getcha, hon?" In addition to her deep Tennessee drawl, the bartender had a blond bouffant and drawn-on eyebrows that rode high above glitter-strewn lids like drawbridges. Last summer he'd watched the oil company's maintenance crews paint the outbuildings at the drill site. They used a pneumatic rig that sprayed paint at two gallons per minute. It looked like she'd used the same rig to apply her makeup. And maybe the same paint.

"Canadian Club." He squinted to read her name tag in the dim light. The pearl buttons of her western blouse strained under obvious duress. "Dolly."

She winked. Something about her bothered him—rather, she looked familiar, and he wondered if he knew her. When she turned to find the bottle, Farley studied her from behind, starting at the red cowboy boots and heading north, past the dark jeans, until he caught her eyes watching him in the mirror behind the bar. He looked away quickly. She laughed.

"The show doesn't start officially start for another few hours, but you go 'head and look all you want, hon."

"No," he said. "I . . ." But once he'd started his sentence, he didn't know how to finish. He decided not to risk his remaining dignity by trying. "What show?"

Dolly turned to look at him.

"You know this is a drag bar, right?" she said, this time in a drawl-free baritone a few octaves lower than before and a full octave lower than Farley's own voice.

He knew a challenge when he heard one.

"Can I still get the whiskey?"

She nodded.

"Then who cares what kind of bar it is?"

Dolly smiled sweetly and poured him his drink. "There you go, hon," she said, her voice restored.

He held a finger up for her to wait, downed the whiskey in a single pass, and pointed to the empty glass. She filled it again, and he raised it to his lips.

"Have we met before?"

"I don't think so. Don't take this the wrong way, honey, but I'm confident I'd remember someone as memorable looking as you."

"Fair enough. You look familiar."

She smiled.

"Give it a minute. You'll figure it out."

Farley sipped the whiskey more slowly this time, trying to remember her. When he could not, he pushed it to the back of his mind.

"Do you mind if I make a phone call?"

Dolly shook her head and walked to the other end of the bar to wipe down glasses, giving him privacy. He took out his phone and checked it for messages. None. He dialed Lissa's number. She answered right away.

"Farley? Do you have her? Do you have Olive?"

"Not yet."

"Oh," she said, her disappointment a knife to his gut.

"But I might have found her. I wanted to check in with you before I go in to get her."

"Where is she, Farley? Where are you?"

"Old Town."

"I'm right near there! I'll meet you."

"No," he said. "Unless we get a ransom request, I don't think you should be there."

She heard something in his voice and acknowledged it by not arguing the point. "Are you all right, Farley?"

He paused before he answered. "Where are you?"

"I've been out looking for her. Searching the camps."

"I need you to be careful, Lissa."

"It's OK. I'm not alone."

"Good. That's good. I'm going to get her, Lissa. I'll bring her home." She said nothing, but he could hear her crying. Why did so many women in his life cry? It couldn't be a coincidence.

"Farley?"

He waited.

"What you're doing for me? For us? I don't think anyone else would do it."

He waited some more.

"Thank you," she said. And then she was gone.

Dolly pretended to polish glasses down at the other end of the bar, but she had clearly been listening to his conversation. He could swear he knew her from somewhere. He pointed to his glass. She came and filled it.

"Everything OK, hon?" she asked.

He looked up at her. "It's been a very long day."

"Working nine to five ain't no way to make a livin'." She grinned expectantly. Farley stared at her long enough for her expression to change to disappointment, another thing he seemed to inspire in women. "Another round?"

"Just the check."

Dolly leaned in close over the bar.

"The day shift here is such a goddamn bore," she said. "I could use a little intrigue. You look like a man who is up to some." Her drawbridge eyebrows opened high. From that proximity he could see the powder makeup, a faint shadow at the beard line. How did he know her?

"There's a building out back. Boarded over. It shares the alley with this bar."

She nodded.

"It's a crash pad. You ever see anyone coming and going from there?"

"Sometimes in the alley when I bring the trash out to the dumpsters. *Unsavory characters*."

"One guy in particular. Face tattoos. Black eyes. Looks like he eats broken glass for breakfast."

"What about him?"

Farley didn't know why he told her about The Ferryman and Olive. Maybe he needed a witness. Maybe he trusted her. Maybe he didn't know if he'd survive the day and didn't want to miss his last opportunity for conversation. But he found himself recounting what he'd been through that day, the path that had led him there.

"I think he's got her in there," he said. "She's in danger. Scared. She's just a kid. A pip-squeak."

"That poor girl. She's your daughter?"

"No." Farley swallowed hard and met Dolly's eyes. "My daughter died. Earlier this year. This is someone else. A friend. A friend's daughter."

"And you're going through all this to get her back from that piece of doody who took her?" She held her hands to her heart; they were nearly as large as his own, hairy, with scarred knuckles and the hint of a tattoo visible beneath the cuff.

"Wouldn't you?"

"You bet your sweet ass, hon," she said, her voice a sweet, sincere flutter. Then it shifted to a deep and distinctively male growl. "In fact, I'll go with you. You can't go in there alone. I'll watch your six, and if that coked-up fucker gives you any shit, we'll end him."

41

STEALTH IS PART OF THE JOB DESCRIPTION

Dolly locked the door to the bar and beckoned Farley to follow. They walked down a hallway to a small room where the dancers dressed for their shows—makeup tables, big mirrors, bright lights. Costumes and dresses hung from a long wire rack. A series of shelves held dozens of high-heeled shoes in a range of colors and styles, most of them big enough to fit Farley.

"I'm not just a bartender here," Dolly said. "I'm the bouncer too. The clientele can get surprisingly rowdy. Especially on Bear Night."

"Bear Night?"

"You have a lot to learn about the world."

"I have some experience with bears."

"So do I, honey."

In the brightly lit room, Farley could see more stubble showing through the foundation on her cheeks and chin, the prominent Adam's apple, the coarse hair sprouting from her ears.

"I can't ask you to do this," he said.

"Why not?"

"It might be dangerous."

"I did two tours in Afghanistan and one in Iraq. I'm not afraid of some pissant addict who takes little girls." She opened a locker and took out an olive-green bomber jacket that she pulled on over her western blouse. "What's your name?"

"Farley."

Dolly removed her bouffant wig, revealing a close-cropped Caesar the color of rust, and draped the wig atop a mannequin head. She pulled on a plain black twill baseball cap and retrieved a sidearm from the locker. He watched her work the slide, removing the magazine and checking the witness hole to make sure a round had been chambered. She returned the slide and locked it into place with a loud click.

"So, Farley." She tucked the gun into her belt and zipped her bomber jacket over it. "You got a plan?"

"Everybody has a plan until they get punched in the face."

Dolly smiled.

"That sounds like a great plan to me."

Farley stood behind the dumpster, staring up at the building. The sun had dropped behind the buildings, and all the streetlights had come on except those outside the fourplex.

"Someone broke them intentionally," Dolly said. "Operational darkness."

"All the doors and windows on this side are covered. We need a way in."

"I'll check the front." She moved briskly down the alley at a pace Farley could not have matched and returned a few minutes later, startling him with her silent approach.

"Front's boarded up too. However he's going in and out, it's from this alley, out of sight of the street. We do the same."

"Won't he know we're coming?"

"No. Stealth is part of the job description."

"For a bouncer?"

"For a Snake Eater," she said. *Special Forces.*

"I was army too."

"Special forces?"

"No."

"Infantry?"

"No. Military Police."

Dolly sighed. "Better let me go first. I've got about an hour before the girls start arriving to get ready. Let's make it count."

She ascended the metal fire escape with a lightness Farley would not have predicted. He followed her, his own angry, tired legs rebelling, and from the top she saw him struggle and turned away. A simple gesture, allowing him to protect his dignity. He wondered how much of her life had been spent fighting similar battles, how easy it should be to allow people such things. He studied the plywood covering the window nearest the landing. The graffiti did not deviate from the standard fare of barely legible tags, crude drawings, and antipolice slogans, but it looked weathered from long-term exposure to the sun and rain. Not recent.

"Some of the nails have been removed," she said when he reached the landing. "See? There's just one remaining along the top."

"What does that mean?"

With one hand, she grabbed the edge of the board and pushed. It pivoted on the nail, opening a gap at the bottom corner.

"It means we have our point of entry."

"Here we go," Farley said, but Dolly put her other hand on his shoulder.

"I go first." She had an iron grip.

"This is on *me*."

"That girl is no more your responsibility than she is mine. We go as a team, but I take lead. You're not moving clean and it's going to take some dancing to get you in that window. That's an operational liability if he's in there. Let me clear the hallway before you come inside, make sure our approach is good."

Farley knew she was right. He just didn't like it.

"You don't have to do this."

Dolly met his eyes. "Neither do you."

He nodded, once.

"What are our rules of engagement?" she asked.

"What do you mean?"

"I mean, are we going to kill this piece of shit or just fuck him up?"

Though her words made real the terms of the situation, they also created a cognitive dissonance delivered from a brightly lipsticked mouth set in a heavily made-up face. Whatever they were heading into, Farley hoped they made it out OK so he could thank her properly.

He closed his eyes to think. In the blackness he saw Olive and Abril, he saw Lissa's fear and Nirva's tears. In that moment he knew there was no length he would not go to, no line he would not cross. He opened them again and met her stare.

"This is a rescue," he said. "Whatever it takes. Just don't let the girl see it. She's been through enough."

Dolly pulled her sidearm from her pants and a small Maglite from an inside pocket of her bomber jacket. With the lit flashlight between her teeth, she climbed through the small window into the darkness. The board swung back into place behind her. Just like that, she was gone.

As soon as she disappeared, Farley's phone buzzed in his pocket. He grabbed it without looking to quickly silence it.

"Lissa," he said.

"You hung up on me, you fat, foul piece of shit."

"Still not a good time."

"You're a goddamned waste of oxygen. You've never done anything useful in your whole pitiful life."

"Hold that thought," he said and disconnected the call. It felt good to hang up on her, and he wondered why he'd never tried it before. The phone rang again almost immediately.

"I mean it," he told her. "This is not a good time."

"Why do you continue to take my calls, Farley? I'm so hateful to you. So *cruel*." The word had two syllables the way she said it. "All I do is insult you."

"Because it seems important to you."

"That's it?"

"That's it."

"Thank you, Farley," she said, shocking him. "Maybe I only blame you because otherwise I have no one else to blame but God."

"I blame myself too."

"That's because it's your fault, you pathetic—" He hung up before hearing how she intended to finish her sentence. As he silenced the ringer, the plywood swiveled on its nail, and Dolly poked her head out. She saw him holding the phone.

"Are you bored?" she asked.

"No. I ordered us a pizza in case we get hungry."

"Hallway is clear. Two doors. Two apartments. One looks like it hasn't been used in a while. The other's got a pretty new-looking hasp screwed into the door and jamb."

"Is it padlocked?"

"No."

"Then he's in there."

"What's your intel?"

"A bunch of people usually use this crash pad. When our guy moved the girl in there, he started locking everyone else out with a padlock."

"He can't padlock it if he's inside."

"Right."

She nodded. "Let's get this fucker, Farley."

"Roger that," he said.

42

A GIRL SCREAMED

Dolly held the board open. Farley stepped over the windowsill with his good leg and lifted his bad leg through with his hands. When she released the board, the hall went dark. She clicked her Maglite and swept the walls with the beam as it came to life. Bags of garbage, food wrappers, empty beer cans, broken bottles. Filth. She grabbed Farley's hand and put it on her shoulder so he could follow her in the dark, and so she'd know his location without needing to speak or look back. Then she raised her sidearm in front of her and advanced toward the door near the end of the hall.

She pointed beside it and held up five fingers. Farley stepped past it and stood with his back against the wall as she counted down silently—four, three, two, one—and then kicked the door, hard, just right of the knob. The wood splintered, but the door did not swing open.

Dolly took a step back and kicked it again, and then a third time, but still the door held.

"Fuck," she said.

Farley crossed the hall, pushed off from the opposite wall, and hit the door with the full weight of his body. It crashed open, swinging violently on its hinges, and he fell sprawling into the dim room, knocking the wind out of himself as he hit the floor.

"So much for the element of surprise." Dolly stepped quickly and efficiently over him, leading with her gun and clearing the corners of the room with the flashlight as she moved without hesitation. Gasping for air on the floor, Farley could see stained mattresses in the beam of her light. A couple of coolers, a metric ton of trash. More graffiti on the walls. The air reeked of sulfur and sweat and mold. She moved through a doorway into another room, and the light disappeared with her, plunging him into darkness.

Flat on his stomach, fighting for breath like a fish on the deck of a boat, he could not believe that for the second time he somehow found himself helpless, powerless, reduced to a spectator by his own initiative at the decisive moment, and hoped he would not fail a second time.

Dolly shouted something from the other room. He heard a crash. She shouted something else, and he saw back-to-back muzzle flashes as two gunshots filled the small apartment with a wall of noise that faded quickly, replaced by the ringing in his ears and the burnt, sour smell of gunpowder.

A girl screamed. High-pitched. Terrified.

"Olive!" he yelled, or tried to, his breath still a stranger to his lungs. Pushing through the pain, he got to his feet, unbalanced, broken, just as somebody came through the doorway Dolly had entered. He could not make out the face or features in the dark, but he could tell it was not her. The figure rushed at him. As it did, it raised something over its head to swing.

For one breathless, oxygen-starved moment, Farley left the decrepit crash pad, left the smell of puke and mold and sweat, and reappeared in the Arctic. Not face down on some piss-stained carpet but in the cold, sharp gravel as the bear rushed at Abril. The air changed, dry on his tongue, his weakened breath visible as it left his mouth. Rebecca's wail pierced the night. As his chest spasmed, he wondered if it was not his lungs at all but his heart exploding as he watched his daughter die again, watched her taken again, his life gutted again, his body destroyed again.

And then the vision released him. Back in the cramped and cluttered apartment, the approaching figure—no longer the dirty ghost white of a bear but a man in a hood—swung something hard and fast. It hit Farley in the head, and he disappeared not just from the Arctic or the crash pad but from consciousness itself.

43

SOMETIMES ALL YOU CAN DO IS WAIT

"What did your friend say?" Freddie asked when Lissa got off the phone with Farley.

"He thinks he found her. My daughter. He's going to get her."

"That's good! That's good. He say where?"

"Old Town."

"Mmm-hmmm. That's mighty close."

"But he doesn't think I should be there."

"I think he's right, miss. I think it might be better if you at home waiting for them when they get there."

"What if something goes wrong?"

The panic inflaming her system had worked its way back into her voice, and Freddie heard it.

"It won't."

He leaned across the table on arms thin as straws. Up close she saw he was older than she'd thought, white stubble beginning to appear on his cheeks and chin, the topographic lines at his eyes and brow.

"This Mr. Farley sounds like he knows what he's doing. Not like you and me, miss. We'd just get in the way."

"What am I supposed to do? Just sit around and wait?"

"I been driving an automobile for a living for most of my life, miss. A big part of what I do is wait around for something. People go into restaurants for dinner, they tell me to wait. People go into stores to shop, they tell me to wait. I sit at the airport waiting for aeroplanes to arrive with my passengers. Sometimes all you can do *is* wait."

"I'm worried something will happen."

"My mother used to say that worry was like a rocking chair, miss. It gave you something to do but it didn't get you nowhere. Now, a 1967 Lincoln Continental automobile like the one we have parked outside? That can get you anywhere you want to go. I'd be honored if you'd let me drop you off at your place on my way home."

"On your way home?"

"I hate to say it, miss, but I worked the airport night shift." He picked up his butter knife and studied his reflection in it. "Maybe it don't show, but I need my beauty sleep."

For the first time, she saw how tired he looked, the redness in his eyes, how gravity seemed to be exerting an increasingly strong pull on him with each passing minute. She smiled and put her hand on top of his. The gesture surprised him, but nearly every gesture he'd made since he pulled up outside her apartment had surprised *her*. It felt good to return it even a little. Lissa knew she'd have been climbing the walls all day without his company.

"Yes, please," she said.

They said goodbye to Rosaree and Walter—a hug and a nod, respectively—and went back out through the kitchen into the wet alley. Freddie helped her into the car and scooted himself across the front seat. Once underway, they rode in silence, but she could see him checking on her every few minutes in the rearview mirror. When they pulled up outside her building, he got out of the car and held her door. A light rain fell on them. Under the building lights, he looked even more frail. Older. He must be in his seventies. Up all night working, and she'd kept him up all day too.

"I'm sorry, Freddie," she said.

"Miss?"

"For being a hysterical mess. For making you miss your sleep. For putting you out today."

"Well, I can't think of a better way to spend a day than keeping a fine young lady like yourself company and eating my favorite meal. Anyway, this is what you do for your people."

"What's that, exactly?"

"Anything, miss. Anything at all."

She surprised him again by hugging him. He felt distressingly thin, birdlike, a skeleton in a suit.

"I'm afraid, Freddie," she said, alarmed by her honesty. "I'm really scared."

"I know, miss." He took her hand between both of his and squeezed it reassuringly. "But your little girl? She's gonna need you to be strong when she gets home. That's the best thing you can do for her. That's the best thing you can do for yourself too."

She bit her lip and nodded.

"You ever need a ride again, you reach me through my cousin. Or anytime you and your daughter just want to eat turkey and pie with an old man."

He tipped his hat.

"Goodbye, miss. And good luck."

Lissa reached for her cigarettes as the big car pulled away. She could smell the rain, could smell Freddie's lingering cologne, a bit of sage from their lunch together. She almost felt good about things. Not good, exactly, but confident in Farley's success. Confident she'd see Olive soon. That everything would be all right.

But the gift of calm that Freddie had given her faded with his brake lights, and the panic quickened within her, the nicotine a catalyst for the guilt she felt about not doing more to find her daughter, about not keeping her safe in the first place. Each angry drag fed that guilt and the ensuing fear, and the fear and the guilt drove her to each successive angry drag like a snake eating its own feelings until she could boil the puddle at her feet with her rage.

When her phone rang, she almost dropped it in her haste to answer it.

"Farley?" she said.
"Who the fuck is Farley?"
"Who the fuck is *this*?" she said, fully engulfed.
"I'm the guy who has your daughter."

44

A WOMAN'S BEEN STABBED

Farley woke for the sixth time that day to find himself face down, nose in something wet and warm and foul-smelling. For a few moments, he could not remember where he was or why he felt a pressing urgency. Once he did, he tried to get to his feet. His entire body in revolt, he managed only to roll onto his back.

His head ached, a dull pain throughout and a focused, sharp pain on the crown. When he reached for it, he felt a lump the size of a walnut crusted with dried blood. The blood ran down along the slope of his nose and covered his lips like a paste. He wiped it on his arm.

"Welcome back." Dolly spoke in a low register, her natural octave. She sounded tired. "Have a nice nap?"

Farley sat up as best he could. The darkness hung close. He could not see very far in front of him, could not make out Dolly or anything else.

"How long was I out?"

"No idea. What day is it?"

"I can't see a fucking thing."

"Still got that cell phone?"

Farley patted his pants pockets for it and found the flashlight app. The bright LED lit up the room. Dolly sat against the wall, legs in front of her, clutching her stomach. Blood covered her hands. He angled the light for a better view and saw more blood soaking the carpet beneath her, a trail leading from the other room.

"Are you shot?"

"No. Fucker ganked me."

"The Ferryman?"

"Maybe. There were two of them. One charged when I entered the room. I took him out. The other got me from behind, tried to let the air out of me."

"How bad?"

"I'll live."

"The one you shot?"

"I don't think he will."

"The girl? Olive?"

Dolly shook her head.

"Took her with him after he knocked you out. She was crying and sounded scared, like she was in shock, but she didn't look hurt."

Aching like a motherfucker, Farley got unsteadily to his feet. The uneven light created a kind of vertigo, or maybe it was all the bumps he'd taken to the head that day. He limped into the other room, found the body slumped in the corner, and aimed the light at it. Not The Ferryman, and not anyone he recognized. A dark stain covered the chest. Farley put his hand on the man's neck, looking for a heartbeat and finding none. It came away wet. He refocused the light on the torso and saw two bullet wounds grouped an inch apart.

"Is he dead?" Dolly asked from the other room.

"He's dead."

"Just call me Double-Tap Dolly." Her voice sounded weak.

Farley saw a folding chair near the door, a mattress against the back wall, McDonald's wrappers on the floor beside it. A couple of empty soda cups. Scrap paper and crayons. Wincing with the effort, he squatted for a closer look. The papers were covered with a child's crayon drawings.

As he made his way back to the other room, he kicked something that rolled across the floor with a clanking sound. Dolly's flashlight.

When he bent to retrieve it, he got dizzy but recovered and pushed the button. Nothing happened.

"Battery's dead," she said.

"I've been out a while."

"He's been gone too long to chase. They're in the wind again."

He stared at her in the dim light. "You know," he said, "one of my mother's boyfriends took us on a road trip to the Great Smoky Mountains when I was younger. We spent a day at Dollywood. I don't have many happy memories from that time in my life, but that's one of them."

"You figured it out," she said, her voice restored. "Maybe that blow to the head made you smarter."

When he nodded, his head played an arpeggio of pain.

"I should be a fucking genius by now."

"You can't be that handsome *and* smart too, honey. That would just be greedy."

It even hurt to smile.

"Let's get you to the hospital," he said.

"Just get me to the alley. Call 911 from there. Nobody will blink at a drag queen getting jumped by a dumpster. Happens on the regular."

Farley looked toward the other room.

"What about him?"

Dolly looked too, though it was too dark to see anything. She thought for a few moments and then closed her eyes. The glitter in her eyeshadow sparkled in the light from his phone.

"Fuck him," she said.

It took some doing, but Farley got her to her feet. With her arm over his shoulder, he helped her down the hallway and over the windowsill onto the fire escape, where they both stopped to breathe in the fresh air. Darkness had fallen. He could see city lights, but the alley remained mostly dark.

She waited while he made a final walk-through of the apartment, looking for any signs that might betray their presence. Then he groaned his own way out the window and helped Dolly down the rusty metal stairs to the street. At the alley her legs gave out. Farley caught her as she fell, lifting her off the ground with a grunt and cradling her.

"You all right, sailor?"

"You're pretty fucking heavy for such a petite little lady."

"I stuff my bra with lead," Dolly said, and Farley laughed in spite of himself. He took the last few steps carefully, his legs a liability, and did not relax until he laid her safely on the ground, her back against the dumpster.

"Are you going to be OK?"

"That shitbird didn't get any organs or arteries. It's a deep gash but it's just a gash. They'll stitch me up, give me something for the pain. I'll be back at the bar in a couple of days." She said it like she believed it but didn't sound like she did.

Farley looked at her with concern.

"We come into this world," she said. "We make our own way. We live with the consequences. A man with scars like yours, I suspect you know that's right."

He nodded.

"What's that look you're giving me?"

"Honestly, I'm not sure. Fondness, maybe."

"It's fucking weird," Dolly said.

"It's new for me too. Not sure I like it."

She laughed her way into a wheezing fit. Farley took out his phone and dialed 911.

"I need an ambulance," he told the dispatcher. "A woman's been stabbed." She smiled. Farley saw he had a missed call and message from Lissa. He put it on speakerphone.

"Farley! Oh my God, Farley, are you OK? He just called me. The Ferryman. He's got Olive! I made him let me talk to her and she said you were dead. She said she saw him kill you. Oh my God, Farley, please call me back, please don't be dead. Please. I don't know what to do."

With the phone still on speaker, he hit the call button. Lissa answered before it finished even a single ring.

"Farley?"

"I'm OK."

"Oh God." He could hear her tears, the scratchy voice. "Thank God. She said he killed you. Did you see her?"

"She's not hurt, Lissa. She's all right."

"He's got her, Farley. He wants money to get her back. He wants to meet."

"When?"

"Now."

"Where?"

"He knows where I work, Farley. He wants to meet there. At work. At the zoo. How does he know where I work?"

Farley pulled Olive's crayon drawings from his back pocket and unfolded them. He recognized the animals in their cages, recognized Lissa in her khaki scrubs.

"Olive told him. Did she know your phone number?"

"Yes. I made her memorize it in case she ever needed me."

"That's how he called you."

"Farley—" Lissa started, but he cut her off.

"Why there? Why the zoo?"

"No one around at night," Dolly said. "Out of the way. Tactically, it's not awful."

"Who is that?" Lissa asked. Farley ignored her.

"What is he asking for? What does he want for Olive?"

"Money. He wants money. He says I got his dog killed and one of his friends killed. He says I ruined his life and he wants money. What friend? What is he talking about?"

"How much does he want?"

"Fifty thousand dollars, Farley. Where am I going to get that kind of money? What's he going to do to her when I can't pay?"

"Let me worry about that. I have a plan."

"I'm home. I'm outside the building."

"Go upstairs. Go home, Lissa. Wait for my call."

"I'll meet you at the zoo."

"No. It's better if you're not there."

"Why?"

Because if anything goes wrong and The Asshole hurts Olive, I don't want you to see it. Because I know what it does to a person to see something like that happen to their child and do not wish it on anyone. Especially you.

"It just is," he said.

"Farley?"

"What?"

"I'm grateful for what you're doing for me. I don't know why you're doing it and I don't know how I will ever be able to make any of it up to you. But fuck you. I'm going to the zoo to get my daughter back and you cannot stop me."

"Lissa, I—"

"I'll meet you there," she said, and hung up.

He looked at Dolly leaning against the dumpster, holding in her guts, and knew it would cost more than the ransom to get Olive back from The Ferryman. He did not yet know what the cost would be or who would pay it, but he knew he had made a promise to her mother and a promise to himself, and nothing would get in the way of that. He was all in. He felt the fire in his legs, the soreness in his back, the welt on his skull, felt the headache like coins in a clothes dryer. The scars on his face tightened, pissed at him for pushing well beyond exhaustion.

They heard sirens nearby, saw the flashing lights approaching the alley. Dolly met his eyes.

"Get lost, handsome," she said. "You don't want to be here when the cops arrive."

"When this is done, I'll come check on you at the hospital."

"You'd better bring me flowers."

"Roger that," he said. She smiled weakly.

"Now go get that girl and make that fucker pay for what he did."

Farley limped toward the shadows at the other end of the alley just as the first ambulance arrived. Dolly called his name, and he stopped and looked back.

"Watch your six, Farley," she yelled. "That drugged-up piece of shit got my gun."

PART FOUR

45

ZOO CLOSED, BRUH

He knew a late-night laundromat a few blocks away and made his way there, stopping only at the first ATM he passed to withdraw as much money as it let him. Inside the laundromat he looked around until he saw an empty duffel bag stuffed in a laundry basket. Someone had left it in front of a running dryer to claim the machine. He filled the bag with the clothes, warm from the dryer but still damp, and stacked the cash—six hundred bucks in ten-dollar bills—on top. Physically, fifty grand wasn't all that substantial, but he didn't imagine The Asshole had ever seen that much cash in one place. To him it would represent a life-changing fortune, and it needed to have substance. Farley liberated a large plastic bottle of hand sanitizer from the unattended counter to give the bag some weight before heading back outside to flag down a cab.

The first three that slowed for him sped away when they got close enough to see him clearly. Finally, a Prius stopped, the driver undaunted by his chaotic appearance. Farley folded himself into the little car.

"Oregon Zoo," he said. "And swing by a drive-through." He hadn't eaten in hours and thought he might need his strength.

"Zoo closed, bruh."

"I know."

The driver shrugged. "It's you money." He kept one bright eye trained on his passenger in the rearview mirror.

Farley looked at the photocopy of his license binder-clipped to the seat. Toussaint Barthelemy. *Haitian*. No wonder he'd stopped for the fare—courage was the Haitian birthright. He wondered if Toussaint knew Nirva. Portland's entire Haitian community could fit in a Cadillac.

Farley devoured two cheeseburgers and a fistful of greasy fries as they followed Burnside through the city and up the winding hill into Washington Park. Not the most direct route, but quieter than hopping on 26W. He appreciated the opportunity to think. He needed some kind of plan.

"You like zoo, bruh?"

"Toussaint? Do you mind if we don't talk?"

"Touie."

"What's that?"

"Name Touie. Toussaint what *ma mère* call me when I in trouble."

"Touie, then."

"Who you, eh?"

"Farley."

"Mistah Farley, zoo closed."

"Just Farley."

The driver smiled, his teeth bright in the dashboard lights.

"OK, Justfarley. We don't talk. You want music?" He reached for the radio, but Farley barked at him.

"No."

Touie's smile disappeared, and he went back to driving with one watchful eye glued to the mirror.

Though it lasted no more than fifteen minutes, the quiet ride calmed Farley. The day had taken a toll on him, and he knew his stubborn will was the only thing keeping him going. He closed his eyes, just for a second, and sleep washed over him. At first he embraced it. He let it come, let it slow his heartbeat. But he saw an image of Olive, and he sat upright, opened the window, and let the cool evening air rush in.

"Let me out here," he said as they neared the Children's Museum on the zoo approach road. Touie pulled over to the curb.

"Museum closed too."

Touie pushed a button on the dash-mounted meter. It spit out numbers.

"Fourteen and seventy-nine, Justfarley."

He'd still have to walk through the zoo's big parking lot, but he didn't want to risk spooking The Ferryman, and it might give him a better chance to spot any backup he'd brought. Of course, if The Asshole wanted to use Dolly's gun to take him out, approaching on foot would make that easier for him too. But you couldn't control every element of risk—sometimes you just have to do the thing even if it blows up on you.

Farley handed Touie two tens from the bag and held up his hand. "Keep the change."

The driver nodded once, grateful but no less apprehensive of his fare, and pulled away immediately.

Farley watched the brake lights disappear around the corner with a weird nostalgia, as if the cab was the final lunar shuttle back to Earth and Touie the last human he would ever see. He'd said goodbye to so many people and lived such an isolated existence that it ought to be easy by now. But it tore at him, the tether cut, the resolve settling in. Generally, he did better on his own—that much he knew. He did not actually miss being a part of other people's lives, but he thought he might miss *missing* being a part of other people's lives. As if he was evolving to be alone and knew that once he did, he could not undo the alterations to his emotional physiology.

He stood in the mist, considering the possibility for a moment.

Then he spit on the curb, shouldered the duffel, and headed into the thin and breathless atmosphere of the quiet zoo.

46

WOULD EVERYBODY PLEASE JUST SHUT THE FUCK UP ALREADY?

Dragging his angry leg across the parking lot, Farley swiveled his head in all directions, watching the shadows, hoping to avoid any surprises. From the nearby highway, he heard the surf-break swell of traffic, crickets or tree frogs in the woods around the park, his own heart hammering in his chest. Near the gate, at the zoo's entrance, he stopped and looked around. He saw no one.

It looked deserted.

Rain began to fall again. Just lightly, but in Portland anything could happen. After a few minutes, headlights appeared on the approach road. The car turned into the lot and drove toward the gate. Beneath the parking lot's sodium lights, it looked like a BMW or Audi, sleek and efficient, well-engineered. German. Dark paint. The kind of car that did not, *could* not, exist in the Arctic. Transporting vehicles to Nanuqmiut cost a small fortune, and most came in through the oil companies—either for field work or when they paid the moving costs for a new high-level employee. Once there, they tended to remain for as long as they could still run. Alaska had no vehicle inspection requirements, but the Arctic had a way of wearing them down, rusting the frames and chassis, cracking the glass, sandblasting the paint. As with everything else up north, function came before fashion, and it was not even close. You saw cars with plywood doors and plexiglass replacement windows, a lot of Bondo and flat primer, missing exhausts. Farley had almost forgotten that a new car could be beautiful in its own way. This one parked a couple of hundred feet away from him with the lights aimed his way.

The driver got out and walked around front. He stopped in front of the car so the headlights created a backlit silhouette, a shadow figure of a man.

"Nice shirt, asshole," he said. "You must be fucking Farley. I remember you. Bitch still has you doing her dirty work for her, huh? You bring my fucking money or what?"

Farley cocked his head.

"What?" he yelled, just to fuck with him.

"I said, did you bring my money?"

"Can't hear you. Too far away."

The silhouette shook its head in disgust, but it also took a few steps closer. "Did you bring my money, asshole?"

Farley pointed at the car. "Is that an Audi?"

"It's a Beemer."

"Nice."

"Right? Five Series."

"Yours?"

"Fuck you, is it mine. It's a fucking Zipcar."

"What?" He raised a hand to his ear. The silhouette shook its head again and closed about a quarter of the distance between them. As he grew closer, Farley could see him better in the cone of the lights—hooded sweatshirt, leather jacket, filthy pants—but his face remained in shadows and he couldn't judge whether he was nervous or confident, aggressive, or unpredictably high.

"It's a fucking Zipcar."

"What's that?"

"You don't know Zipcars? Fuck. They're parked all over town. You reserve them with an app on your phone and just dump them wherever you want when you're done. All you need is a credit card."

"*You* have a credit card?"

"Fuck you. Of course I do. I'm homeless, not fucking useless."

Farley considered it. "Stolen?"

The Ferryman shrugged.

"Never heard of them. Zipcars."

"They're great, man. Beats the fucking bus."

"What about cabs?"

"Fuck you, what about cabs. Fucking immigrant cab drivers committing highway fucking robbery. Uber's driven the whole fucking market into chaos."

A silence followed. They stood under the sodium lights, forty feet between them as the rain turned to mist and then back to rain.

"So," Farley said. "Where's the girl?"

"In the car. She's in the fucking car. Do you have my money?"

He lifted the duffel bag. "Is she hurt?"

"You think I'd hurt a fucking kid?"

"You did kidnap her."

"Fuck you. It was for ransom. Just for ransom."

"Just for ransom? So, what would you have done if you didn't get the money? Just let her go?"

"Fuck you, man." He sounded exasperated, maybe insulted. "I wouldn't hurt no kid. That bitch got my dog killed. Smoke. I fucking loved that dog. I fucking miss her. A lot. I just wanted that bitch to feel that way too, just for a while. But I wouldn't hurt no kid. I just want us to be even."

Farley stared at him long and hard, not so much considering what he'd said as assessing the situation.

"I don't believe you," he said finally.

"Fuck you."

"Where is she?"

"In the fucking car."

"Show me."

"Give me my money."

Farley threw the bag on the ground at his own feet.

"Let me see it, asshole."

"Not until I see her. Not until I talk to her."

Increasingly irritated, The Ferryman took an angry step toward him and reached for his belt—Dolly's gun, Farley figured—but stopped short. He looked back at the car and signaled with his hand. Someone got out of the back seat and helped Olive out. Farley could not see her clearly, but she had a blanket over her shoulders and looked like she might be barefoot; he couldn't be sure.

Olive yelled his name when she saw him and tried to run to him, but the second figure held her back.

"Farley!" she said, a hitch of tears in her voice. "I thought you were dead!"

"Hi, Pip-squeak. Are you OK? Did they hurt you?"

"I want to go home, Farley."

"Soon." He hoped he was right.

The other figure stood behind her with his hands on her shoulders, rocking back and forth from foot to foot. "Hey, Farley," he said, not unfriendly, lifting a hand to wave. "Hey, man."

Farley squinted through the rain. "Wayne?"

"Yeah, man. How are you? How have you been?"

The Ferryman turned to look at him and the girl.

"Shut the fuck up," he said. Wayne lowered his hand.

"What are you doing here, Wayne? Why are you with this asshole?"

"Well, he said he needed help babysitting. He said we were going to the zoo."

"I said to shut the fuck up, you crazy old fuck."

"Kevin told me I should help her, Farley. He told me I needed to help keep her safe."

"OK, asshole," The Ferryman said. "You've seen the girl. Now show me my fucking money."

Farley opened the bag and pulled out some of the bills, fanned them like a poker hand, held them up for The Ferryman to see. Then he put them back in the bag and zipped it shut, limped a few steps closer, and dropped it on the asphalt in front of him.

"Wayne," he said. "Take the girl somewhere safe."

"Don't fucking move, Wayne."

"Take her, Wayne. Get her out of here."

"Where to, Farley?"

"Just take her away from here. Away from *him*."

"I said don't fucking move." The Ferryman pulled the gun from his pants and waved it at Wayne and the girl.

That changed things. Farley considered his next move, but every line of action led to the same result—he could not outrun The Asshole, and he couldn't just hand over the duffel bag without him figuring out he'd been shorted. He knew there was still a chance that Lissa would show up, and if she did, her presence would only complicate things. Seeing her might set Olive off, and her tears might garner some sympathy—but he thought it just as likely that seeing her would set The Ferryman off and inflame the situation further. He tried to focus over the pain, to formulate a plan, but it felt like trying to tune a distant radio station with a broken antenna. Too much static.

Another set of headlights appeared on the zoo road. They all watched as it turned into the parking lot and approached, the lights rolling across the scene hypnotically.

"What the fuck is this now?" The Ferryman said. "Better not be fucking cops."

The car—a small SUV, Farley thought, maybe a Honda—stopped a hundred feet away from the BMW, its windshield wipers sweeping back and forth, back and forth, back and forth against the rain. One of the back doors opened. Lissa all but flew out, running toward the other car.

"Olive! I'm here, love!"

"Mom!"

"Stop." The Ferryman pointed the gun at her, and she came to an abrupt halt, raising her arms over her head and stumbling forward, off-balance. At the sight of the gun, the Honda's driver hit the gas and peeled out of the parking lot. "Your friend is a chickenshit."

"It was an Uber," Lissa said.

"You should have gotten a Zipcar."

"Stay there, Lissa," Farley said. "Wayne, take Olive to her mother."

"The fuck you will, Wayne." The Ferryman waved the gun between them.

"I have your money," Farley said. "Right here." He held the duffel in front of him.

"What are you talking about, Farley?" Lissa said.

"Deal with me." He shook the bag. "Not her."

"Just everybody shut the fuck up," The Ferryman said. When he pointed the gun at Lissa again, Farley took a step toward him to get his attention. He swung the barrel back toward Farley. Seeing him handle the weapon, Farley could tell he had not been trained and did not have any useful experience. He knew guys who could tell the make and model from fifty yards, guys who romanticized firearms, elevating them to a state of taxonomical worship like a lepidopterist with butterflies, but he couldn't tell the caliber, just that it was a semiautomatic with a clip. From what he knew about Dolly, he could assume it was a cannon, but it didn't much matter—even at forty feet, The Ferryman had a pretty good chance of hitting such a big and slow-moving target.

"Tell us a joke, Wayne," Farley said, trying to buy time to think.

"Really?"

"Just one. To lighten the mood."

In the darkness he couldn't be sure, but he thought he saw The Ferryman roll his eyes. He waved the gun as if to say, *Go ahead, get on with it*. Wayne scratched his head, maybe thinking of the best joke for a hostage situation in the parking lot of a zoo.

"OK," he said finally. "Lemme ask you something. What's the difference between a hippo and a Zippo?"

"Jesus Christ. I have no fucking idea."

"One is really heavy," Wayne said, "and one is a little lighter."

The Ferryman spit on the ground in his general direction. "There's something fucking wrong with you," he said.

But Farley looked at Wayne like an oracle. "You're a beautiful genius," he said to Wayne, and then to The Ferryman, "Hey shitbird—pay attention."

Wincing against the effort, he bent down and unzipped the duffel, took out the big bottle of hand sanitizer, and poured it all over the bag and its contents. Then he took Sister Isaiah's Zippo lighter from his pocket and spun the wheel to produce the flame, hoping like hell the rain would not put it out.

"What the fuck are you doing?"

"I told you, I don't trust you. Let the girl and her mother go, or I torch your money." He held the lighter closer to the bag. "There's no other way out of this, Asher."

"How about I fucking shoot you? How about *that* for a way out?" If the use of his given name bothered him at all, it didn't show.

"See what I mean?"

"What?"

"That's why I don't trust you."

"Shut the fuck up. Back away from the money or I'll blow a fucking hole in you."

"You can't shoot us all."

"I don't fucking have to. I just have to shoot *you*."

Shit, Farley thought. *He's right.*

"You shoot me, I drop this lighter into the bag and all your money goes up in flames." He held the Zippo closer to the duffel. "You going to shoot the fire out too?"

Indignant—and starting to panic—The Ferryman put his hand to his head, thinking, waving the gun barrel as he went. Clearly, events were not going as smoothly as he'd pictured, and his drug-addled brain was beginning to short. After a few strenuous seconds, he pointed the gun at Olive.

"Fine. I'll just shoot the girl. That would make us fucking even."

"No!" Lissa screamed. Farley could hear the fear in her voice, could feel it, not just how it shook and broke but the desperation in it too.

"Didn't you just tell me you wouldn't hurt a kid?" he said, and The Ferryman pointed the gun back at him.

"You don't have to shoot anyone," Lissa said, her voice frantic. "Please. Just let my daughter go. She didn't do anything. Please."

"Hey, you can't hurt the girl, man," Wayne said. "She didn't do anything."

"They're right," Farley said. "Nobody has to get hurt. Just come get your money. But first, let the girl go or I torch it."

The Ferryman swung the gun from Farley to Wayne to Lissa and then back to Farley.

"Shut the fuck up," he said. "Just everybody shut the fuck up so I can think."

The flames were beginning to heat the metal of the lighter, and already Farley found it uncomfortable. Soon it would be unbearable, impossible to hold.

The Ferryman swung the gun back at Olive. "Put out the lighter and step away from the bag or I shoot the fucking kid. Final offer."

"No!" Lissa said.

"Mom!" Olive yelled.

"You can't do that, man," Wayne said. "You said you wouldn't hurt her."

"Shut. The fuck. Up," The Ferryman said.

"You can't hurt a kid, man. You said you wouldn't."

"I also said to shut the fuck up."

The lighter had begun to burn Farley's fingers. He watched Wayne step in front of Olive, turning his back to The Ferryman so that he faced her. He reached down and lifted her into his arms.

"Trust me, man," he yelled over his shoulder. "You don't want to hurt a kid. You don't want to do that." Keeping his back to The Ferryman, his own body between the gun and girl, he walked sideways toward Lissa.

"Put her down, you crazy old piece of shit."

"Good job, Wayne." Farley could smell the flesh on his fingers burning, and it took a deep-reaching stubbornness not to let go of the lighter.

The Ferryman held his hands to his head and pounded his forehead with the butt of the gun.

"Would everybody please just shut the fuck up already?" he screamed. "I can't even hear myself fucking think."

Lissa paused for a moment. Then she began to run toward Olive and Wayne. He reacted quickly and pointed the gun at her.

"Stop. Now."

He took a few steps her way.

"Put the kid down, Wayne, or I'll shoot her fucking mother."

"Mom!"

Farley yelled for his attention and dropped the hot lighter into the bag. The vapors from the hand sanitizer caught fire immediately, even in the rain, and a cloud of blue flame appeared, devouring the oxygen in front of him and singeing his eyebrows and the hair on his hands and arms.

"Fuuuuuck." The Ferryman began running toward him, gun raised. The flames turned yellow and orange as the clothes in the duffel caught fire, the heat already intense and unpleasant. Farley grabbed it by the handles, burning his hand. He shifted his weight to his good leg, pivoting on his heel like a chewed-up, ungainly compass tracing unsteady circles on the blank page of the parking lot, and spun once, twice, three times. Timing his release as best he could, he let go, launching the bag as far across the parking lot toward the zoo's gate as he could. His momentum and weight and unhappy legs and gravity all conspired against him, and he fell, landing hard on his side on the pavement.

The Ferryman raced past him toward the flaming bag.

"Get them out of here, Wayne," Farley yelled. "Go. Take the car."

But Lissa, moving with adrenaline, with a mother's instinct, had already snatched Olive from Wayne's arms. Farley watched as she rushed her into the BMW's back seat like a presidential security detail. She held the door open and yelled to them, to Farley, to Wayne.

"Get in!"

She circled around the car to the driver's door. Wayne looked unsure about how to proceed. He looked at the car and then back at Farley, lying on the ground, and then back at the car.

"Go, Wayne," Farley said, but Lissa was already on it.

"Get in the fucking car," she yelled, an angry mother's tone that said she meant business. Without further hesitation, Wayne sprinted to the BMW and dove into the back beside Olive.

"Farley!" Lissa yelled. "Come on."

Unsteadily he climbed to his feet and began limping toward her, toward the car, as fast as he could. But his legs had nothing left—furious, broken, a betrayal in wet fatigues—and he fell again. He looked at Lissa.

"Go," he said.

Behind him, The Ferryman screamed a protracted curse with enough heat to boil water.

"Fuuuuck."

Three more followed it, each successively longer.

"Fuuuck. Fuuuuuuck. Fuuuuuuuuuuck."

He'd reached the duffel; maybe he'd put out the flames or had seen the burnt laundry inside. It didn't matter now. Farley did not turn around to look. As he got to his feet again, he did not take his eyes off Lissa.

"Farley?"

"Go," he said again. Even with the distance between them, in the misty darkness, he saw the alarm on her face, saw how her jaw and brow tightened in unison, saw the tears in her eyes as she raised a finger and pointed behind him. Rising slowly to his feet, before he could even turn to look, he felt the bullet rip into his lower back. A fraction of a second later, he heard the gunshot. Though not long, the gap was enough to confuse him.

He did not feel pain. Not exactly.

Momentum, maybe. Brute force. Like being clubbed by a canoe paddle. A board.

It felt more like something blunt than a bullet's surgical entry. When it hit, he stumbled forward, legs like cast iron. Inflexible. Heavy. But he did not fall.

Not at first.

Lissa's voice broke as she screamed his name. She doubled over as if the bullet had hit her instead of him. She tried to scream again but seemed unable to find her breath, panic and fear confounding her. Farley took a step toward her but could not finish it. Falling again to his knees on the wet, rocky pavement, he looked down at his hands, at the blood covering them, and at that moment the pain arrived, as if the bullet had moved faster than the sound of the gunshot and the sound had moved faster than the pain it caused.

He could hear Olive crying from the open car.

"Farley?" Lissa said, her voice desperate.

"Go," he told her one last time.

The sky chose that moment to open up. Rain poured down on them like a building collapsing. In a chaos of limbs, Lissa got into the car and gunned the engine before she'd even closed the door. The BMW's six cylinders roared like a planet being born, and the car spun in a tight arc, the unlatched door swinging open and slamming shut as the car whipped around, the halogen headlights carving a sweeping path across the nearly empty lot. When it turned for the exit, Farley saw Olive's face at the back window, saw the whites of her wide eyes. Then Wayne put a hand on her head, pushing her safely out of sight. He raised his other hand to Farley, who tried to raise his own in response but could not.

It felt like the muscles had been disassembled and reassembled incorrectly. He took a wincing, pained breath. His chest burned. He'd suffered a lot of pain in his life. Inordinate amounts of it. Today alone he'd added to the aggregate, as if he'd set a goal of finding the boundaries of punishment his body and mind were capable of withstanding and exceeding it. But the day was not over yet, and he had a feeling that a lot of hurt still lay in store for him.

The car swung a hard left onto the exit road, tires squealing like a wounded animal. All he saw were taillights vanishing. The sound of the engine vanished with it, and then only silence remained, as if the car had sucked all the ambient noise and the air out of the night and carried it with it, trailing it all behind like a vapor trail fading to oblivion. The silence brought a moment of calm as surprising as it was necessary.

The Ferryman broke it first, shattering the night once more.

"You stupid fucking asshole. You fucking stupid, cut-up, ugly piece of shit. I'm gonna fucking kill you. This could have been so easy. All you had to do was give me the fucking money. Now I'm gonna fucking kill you. And then I'm going back to that bitch's apartment."

Farley tried again for a breath. This time it came a little more easily, the pain still there and no less intense, but no longer a shock.

Expected. Familiar. A comfort, almost.

Blood soaked his shirt and hands. His insides felt like broken glass, muscles and limbs and nerves like metal shavings beneath the skin. Before he'd been shot, he'd been beat up, knocked unconscious, had fallen down stairs. He'd walked dozens of miles. He'd rowed a few more. "You look like you've been through some shit," his mother used to say when he'd come home on leave from the army. "Let me make you a meatloaf." Today he'd been through all the shit, all of it, with no meatloaf even to show for it. The Ferryman pointed the gun with a loose wrist and lazy hands, what his marksmanship instructor would have called "weak muzzle discipline." But by Farley's count, Dolly had fired twice in the crash pad, and he'd fired just once since then, which meant enough rounds remained in the clip for even a shitty marksman to do the job. Farley knew he couldn't outrun or dodge them. But he knew, too, that he didn't have to. He got to his feet and turned to face The Ferryman.

"You can't kill me," he said.

"Why the fuck not?"

Farley stood as straight and tall as his shattered body would allow, widening his shoulders, stretching his arms, cracking his neck. Taking a deep breath and locking eyes with The Ferryman so his body movement would not betray him any earlier than necessary, he lowered his center of gravity and shifted his weight to his good leg.

"Because fuck you," he said. "That's why."

Muzzle blasts lit up the night as he charged. A concussion of gunshots rent the air, scattering night birds from the trees and waking the sleeping animals as the sound echoed throughout the habitats of the dark zoo. As the pain within him expanded, embracing the new pain, it gave him comfort to know that nothing else remained to do, that he would not fail in his task—not this time—and to know, too, that he did not need to survive this. He just had to stay alive long enough to see it through.

47

A GIRL, HER ARMS OPEN WIDE TO EMBRACE HIM

Farley made his way along the fence behind the zoo with one hand, using the other to apply pressure to his wounds. He left blood along the top rail and a trail of it in the dirt behind him, and the sharp wire cut his palm, but he did not feel the pain. Even in the dark, he found the gate Lissa had shown him. With some trouble, he disengaged the lock. Once inside, he stumbled and fell, and then again, getting back up somehow and moving forward each time and shuffling inexorably toward his final destination.

The rain had stopped. The sky had cleared. The moon threw enough light for him to see by, but he had walked the zoo enough times by now to know his way even without it.

The animals of the Great Northwest habitat were restless, provoked, maybe, by the sound of gunshots. Some cages were empty, their occupants kept indoors, but the animals that remained outside seemed aware of him. His presence made them anxious, the scent of a wet and filthy human, the scent of blood. The condors paced their cage, grunting and coughing, and the sea lions circled and barked in their pool, splashing water in their huffing excitations. Farley could smell what they smelled too—it was not just blood that leaked out of him, but his past. Life itself. As he went, memories of all the people he'd known spilled out of him, memories of the places he'd been. Nirva and their polar highs and lows, Abril's birth, their fluid definition of a family. Mayor Nell spitting tobacco, her laughter echoing across the icy dump. Rebecca and Pastor John at his door with a Bible and a chess pie she'd made to welcome him to the village. Wilson Mequssuk cheating at poker, cards tucked beneath his Barrow Whalers cap. With each step he lost more, first remembering and then forgetting as his past leaked out behind him and soaked into the ground. Dolly. Edge. Sister Isaiah. Flex. Lady MacDeath. Even Skelly and Chad. The relentless darkness of an Arctic winter, northern lights shimmering over the sound. The communal joy of spring ice-out, mosquitoes the size of crows. Suffering in the South Carolina humidity as the army beat years of accumulated behavioral knowledge into him at Fort Jackson, like metal hammered in a forge. The physical exhaustion of basic, the cruel and methodical way the instructors stripped them of their identities. One by one he remembered the soldiers he'd trained with, those who'd survived it, those it had broken. Their time together and the time he had left dripped out onto the path he followed, the past and present indistinguishable, the future impossible. The further he went into the zoo, the more he remembered; the more he remembered, the more he lost. The two years he'd been stationed in Wiesbaden, the steady trauma of soldiers passing through. His mother chain-smoking cigarettes and cursing at the world and its many disappointments. His high school football coach, the classmate he shared a locker with, the goldfish he'd won at the Pendleton Round-Up. As his strength ebbed, his legs failed, and every few yards he stumbled again.

But he didn't have far to go.

He did not know if the zoo employed security guards at night. He assumed it did, assumed they would eventually find him on their rounds, spot him on their cameras, but it didn't matter. He wouldn't be long.

Several times he thought he might lose consciousness. He knew he would not regain it once he did. He thought he'd taken a second bullet before he reached The Ferryman. Maybe another one after. Maybe not—maybe none after the first, just one enough to hollow him out. He marveled at the not-knowing, the chaos and disorder of the moment too much for either of them—the *fog of war*, they called it—the pain subsumed by adrenaline, by anger, by purpose. Maybe pain was like water, how you could only be so wet once you were submerged in a dark sea, no matter how long you were under. But the pain didn't matter. He'd been able to put an end to it—to the shooting, the kidnapping, the bullying, but also to the addiction, the mental illness, the lifetime of misery. He had put an end to The Ferryman himself. All that remained when he'd finished was Asher, an unloved boy who'd become an unloved man, and who'd then made himself into something more. Something so foul and ugly and cruel that he did not have to wonder why no one loved him. Just like that, a life gone. Farley had never killed anyone before. He had no taste for it, but neither would he mourn him. Nobody would. An unwiped ass of a human being. Nor would he be around long enough to feel either guilt or remorse.

Would anybody mourn *him*? If a judgment was coming, he'd made his decision and would stand by it.

He reached his destination and collapsed, smearing blood against the glass wall as he slid to the ground. The pain was exquisite, all-encompassing, his body nothing but torn muscles and shredded nerves, burnt flesh stitched together with calcified bone repairs and thickened scar tissue, now shredded and torn anew.

What remained of his life felt like even less. He'd accomplished nothing in his years on this earth. He'd built nothing, created nothing. Less than nothing.

What about Abril?

Yes, he'd created a daughter. There was a daughter.

And then there was not.

Farley could see inside the enclosure but did not see any movement or signs of life. He raised a bloody fist and banged on the glass. Where were they? Couldn't they smell the blood? Couldn't they smell the death? They'd marked him that night in Nanuqmiut, a scent on his skin, spittle in his wounds—couldn't they smell it even now? He banged again and thought he saw something moving at the far end of the enclosure. A glimmer of dull white.

A bear.

A ghost.

It grew closer, growing until its form became clear as it waddled toward him with lazy interest, a bothered look at the late-night disturbance. It approached the glass slowly, with curiosity but without fear, and put its nose to the glass where he'd smeared blood. As it sniffed, he watched its nostrils expand and contract, great gaping holes of darkness. Only an inch of plexiglass separated them. The bear looked at him for a long moment, its black eyes focused, jaw muscles quivering.

Then it sat, heavy on its haunches. Farley could see it clearly, every inch of it. He could see himself too, his own reflection overlaying the bear, distorted, warped by the glass, by the rain, by the world, by his time on Earth and the path he'd followed. The bear lifted a huge paw and pressed it against the glass. Farley saw the long claws, the pads an archipelago of black islands in a dirty white sea, and put his own paw up against it, the glass cool and damp with night. He had big hands, giant hands, but they looked insignificant against the bear's paw.

Blood dripped down the glass. It covered not just his hands and wrists but his forearms, his sleeves, most of his shirt; it spanned his lap and his legs, thinned and mixed with the rain, burdening him with its weight. His breath came only in spurts now. Brief and jagged heaves. He couldn't feel anything below his waist. A blessing, maybe, but also another mile marker reached, the destination close. The pain had reached a singularity. He could no longer distinguish it from anything else, not his breath or his heartbeat, not his thoughts, not the cold cement he sat on or the quiet air surrounding him.

The bear studied him through the glass, thick of limb and broad of snout. In its big eyes he thought he might see ferocity or anger or hatred, even—he *wanted* to see it—but he saw nothing. He looked more deeply, hoping to see *anything*. Recognition. Familiarity. Kindness. Pity. Pride. Anything at all.

But all he saw was boredom.

The bear sniffed the air. It withdrew its paw from the glass. It got to its feet.

Farley wanted to be mad at it. He wanted to hate it. He'd hated it for so long already that the anger had festered within him. But the anger had done him no favors, and he regretted holding it so tightly. It leaked out through the wounds in his body and dissipated into the night like steam.

The bear shook its head. It scratched its flank. It turned and ambled away—not a predator, not a demon, not a killer. Not a beast. Just a tired old bear trapped in a cage for all the world to stare at.

Not even a mean bear. Just an ordinary bear.

Like you, Farley.

He could not believe how heavy his own head had become. How he could not even support its weight anymore. Holding your head up, it's like breathing—something you take for granted. Until you can't do it anymore.

The cold cut through him like a knife. Like bullets.

Like teeth.

Time passed. Or it didn't. Maybe he dozed off.

Maybe he didn't.

Slumped against the glass in a puddle of his own blood and urine and drool, he sat and waited, and as he waited, he grew weaker. More tired. Waiting.

Waiting.

Waiting.

More time passed. Or it didn't.

And then something changed. Something was different. He *felt* different. Or the night did. Just a feeling. A sense. No.

A sound.

His phone, buzzing. He could not feel it against his leg because he could not feel his leg. But he could hear it. Barely. He'd silenced the ringer before following Dolly into the Old Town crash pad, and now it vibrated to announce a call.

Answer it.

Instinct. Muscle memory. Cause and effect. Pavlovian response. Maybe Lissa calling to see if he would answer. To see if he *could* answer. To see if he survived. Maybe Rebecca calling to berate him, to tell him she wished him dead.

Answer it, his brain said, but his fingers did not work, no longer individual digits but clubs where once he'd had hands, blunt instruments, bloodied and useless like stubs of frozen meat. He dragged them near his pocket, the rain-soaked pocket of his bloody pants. He stabbed at it and his phone slipped out onto the ground. It clattered against the cement and vibrated again, louder now, freed from his pocket, and he squinted at the rectangle of glowing light but could not read it, could not make out what it said.

Everything blurry. Everything dark. His vision failing.

Everything failing.

He pushed at the screen with a numb hand, smearing it with blood. The buzzing stopped and the night went silent again. He thought he heard sirens in the distance. Were they getting louder? Growing closer? The rectangle of light changed, blinked once, shifted color. Slumping against the wall of the enclosure, he slid onto his side on the cold, wet ground and lay his head next to the phone. As he did, he thought he saw movement in front of him, someone running toward him out of the shadows at the other end of the bear-viewing area near the bench where he liked to sit.

A child running toward him.

A girl, her arms open wide to embrace him.

He heard a voice from the phone, tinny and distant and weak. "Farley?" it said. "Farley?"

EPILOGUE

ORDINARY BEAR

Olive sat at the kitchen table coloring, the TV on and tuned to the Cartoon Network. Lissa didn't know why she paid for an entire package of cable channels when they only ever watched the one. She could probably lose her remote control and it wouldn't matter. Olive's new therapist had assigned the coloring as a means of dealing with the trauma. Still in his twenties, with a boyish face and a child's voice that probably made him more relatable to children, he had a youthfulness Lissa found disconcerting. Derisively, she referred to him as "Carl Young" and suspected him of choosing crayon therapy for the sole reason that he, too, liked to color.

The cartoons weren't part of it. But they made Olive happy. Lissa desperately wanted her to be happy. She wanted her to be her old self again. She just wanted her to be OK.

Even six months later, she still didn't really understand what she'd been through. In the aftermath, Lissa had shielded her from as much of the truth as possible. The day had simply been a kind of adventure with strangers who took her to unusual places. She'd mostly forgotten the chaos and violence, or had buried it, though the fear and trauma had changed her in ways not clearly visible. Some nights Lissa heard her crying in her sleep, and occasionally she asked questions about what had happened—questions for which her mother had no good answers—but the memories remained subsurface. She seemed mostly unaware of them. To Lissa that felt like a blessing. A small one, maybe. But *she'd* been through something too, and it had also changed *her*—from here on out, she would be grateful for every damned blessing offered her, no matter how small.

The two officers who had come to her apartment when she first reported Olive missing returned the next day. They had an apologetic solicitousness, which she wanted to shove up their asses along with their notebooks, pens, and batons, and brought her to the station with Olive to take her statement. The man who took her from her bedroom had been nice, she told the therapist in a windowless interrogation room as her mother held her tightly and detectives watched from behind mirrored glass.

"He was nice to you?"

"Well, he was a little scary. And he was mean to Farley. But he let me draw. And he let me get McDonald's. I got chicken nuggets and fries and a shake. My mom never lets me get McDonald's."

She will now, Lissa thought. *Every last Big Mac you want.*

As soon as they'd gotten clear of the zoo that night, a frantic Lissa had called the police and begged them to send an ambulance for Farley. She barely remembered driving, just white knuckles and adrenaline. How had she not crashed the car? A blur of panic and terror, zigzagging through the streets in case they were being followed, watching the man called Wayne in the mirror as he tried to console Olive in the back seat. When she couldn't breathe anymore, she'd pulled to a curb somewhere downtown and made Wayne get out of the BMW. In that moment she needed to know they were safe, and she wanted him—everyone—away from Olive. She'd driven blindly for another half hour until she thought her heart jackrabbiting in her chest might kill her right then and there, and she parked beneath a highway overpass to climb over the center console and hold Olive tightly in her arms. They'd stayed there crying together in the dark, bodies and voices and tears intertwined, inseparable, shaking with the traffic passing high overhead until Lissa's phone rang and the police assured her it was over.

"Wayne was nice too," Olive told the therapist. "He was funny. He told a lot of jokes and did funny voices. I didn't really get the jokes but I liked the voices."

Lissa had not recognized him at first—there had been too much chaos—but later she remembered Wayne from the homeless camp. When the police told her about his history, about what he'd done to his own children, she could not reconcile it with how he had treated Olive that night. But the police considered him a coconspirator and arrested him on the streets a few days later. Lissa wanted to believe that people weren't defined by the worst thing they did in their lives but by what they did afterward—by how they tried to make it right—and she refused to press charges. But he'd violated his parole, and that was it.

"What happened to Wayne?" Olive had asked.

"He had to go away, love."

"With Farley?"

"No. Somewhere else."

"Will he be back?"

"I don't know, love."

"What about Farley?"

Olive still drew pictures of them, both of them: Wayne with his yellow teeth and scribble of hair, giant Farley with a white eye and cane. How many people would she have to say goodbye to in her life? How many people would she have to grieve?

Sometimes Lissa wondered what it had been like for Farley after she left him at the zoo that night. Whether he'd been afraid. How much pain he'd felt. She wondered, too, if she'd have been able to do what he did if she'd been in his place. What it might have felt like.

She owed him everything. Olive wasn't the only one who would miss him.

The phone startled her out of her reverie, a text message vibrating it across the countertop, and she looked at the screen.

I'm outside.

"Time to go, love," she said. "Why don't you go get your hat and coat?"

"OK, Mom." Olive gathered some of her crayons in a red plastic cup and disappeared down the hall.

Carl Young had said it would take some time for her to heal completely. It would also take work, patience, and a little bit of luck. "Kids are remarkable," he'd promised, sounding both unconvincing and unconvinced, as if talking about himself and his own potential. Unrealized; aspirational. "They're resilient." But hadn't The Ferryman been a kid once? He had not been resilient enough to survive whatever had happened to him, and it turned him into a monster. And Wayne—what about *his* children? What had become of them? Maybe they were fine. Maybe Olive would be too. But a cupful of crayons and a couple of maybes didn't feel like enough to bet on.

The TV had gone to commercial, fast-talking voices and chaotic music filling the small kitchen with noise. Lissa found the remote on the couch, next to the stuffed bear, and when she pushed the button to shut the TV off, the silence felt like a gift. Another tiny blessing. Then she put on her coat to wait for Olive.

Together they took the elevator to the lobby and stepped outside into the day. There was no rain, not yet, but it would come. It always did. Even without it the air felt wet, the wind cool, spring still new enough to be hesitant and unsure. The car appeared immediately, big and black and shiny, and cast them into momentary shadow as it pulled alongside the curb. The driver hurried around to their side and bowed deeply.

"Good afternoon, Miss Olive."

She dropped her backpack and hugged him, wrapping her thin arms around his camel-colored coat, and he winked at Lissa.

"Ready to go, miss?"

"Hi, Freddie," she said.

Olive liked to ride up front on the Lincoln's big leather bench seat. He let her push the buttons on the old radio, and they would talk the entire way, Olive telling stories and Freddie not just indulging her but peppering her with questions like an interviewer. Even after they arrived, she knew they'd sit together at a table in the back and talk some more. It had become a weekly routine, serving meals at one of the shelters with volunteers from his church. Members of the congregation helped cook and serve food and mingled with the diners over coffee and donuts. Making conversation. Building community. Freddie had invited Lissa and Olive to join them one weekend. Carl Young thought it might be good for Olive to be around other people and to interact with some of the city's homeless in a more positive way to minimize the stigma from the trauma. Though she'd been hesitant at first, Lissa had to admit, it had been good for Olive. Freddie and his family doted on her. She liked riding in his big car. Sometimes they all went out for sundaes after, and he promised her that in the summer they could ride with the top down.

The real surprise was that it had been good for Lissa too. How it felt good to help. To be part of something.

The fear still clung to her in all the insidious and annoying ways that fear does. So did the anger. Sometimes she thought she recognized someone from the bus shelter camp passing through the shelter line with a lunch tray, and that would trigger something within her. An artifact. A memory. But she didn't want to live with fear, and she did not want to live with anger. She would ask one of Freddie's cousins to keep an eye on Olive and go outside to the loading dock, where some of the other volunteers, shelter residents, even the little nun who ran the place stood together to smoke in silence and watch the rain fall. She felt a kind of connection with them. An understanding, maybe, each of them haunted by something different, a fear or anger of their own, but linked by the fact of the haunting itself.

Find your people, Freddie had told her. For so long it had felt like all she'd done was lose them; it felt good to find new ones again. To expand her world rather than shrinking it further. Another blessing.

She and Allie had been talking again, and she was coming to town in a few weeks—even staying with them. Lissa would give her a behind-the-scenes tour of the zoo, and they'd do a few Portland things together. Saturday Market. Brunch. Maybe even take in a roller derby match. Olive would get to know her aunt a little better, and Lissa might too.

She put out her cigarette and went back to the kitchen, where Olive sat with Rosaree and some of the other women, drawing with crayons on a paper tablecloth. She stepped up behind her daughter and circled her in her arms, hugging her for a long, long time. Olive didn't seem to mind. That was a kind of blessing too.

"Mom?" she said finally.

"What?"

"Can you let go now?"

"No, love," Lissa said. "I'm never letting go."

Long ago, the Iñupiat people would lay their dead out on the tundra and cover them with driftwood to protect them from predators and scavengers. Though the ways had changed, Wilson Mequssuk and some of the villagers had erected a pair of monuments at the base of the spit for Abril and Pastor John. The men hauled stones on sleds and piled them into mounds on which they built weathered lean-tos and rough crosses of whalebones tied with sinew from a years-ago hunt. They were visible for miles across the unbroken land.

Nell sat behind Jeffrey on his big snow machine, looking out over the spit where the wind whipped spindrifts of snow around a solitary bear as it shuffled around the memorial site, sniffing at the bones. The ice pack had been thick this winter, the sound frozen enough for the bears to wander more widely than in recent years. The village elders felt this to be a return to normal. The mayor was less certain.

"I think maybe it will keep changing," she said. "The weather. Good ice one year, bad the next, maybe. Maybe it's changing all the time."

They took turns drinking from a thermos of black coffee with lots of sugar, picking at the meatloaf sandwiches she'd brought and reveling in the weak but persistent April sunshine. Nanuqmiut would gain about ten minutes of light every day that month. It already saw nearly sixteen hours a day, though the temperature had yet to climb even into double digits.

"The people can never be sure of it no more," Nell said. "That's the trouble with the ice now."

Jeffrey shrugged to acknowledge that this, at least, seemed to be one of the good years. His mother sucked her teeth and spit tobacco onto the snow at their feet.

"Even broken clocks are still right twice every day," she said, unconvinced.

Soon the sun would find its strength and breakup would come, turning the sound into a patchwork of white and blue. The caribou would return, the snow would melt, and the village hunters would set out in their boats once more. The bowhead whale was the cultural heart of the people. According to their traditions, neither could exist without the other, but the sacred whale had become increasingly difficult to find. The hunters had failed last year, and all winter an anxiousness had rippled throughout Nanuqmiut like a whisper or a wave, passing from person to person and house to house. The village was overdue for something good, for some bounty from nature. For a bit of good luck. The low sun cast long shadows over the ice, and the people had been living in those shadows for many years now.

"Maybe we get a big whale this year," Nell said. "We better hope so. The old ways, they're going away even faster than the ice." She took a sip of coffee and winced at its bitterness. "You know what your grandma used to tell me? In the olden days, the people used to live underground, in igloos, and put our dead above it. Once the white men came here, we started burying our dead underground and living ourselves up above. Everything got upside down."

Shivering, she spit into the snow again and watched the brown stain spread beside the snow machine's track.

"Maybe we've never been warm ever since," she said. "Maybe we'll never be warm again."

Jeffrey took her gloved hand in his and squeezed it.

Down on the spit, the bear stood up straight and sniffed at the wind, catching their scent. It turned and looked their way, and slowly it began to make its way toward them, limping and unsteady in the snow. Injured. Tired. Old.

For a long time, they watched it approach, silhouetted against the low sun. When it finally reached them, Jeffrey nodded.

"You look cold," the bear said, stepping out of its fur and draping it over Nell's shoulders. She grinned.

"Hi, Farley. Welcome home."

ACKNOWLEDGMENTS

The publishing world can feel, at times, like a machine engineered to efficiently crush the human soul. And I've been writing for a long time, which means I've accumulated many debts of gratitude to friends and family who have championed me and my work, consoled my rejections, and kept me distracted along the way. This is at best a partial reckoning.

My wife, Kim, sets all records for being supportive, and then breaks them. It's no coincidence that my books only found traction when I found her.

Laura Strachan has been my agent through many successes and even more failures. She's also become a friend, and I'm grateful.

This is my second book with Blackstone, and there are no superlatives up to the task of explaining how I feel about the people there. I wish I could name them all. Thank you to my remarkable editor Marilyn Kretzer, publicist Sarah Bonamino, the amazing Josie Woodbridge, Caitlin Vander Meulen, Naomi Hynes, and all of the others who've worked with me and behind the scenes to make Blackstone the exception to the rule about publishing's intentions for writers' souls.

Everyone who read a version of *Ordinary Bear* made it better. Editor Michael Signorelli was the pilot boat that guided me through a field of deep-water mines. Armin Tolentino was a convincing voice for a change that needed making (read Armin's book, *We Meant to Bring It Home Alive*, next). Jeanne Nebeker Hilderbrand helped me align how children and parents act in my fiction with how they act in the real world—for the second straight book. And Chris Crowley shared visions of what the book could be, a gift for a writer mired in what it was. Thank you.

As a novelist, I come and go between real and imagined worlds. I make up the people who live in one of them, but even if I tried, I could not imagine better friends than the ones who occupy the other.

Dan Tuohy and J.L. Stevens, James Norcott, Scott and Nancee Morrissey, Jeff Gibson, Dan Murphy, John Drake, Gavan O'Shea, Kurt Mullen, Kate Gray—more than friends, you're family. Nicole Lagace, how is it possible we've been walking beaches together for three decades?

To all the friends and strangers who read, promoted, shouted about, or shared *Small Animals*—each of you changed my life in a very real way. Thank you, Ernie Stone, Jon Sering, Jackie Shannon Hollis, Dale T. Phillips, Brendan Jones, Tom "Recommender in Chief" Dooley (@Duells06), James Burg, Caroline Leavitt, Erin Popelka, Andrew Furman, Nicole Walker, John Pukstas, Ann Cereghino, Tracy Connor, Rebecca McDevitt and Cindy Ahrens, Jim Thomsen, Adam Shafer, Karen Graham, Amadie Hart, Michele Tomlinson, Jeff Shoemaker, Katrina Woolford, Kim Heacox, James Payne, Jill McArthur, Ben Stuart, M. Michael Armstrong, C. Matthew Smith, Audrey Schulman, Kristin Bair, Suzanne DeWitt Hall, Diane Josefowicz, Pedro Hoffmeister, Liz Michalski, Justin Tussing, and so many more. And thanks to my neighbors and friends who run dogs, boats, and mouths with me: Mike "Mike One" McCrary, Mike "Mike Two" Norklun, Captain Greg Houde, and Susan Estabrook.

I'm especially thankful for my family's love and support: Shawna and Anthony, Chris and Barbara Pukstas, and my sisters- and brothers-in-law and beautiful nieces. And to my parents, who maybe didn't always understand my relationship with writing but who could not be more supportive. Thank you.

This is my third book. All three have been set in Alaska, Oregon, or—in this case—both. I am lucky enough to have called each of those places home, and their landscapes and people struck me like a tuning fork—all these years later, I'm still making noise. To everyone there with whom I shared experiences and adventures, know this: I remember you fondly and think of you often.